THE
OCEANIC PRINCESS

ALSO BY DAVID DELEE

Grace deHaviland Bounty Hunter series
Too Far
Stare at the Moon
Takedown
With Intent to Deceive
Pin Money
Fatal Destiny

Brice Bannon Seacoast Adventures
Crimson Storm
Siege at Tiamat Bluff
The Yakuza Gambit
Strike of the Stingray
The Oceanic Princess
Facing the Storm

Nick Lafferty Crime Thrillers
Cold Cases
Out of the Game
Crystal White

Flynn & Levy Police Thrillers
Between Truth and Lies
While the City Burns
Moral Misconduct

THE
OCEANIC PRINCESS

A BRICE BANNON
SEACOAST ADVENTURE

DAVID DELEE

COPYRIGHT

THE OCEANIC PRINCESS
Published by Dark Road Publishing

ISBN: 978-1-962241-01-4

For information, contact us at www.darkroadpub.com.

For more information about new releases, special events, and exclusive content only available to subscribers, sign up to get David's newsletter.

https://www.subscribepage.com/daviddelee

Thank you for purchasing this book. We hope you enjoy it.

Dedicated to the brave men and women who serve in the U.S. Coast Guard, past and present.
Thank you for your service and your sacrifice.

Semper Paratus
"Always Ready"

THE
OCEANIC PRINCESS

THE DARK TURQUOISE EXPANSE of the North Atlantic Ocean stretched out below them for as far as the human eye could see. Smooth and flat as a tabletop, the water reached to the ruler-straight line of the horizon, due east. The untouched sea swept past underneath them, fast and relentless, with only the gentle whitecaps and the bright sparkle of the glinting sun shimmering across its majestic surface to distinguish it from the azure sky. Pristine and unchanged since the oceans were formed, undisturbed by man this far from land.

A few cotton ball clouds marred an otherwise unspoiled bright blue sky in the distance. A school of dolphins breached the water to chase the racing shadow of the helicopter as it skimmed the surface of the sea below.

In the copilot seat of the white, red, and blue Sikorsky MH-60T Jayhawk helicopter, Coast Guard Commander Brice Bannon lowered his binoculars and pointed in a southwesterly direction.

"There!" He shouted over the chomp-chomp-chomp of the main rotor overhead.

The Coast Guard twin-engine, medium-range, interdiction helicopter flew at a brisk one-hundred-forty knots. The engines thrummed smoothly through the decking, vibrating up through the soles of his boots. It was a feeling as familiar to Bannon as the rolling deck of a ship at sea or the grip of an M16 rifle in his hands.

"Where?" Skyjack McMurphy growled from the pilot's seat even as he gently urged the powerful bird in the direction his old friend pointed. He scowled behind a pair of mirrored sunglasses. Nicknamed Skyjack, John "Jack" McMurphy was a large, ruddy Irishman who'd easily be mistaken for an albino walrus if not for his bright red hair and a cigar almost always clutched between his teeth, lit or not.

The two men had served in the Coast Guard together going on fifteen years. Both were retired from full-time service but remained active reserve. McMurphy glanced at the clock on the instrument panel. They'd been at it for over two hours and forty-nine minutes without a hint of even a false alarm.

That was about to change.

"Near the horizon." Bannon returned the field glasses to his eyes. "Barely a black smudge from here but trust me. That has to be it."

Trust had never been an issue between these two men. Fifteen years earlier, the Coast Guard had brought them together. After so many years, they'd become best friends, closer than brothers. Each, having saved the other's life more times than either man could count, made them comrades-in-arms.

"About damn time," McMurphy groused.

They crewed with three Coast Guard Maritime Safety & Security Team members: a Chief Petty Officer named Johnson and two seamen, Reyes and O'Neil.

Bannon twisted around in his seat, looking back into the cabin.

The three men were strapped in padded black bucket seats. The side doors were open. The roar of the rotors and the wind were an assault on the ears. Each man wore a dark navy jumpsuit and tactical gear, including a fully loaded equipment vest and helmet. They wore Beretta M9 pistols strapped to their thighs and carried M16 assault rifles.

"Chief," Bannon said, adjusting the radio mouthpiece. "Coming up on our target in ten."

Johnson gave him a thumbs up.

"I don't like it," McMurphy said.

Bannon switched off comms. "You always say that."

"That's true, but this time's different."

Bannon smiled. "You always say that, too."

"We have no idea what we're flying into. Lizzy didn't tell us squat."

Lizzy was Elizabeth Grayson, the Secretary of Homeland Security and their boss. She didn't like being called Lizzy, but over the years, McMurphy had worn her down.

Bannon frowned. His friend had a point. It seemed Grayson had been even more cryptic than usual with this mission. Bannon played it off as routine. "There's a boat with some bad guys on it, planning to do something bad. We board 'em and we stop 'em." There it was. A simplistic, barebones description of the op. "What more do you need to know?"

"How many are on board? What level of resistance can we expect? Are they going to try and kill us?"

"That last part," Bannon said with a playful grin. "You can probably count on."

"Yeah," McMurphy said, resignation in his voice. "That's the part I don't like."

Ahead of them, the boat had grown from a black line on the horizon to a medium-size cargo ship. The *MV Naeem* was a handysize ship with a 32,000 DWT or deadweight tonnage. Five hundred twenty-five in length, it had five cargo holds, hydraulically operated hatch covers, and four 30-ton cranes. The accommodation section and bridge castle—that part of the ship that looked like an apartment building had been plopped down on the deck—was located at the quarterdeck. It housed the crew and officers' quarters, the mess, the bridge, navigation, and communications.

Handysize vessels were most often used as dry bulk carriers, as the *Naeem* was, or as oil tankers. They had a shallower draught than larger supramax and Panama ships, which allowed them to operate in most ports and terminals around the world. An added benefit, most were geared, meaning they had on-deck cranes. Like the *Naeem* had. This made it possible for them to operate in ports that lacked their own transshipment infrastructure.

Bannon unsnapped his harness. He clasped McMurphy on the shoulder. "See ya downstairs."

"Try not to get yourself killed before then."

"That would be the plan."

Bannon pushed through into the cabin. Also dressed in a navy blue jumpsuit, he donned his equipment vest and strapped a thigh holster to his leg. He tucked two full clips into their pouches, dropped a third from his old Colt Army .45, checked it, and slapped it back home before holstering the weapon. The .45 wasn't a sanctioned Coast Guard weapon, but it was Bannon's favorite. He preferred its stopping power over the Beretta M9 and Sig Sauer P229 nine-millimeter. He strapped a black-bladed, five-inch titanium diving knife to this opposite calf.

"What more can you tell us, Commander?" Chief Johnson asked over the roar of the Jayhawk's main rotor. His men looked eagerly at Bannon.

"Not much, I'm afraid. Homeland Security picked up reliable chatter the *Naeem* is transporting something they don't want to reach the U.S. My best guess is it's some kind of contraband cargo to be used in a possible terrorist attack. The mission is simple: secure the vessel and prevent the destruction or disposal of any contraband items until the *Bowman* catches up."

The *USCGC Dixon Bowman* was a 154-foot long, Sentinel-class Coast Guard cutter, often called a fast response cutter, assigned to back up Bannon's interdiction effort. The ship crewed with twenty seamen and four officers and had a top speed of twenty-eight knots. It was armed with one MK-38, mod-2, 25mm chain-driven autocannon, and four Browning M2 machine guns. Onboard was a twenty-three-foot rigid hull, short-range, inflatable boat that could be launched at speed for rapid deployment if necessary.

"We've radioed them our position," Bannon said. "They're twenty minutes out."

Seaman Reyes asked, "Do we know what the cargo is, sir?"

"No, we don't."

"Can we expect resistance?"

Bannon tucked the compact Sig P229 9mm he carried as a backup into a side pocket—this one the Coast Guard allowed—and zipped it up. "We can count on it."

"Saddle up, boys and girls," McMurphy said over the chopper's comms. "We're here."

The MSST team came to their feet and took their positions at the open cabin doors.

They were approaching the *Naeem* from the port bow side. Bannon leaned out and, fighting the wind, saw no one visibly on the forward deck. Stacked red and blue cargo containers filled the midsection, but the bow deck was clear for landing.

"Once we touch down," Bannon told Johnson, "McMurphy and I will secure the bridge. You and your team secure the crew and get control of the engine room."

"Roger that."

The chopper decelerated, losing altitude. McMurphy was the best pilot Bannon had ever known, and he's worked with many of them over his military career. The Jayhawk hovered over a closed cargo hatch cover, nose slightly raised, before quickly dropping the last few feet to the deck below. Bannon stood with Seaman O'Neil while Johnson and Reyes held on and prepared to leap from the other open cargo door. McMurphy steadied the chopper. The winds were less than five knots out of the southeast. As the landing skids were about to touch down, they suddenly took on a barrage of small-arms fire.

McMurphy cursed. "Son of a—"

The chopper wobbled. Bullets pinged off the metal skin. The chopper rose sharply. Bannon and the others got tossed to the back of the cabin as the chopper tilted, tail down and away. Caught by surprise, O'Neil clutched for the side of the open door, almost falling out. Bannon grabbed his vest and pulled him back in. The engines whined with the strain of the fast acceleration as they peeled off and to the left.

"Everybody okay back there?" McMurphy asked.

"All good," Bannon shouted over the comms. "We need to go back."

"I was afraid you were going to say that," McMurphy complained, but already Bannon could feel the chopper banking, swinging around to line up for a return trip. "Plan B?"

"Plan B," Bannon confirmed.

"What's plan B?" Johnson asked. Reyes and O'Neil looked at Bannon, curious as well.

Bannon grabbed an M16 from the bulkhead rack. He slapped a magazine in and jacked a round. "We rappel."

Johnson nodded, repeating McMurphy. "I was afraid you were going to say that."

His team hooked up their harnesses and guidelines. The metallic snap of D-clamps filled the air. Each man readied his M16. With a nod, each was cocked and locked and ready to rock and roll.

McMurphy brought them around. This time, he hovered twenty feet over the deck. Over the comms, he said, "Don't dawdle, gentlemen."

Without comment, Reyes and Johnson dropped from the port side. Bannon and O'Neil did the same from the other side. Wind and the updraft from the rotors buffered them, twisted them around as they descended. Communication was impossible. Not that there was any time for talking. The descent would only take seconds.

The crew of the *Naeem* opened fire on them immediately.

They were dug in pretty well, Bannon noted, while he and the others were completely exposed. Bannon held the butt of his rifle against his hip, using his elbow to pin it there. With his hand squeezed around the weapon's pistol grip, his finger on the trigger, he shot one-handed while controlling his descent overhead with his other.

Muzzle flash gave their opponents away. Small arms, pistols. No automatic weapons.

Bannon counted six men in all, shooting from three positions.

He aimed at a dark figure crouched behind a red steel cargo container. With a squeeze of the trigger, the figure fell back, shooting off a short burst of gunfire. Bullets whizzed by Bannon's ear. He tracked another figure lying under a canvas-covered lift boat. Bannon's rounds sparked across the metal deck, looking like a line of firecrackers. The prone figure jerked and twisted onto his side. His gun fell silent.

Johnson and Reyes exchanged gunfire with three men they had pinned down along the port railing. Bannon swung the barrel of his weapon around, about to give them an assist, when behind him, O'Neil cried out. Instinctively, Bannon knew the kid had been hit.

The shooter ran across the deck directly under them. A rifle pointed straight up. He fired blindly into the sky as he ran. Bannon put him down with a squeeze of the trigger.

The team landed.

Bannon quickly released his gear. Then twisted around to tend to O'Neil.

The young man was having trouble disconnecting from his line. He was only using one hand. His other arm hung limp, the sleeve of his jumpsuit wet with blood. He'd taken a round in the arm. The others had disconnected successfully. Johnson and Reyes scurried for cover, returning fire to keep the last remaining shooters pinned down.

The chopper jerked upward suddenly.

From the corner of his eye, Bannon saw why.

A crewman had climbed on top of a cargo container. He knelt on one knee, cradling a rocket launcher on his shoulder. The sights were flipped up. He tracked the chopper with the weapon and fired.

McMurphy banked hard to port, still rising. The chopper whip shot around in a spin. The rocket-launched missile streaked past the tail rotor, just missing it. A narrow escape by McMurphy, but O'Neil was still attached to his line. The maneuver had jerked the young seaman across the deck.

Bannon scrambled and dove for him.

He caught him, wrapping his arms around the man's waist. Together, the chopper dragged them across the deck as it continued to rise and turn to avoid a second missile. In seconds, they'd be slammed against the ship's railing. Bannon tried to release O'Neil's harness, but the tension on the line made that impossible.

Still holding O'Neil by his vest, Bannon reached for the dive knife strapped to his calf. He unsnapped the sheath with his thumb and pulled the knife. He swung the blade at the rappelling line. The sharp edge cut deep but didn't slice entirely through.

With a downward swipe, Bannon cut at it again. This time, the line snapped.

The chopper pulled away.

Clutching each other in a tight bear hug, Bannon and O'Neil tumbled across the deck like they'd been shot from a cannon. They slammed into the metal gunwale. Bannon took the brunt of the crash. He hit his head and saw stars. His breath exploded from his lungs. He grunted. O'Neil groaned.

Bannon opened his arms, letting O'Neil spill from his grasp.

"Let's not ever do that again," Bannon said between wheezing gasps.

Breathless, O'Neil said, "Agreed, sir."

Bannon heard the continual pop of gunfire.

Johnson and Reyes were crouched behind tarp-covered cargo strapped to wooden pallets. The man who had launched the shoulder-fired missiles was dead. His body lay draped over the edge of the container. Amid the sound of dropping guns, the rest of the welcoming committee gave up the fight and retreated. Johnson glanced over at Bannon with a wide grin.

"Five down," Johnson reported. "Last one's high-tailing it out now. You good, sir?"

Bannon raised a hand, groaned, and gave him a thumbs up. Through clenched teeth, he said, "Peachy."

CHAPTER TWO

BANNON GOT TO HIS feet as McMurphy landed the Jayhawk on the deck. Johnson and Reyes took up cover positions, watchful should any hostiles return. The chopper's skids touched down. The rotors slowed and McMurphy climbed out of the cockpit. He took his helmet off and tossed it on the pilot seat. With a grin, he said, "That wasn't so bad."

O'Neil sat on the deck with his back to the gunwale. He held his bloody arm in his lap. He looked at Bannon. "Can I shoot him, sir?"

Reyes grabbed a first aid kit from the chopper and field-dressed O'Neil's wound while Johnson kept an eye out for returning crewmembers. McMurphy strapped on his Beretta M9, grabbed an M16, and a few spare magazines.

"Ready?" he asked.

Bannon checked his dive watch, an Omega Seamaster, one of the only things left from his childhood. "The *Bowman* is ten minutes out, Chief. Do what you can to round up the crew. Skyjack and I'll secure the bridge. You and your men shut down the engine room."

"Yes, sir," Johnson said.

Bannon turned to O'Neil. "You up for finishing the mission, seaman?"

Reyes helped pull O'Neil to his feet. "Try and stop me, sir."

Bannon clasped the shoulder of his uninjured arm. "Good man. Let's move out."

Crouched, he ran across the deck toward the accommodation section. McMurphy fell in step behind him. Johnson barked orders to his men, directing them to the nearest passageway that would lead them below deck.

"You got a plan?" McMurphy called out.

"Nope." Bannon reached the accommodation section. It rose four stories from the *Naeem's* main deck. Attached to the port and starboard sides were exterior metal stairwells. They resembled a building's fire escape but were painted battleship gray, not black. Their boots hitting the metal treads clanged loudly as they clamored up the steps. Stealth wasn't a concern.

Bannon reached the bridge door at the top level first. His .45 clutched in two hands, he waited half a beat for McMurphy to join him. Huffing, McMurphy threw his back to the wall on the opposite side of the door. He held his Sig in two hands and nodded his readiness.

Bannon charged through the door. "U.S. Coast Guard. Hands where I can see 'em!"

There were three men inside.

The captain was a thin man with dark Middle Eastern features, a narrow face, and white two-day stubble. He wore a light blue shirt with black shoulder board epilates. He held his hands high in the air, a walkie-talkie in one. Two crewmen sitting in chairs near the bridge controls did the same. Bannon crossed the room and patted the captain down while McMurphy circled the console and loomed over the two frightened men.

"On your feet. Stand up." He repeated the command. "*Kharē hō jā'ō!*"

The men stood and put their hands on their heads. McMurphy patted them down. "They're clean."

"We are a simple merchant ship," the captain said. "Of course, we have no weapons."

"No?" Bannon asked. "What was your crew using to shoot us out of the sky? Water pistols?"

"They are not my crew," the captain insisted. "I was forced to bring them on board."

Bannon didn't believe a word of that. He pushed the captain around the console to join the others. "What's your name?"

"I am Captain Karim Amar. A legitimate ship's captain in the employ of the Oceanport Shipping Company from Durban, South Africa."

"And I'm Santa Claus," McMurphy said.

"Skyjack, bring us to all stop." To Amar, Bannon said, "You're under suspicion for transporting dangerous cargo into the United States. I want to know what it is."

"I don't know what you mean."

Bannon shoved him into a chair. "Don't play games with me. What is it?"

"No games. I swear. I do not know what you speak of. We have no dangerous cargo. You can check our manifest. It is on the computer." He started to get up, but Bannon pushed him back down in the chair.

"Tell me," Bannon said. "What is it?"

The bridge had a broad one-hundred-and-eighty-degree view high over the ship's midsection and bow deck of the surrounding ocean. Before the captain could answer Bannon, McMurphy called out, "The *Bowman's* making its approach."

"You got these three?" Bannon asked.

"In my sleep. Where are you going?"

"To take a look around." Bannon slipped out the door and, using the metal railings slid down the four flights of stairs to the deck below. There, he ducked through a passageway and proceeded into the bowels of the ship. He was curious about what the *Naeem* was transporting and why Grayson had been so cagey about it.

Familiar with the basic layout of a dry goods hauler, Bannon made his way quickly to the forward cargo holds. The low, cramped corridors were eerily quiet. His footfalls echoed loudly. The normal hustle of crewmen going about their day was absent as the companionways were void of people. Had Chief Johnson and his men been that good at clearing the ship? Or had the crew of the *Naeem* seen the writing on the walls and surrendered without further resistance?

Either way, it didn't matter.

He could feel the ship slowing down. The vibration from the engines through the metal decking had ceased. The *Bowman* would be slipping up alongside the *Naeem* any minute. Dozens of Coast Guardsmen would be aboard, securing the ship from stem to stern. The contraband, whatever it was, would be found. The threat it posed had been neutralized.

Still, Bannon's curiosity sent him deeper into the holds. He wanted to know what they were smuggling into the U.S. What dastardly plan had been hatched, even if they had successfully thwarted it?

A bullet plinked off the bulkhead inches from his head. The gunfire boomed in the narrow chamber. He ducked, though his instinctive reaction had little to do with not getting shot. He had the shooter's bad aim to thank for that.

He drew his .45 and jogged down the corridor toward where the shot came from, crouched and a hell of a lot more cautious than he'd been minutes earlier. He heard footsteps running on the metal plates ahead. The sound reverberated in the metal corridor. He caught sight of a figure in an all-black outfit darting through a passageway and into a cargo hold up ahead.

He reached the open passageway and stepped through.

He was rewarded with a kick in the gut that tumbled him back into the corridor. He landed on his backside with a grunt. His already bruised ribs voiced their protest at the abuse.

The figure, clad in black slacks and a billowing black top, leaped through the open passageway holding a pistol aimed at Bannon's face in two gloved hands. "Who are you?"

Bannon hesitated for two reasons. First, realizing his adversary was a woman. Like the captain, she had dark Middle Eastern features. Her long black hair was loose and a wavy mess. She wore a black shawl that had covered her head but now only draped her shoulders. Loose bangs covered her forehead. She brushed the hair from her face. The stern look in her green eyes told him she'd have no problem pulling the trigger.

But what struck Bannon and caused him to freeze was the woman's more than passing resemblance to Tarakesh Sardana, his co-worker and long-time friend.

As time slowed around him, the woman's eyes narrowed. Bannon could hear the creak of her slim, black leather gloves as she tightened her grip around the gun as she began to squeeze the trigger. He twisted to his right and savagely swung his leg to the left, kicking the weapon from his would-be assassin's hands as it went off. The bullet struck a pipe, releasing a surge of hot steam near his head. That was two close calls, he thought. Two too many. The woman's gun went flying. It clattered into the bulkhead and skidded out of reach of both of them.

Before the woman had a chance to react, Bannon kicked his foot straight out, crippling her knee. It popped. She cried out and went down on her good knee. He scrambled to his feet but was quickly doubled when she swung her arm up, delivering a vicious karate chop to his manhood. He cupped himself and dropped to his knees. The woman swung a fist at his face. He blocked it with his arm. She connected with a follow-up punch that landed from the opposite side.

Between the cheap shot and the well-placed punch to his jaw, Bannon saw stars—again. He twisted, putting his arm out to arrest his fall. He spit blood and cursed.

The woman used the open passageway to pull herself up to her feet. She turned and awkwardly limped into the cargo hold.

"You've got to be kidding me." Bannon scrambled to his feet and hobbled after her.

The hold was filled with cars. Rows of them, parked. Brand new luxury BMWs.

He lost sight of the woman for a moment but picked her up again as she darted out from behind the front fender of a black BMW M6 Hurricane. He ran after her, if you could call it that. More of a hobbling shuffle as he pushed off the fender of car after car. He winced with each aching step he took. Still, he closed the gap between them relatively quickly. Fortunately, her injured knee slowed her down way more than his did him.

At the far passageway, he grabbed her by the shoulder and spun her around. "End of the line."

"Unhand me!"

She threw a straight jab aimed at his throat. Her knuckles slammed into the side of his neck as he turned, avoiding the worst of the punch. It still hurt like hell.

He lashed out and grabbed her by the throat. He drove her back, slamming her into the bulkhead behind them. She hit the wall with a thud. She grunted. Still, she swung her arms and kicked at him like a wild beast. With his free hand, he blocked her swinging arms. By twisting his hips as quickly as she could kick, his thighs absorbed the worst of her ferocious footwork.

He tightened his grip on her throat and shook her. "Settle down. I don't want to hurt you."

She snarled. Her eyes began to bulge.

"Quit it. It's over." Bannon struggled to keep her pinned against the wall while not getting his bell—or other parts of his anatomy—rung a second time. He had no zip ties or handcuffs, no way to secure her except by physical restraint.

From the far side of the cargo hold, he heard the rushed footfalls and the clicking military equipment made when soldiers rushed into a space, looking to secure it. The question was, were they his people or members of Amar's crew coming to finish the job they'd started up on the ship's deck?

He risked a glance over the roofs and hoods of the BMWs and smiled with relief.

Tarakesh Sardana led a group of armed, urban-camouflaged Coasties into the room. He gave the woman he held pinned to the bulkhead another look, again struck by the resemblance between his friend and this woman.

Egyptian and in her early thirties, Tarakesh Sardana had dark skin bronzed by the sun. Long, raven black hair, a narrow, straight nose, and a lean physique that was deceptively strong. And a fondness for edged weaponry that had earned her the nickname Blades.

"This way," Tara said to the squad she led.

"About damn time," Bannon complained as he released his hold on his prisoner. He leaned over breathless, holding his hands to his knees.

Tara kept the woman pinned in place with one side of a double-bladed knife pressed to her throat. She fisted the weapon, known as a haladie, holding the bone-carved center grip between its two curved blades. The weapon was a favorite of the *Raput,* India's ancient warrior class known as the samurai of India.

"Who told you to go charging off all by yourself," Tara asked, "without backup?"

Bannon looked up at her and arched an eyebrow, wondering as he often did, who was really in charge between them? Grateful she was on his side, either way. "Good to see you, too, Blades."

"Are you hurt?"

"A few bumps and bruises." Bannon straightened up and winced. "The landing was a little bumpy."

"So I heard." Tara handed the woman off to two Coasties. They pulled her hands behind her back and ratcheted handcuffs around her wrists.

"Which is why you should have waited for the *Bowman* to catch up before you dropped in here guns blazing." The new voice came from behind the remaining Coasties, who parted like the Red Sea—and snapped to attention—for the approaching Secretary of the Department of Homeland Security, Elizabeth Grayson.

A former senator from Louisiana and four-star General in the U.S. Army, Grayson had served the current administration as the Deputy Secretary of Defense for two years before being tapped to head up Homeland Security. A formable woman in her early sixties, she had friends and enemies in equal measure on both sides of the aisle and enough political clout to get stuff done without compromising her position or her principles. That was something Bannon admired in great measure and was probably the single biggest reason he'd agreed to work for her when she'd asked.

"Madam Secretary," Bannon said in greeting. "I take it the rest of the ship's been properly secured." In charge or not, she wouldn't have been allowed aboard the *Naeem* if it hadn't been.

"It has."

"Then the only thing left to do is find this dangerous cargo everyone's so worked up about."

"Which you have done quite admirably, Brice."

Surprised by that, he said, "I have?"

Grayson waved a hand toward the dark-skinned woman, now properly secured. "Allow me to introduce Miss Safiyyah Zayd. She's the reason we're here, Brice. She is the dangerous cargo we're after."

CHAPTER THREE

THE COAST GUARD TOOK control of the *Naeem*. The crewmembers still alive were held under armed guard in one of the cargo holds, the bodies of the dead were covered, and with the *Bowman* providing escort, they altered the ship's original course. Rather than proceed straight to Boston Harbor as scheduled, Secretary Grayson ordered the ship to dock sixty miles north in Portsmouth, New Hampshire.

Back on the *Bowman*, Grayson ordered Bannon to see the medic they'd brought aboard. Along with his objections, he peppered her with questions about the mission, which she refused to answer. She assured him there would be a mission debrief when they reached Portsmouth. With a stern finger, she directed him to sickbay while she commandeered the CO's private cabin and remained behind closed doors the rest of the trip.

After diagnosing Bannon with a possible cracked rib and assuring him he'd still be able to have children, the medic prescribed a few days' rest. Bannon went to the galley for a cup of coffee. There, he found Seaman O'Neil with his arm in a navy blue sling, sitting alone at the long mess table enjoying a glass of orange juice.

With his coffee in hand, Bannon joined the young man.

O'Neil told him the medic had removed the bullet from his arm. "Said it wasn't very deep. Used a pair of tweezers to pluck it right out of there." O'Neil grinned. "Told me the damn thing might've fallen out on its own if we'd let it be."

Bannon doubted that but was glad the kid was okay.

O'Neil said, "Still gotta get checked out by the real docs at the Naval Hospital when we reach port. Otherwise, a clean bill of health."

"That's good to hear. How long you been in the Guard?"

"Less than a year, sir. I'm stationed out of Cape Cod Air Station. It's been a dream of mine since I was a kid."

Bannon smiled at that. To him, the boy was a kid still, barely old enough to drink.

"Where's home?"

"Nebraska."

"The most landlocked state in the country," Bannon said. "Did they have to teach you how to swim at Cape May?"

Training Center Cape May, New Jersey, was the Coast Guard's eight-week boot camp. O'Neil laughed. "Pretty much. Guess that's why I wanted to be on the water so badly. I never had it growing up."

"Well, you did good out there, O'Neil. And now you've got a hell of a war story to tell."

Bannon got to his feet, holding his arm around his ribs as he got up. He patted the kid's shoulder. "You're ever in Hampton Beach, look me up. You can find me at the Keel Haul. First round's on me."

"The Keel Haul, sir?"

31

"It's my bar." At O'Neil's quizzical expression, he added, "It's a long story. Take care of yourself, Seaman."

"Yes, sir." Before Bannon reached the door, O'Neil called out, "Commander?"

Bannon turned.

"Thank you, sir. You saved my life out there today."

"And you'll do the same for the next guy."

O'Neil grinned. "You can count on it, sir."

Bannon smiled. "I'm sure I can."

After leaving O'Neil to go up on deck, Bannon bumped into Chief Petty Officer Johnson exiting the pilothouse. The Chief had changed from his tactical gear and jumpsuit to his ODU, the solid, dark blue operation dress uniform that was standard dress for the Coasties. He wore a bush-style Boonie hat rather than the regulation baseball-style ball cap. They had gained in popularity in recent years. A folded pair of sunglasses hung from his left breast pocket.

"Commander."

"Hey, Chief." Bannon shook the man's hand. "Glad I ran into you. Wanted a chance to thank you again. You and your men did good work out there."

"Our pleasure, sir."

"No problems securing the rest of the ship?"

"None at all." He grinned. "Once word spread about what took place on the deck, the rest of the crew fell all over themselves trying to surrender after that."

"How many?"

"Twenty-two, not counting the five dead on deck. That includes the captain and his two-man bridge crew."

Bannon clasped the man on the shoulder. "Like I said, good work all around."

"Thank you. May I ask you a question, sir?"

"Sure, Chief. What is it?"

"I heard…was just wondering if it was true. You commanded a DOG unit?" He added, "Back in the day."

Johnson was referring to the Deployable Operations Group. A command created over a decade earlier. They'd been the Coast Guard's answer to the Army's Special Forces and the Navy's Seal program, born out of the aftermath of 9/11 to assist in the War on Terror. They ran high-risk, high-profile counter-terrorism missions, dive operations, and shipboard takedowns. They conducted thousands of threat assessments involving nuclear, biological, and chemical concerns and combatted Middle Eastern piracy operations overseas. The group had been decommissioned after six years. That had been the catalyst for Bannon to put in his papers and retire from the full-time Guard.

"I did. Why?"

Johnson shook his head and grinned. He shook Bannon's hand again. "No reason. It's just I admired those guys. What they, what you, all did. I was bummed when I heard they decommissioned the command."

"Me, too, but what you're doing in MSST isn't much different."

"No, I suppose not," Johnson said. Then he smiled. "Except the work you all did, that was the stuff of legends."

Bannon didn't see it that way. "Just a bunch of Coasties doing our jobs."

"If you say so, sir. Anyway, I just wanted to say we enjoyed working with you today. If you ever find yourself in need of MSST support again, just give us a holler. It's been an honor."

"Same goes for me, Chief."

After watching Johnson disappear inside the pilothouse, Bannon smiled and slipped on a pair of Ray-Bans. He spent the rest of the trip on the bow deck, enjoying the warm sun on his skin, the spritz of cool water, and the salty breeze gently blowing through his hair. Nothing made him feel more alive than when he was on the open water. This was as close to heaven on Earth as it got.

But his questions nagged at him, kept him from fully enjoying the sun and sea. Who was this Safiyyah Zayd? Why was she so important? What made her a terrorist threat? Why had Grayson kept them in the dark about their real objection?

The two ships entered Piscataqua River and slipped past the Portsmouth Harbor lighthouse on New Castle Island. A quintessential New England coastal fixture, the fifty-five-foot, white cylindrical tower had stood quiet sentry in one form or another on that rocky shoal since 1771. Fort Constitution, a military outpost dating back to the Revolution, was close to the lighthouse. It was a state historical site, sharing real estate with the Portsmouth Harbor Coast Guard Station.

They were to dock alongside the wharf extending out from Sullivan Lane. It would be closed to civilian boaters for however long they'd be there. Bannon wondered how long that would be.

"Hey." McMurphy joined him on deck, a thick cigar jammed in the corner of his mouth. He carried two Styrofoam cups. He handed one to Bannon. "Sorry, I bounced you guys around like that today."

"Sorry they were shooting rocket-launched missiles at you."

McMurphy shrugged. "Not the first time, won't be the last."

Bannon laughed. "Probably not."

"Gotta ask. What's the deal with that chick? She looks like she could be Blades' twin sister."

"No clue. And Grayson's not talking."

"Typical bureaucrat." McMurphy puffed out a cloud of cigar smoke. "When we started this thing way back when. She was supposed to be different. Guess not."

"That's a little harsh. She's not like that bunch in Washington, you know that."

"You're right. She's not," McMurphy said, amending his stance. "I just hate being kept in the dark. At least she's been in the trenches like the rest of us. Maybe the rest of 'em are rubbing off on her. Like being a bureaucrat's contagious."

Bannon hoped that wasn't the case, though he'd seen it before. "It sure does feel like she's holding something back. That's not like her." He tried to put a positive spin on it. "I'm sure she'll explain it all at the debrief." Bannon mulled it over more before adding, "She's never steered us wrong before."

But was he trying to convince McMurphy or himself?

"I'll give you that. But remember, there's a first time for everything."

Bannon grinned. "Careful. Your pessimism's showing, old friend."

"Other than you and Blades, my pessimism's the only thing that's never let me down."

"I'll drink to that." Bannon tipped the coffee cup back and drank. He blinked and sputtered. "Jesus, Skyjack. This isn't coffee."

McMurphy laughed. It was straight Kentucky bourbon. "Never said it was."

"Guard vessels are supposed to be dry." No pun intended.

"When did that ever stop me, brother?"

The man had a point. Never had Bannon met a bigger rule-breaker than Skyjack McMurphy. The whole time Bannon had known him, it seemed as if the man went out of his way to thumb his nose at authority. Like it was a source of amusement for him, a game to see how much he could get away with. Be that as it may, Bannon had also never met a more skilled pilot, a more able seaman, or a more compassionate man than Skyjack McMurphy either. He trusted the man with his life. And had a dozen times over.

McMurphy puffed and squinted up at the sun as seagulls circled overhead and cawed. "So, while you're singing Lizzy's praises, riddle me this. If she's not hiding something important from us, why's the debriefing at the FBI offices in the federal building on Daniel Street?"

"The FBI's involved?"

"It's what I hear." McMurphy looked around the deck as if he'd lost something. "And by the way, where the hell's Blades been all this time?"

CHAPTER FOUR

AN HOUR AFTER THE *Bowman* and *Naeem* docked, Bannon and McMurphy returned to the main deck freshly showered, shaved, and changed into civilian clothes. For Bannon, that meant a black Polo shirt, khakis, and boat shoes. McMurphy wore white painter's pants, an untucked plaid work shirt, unbuttoned and loose, and a novelty T-shirt, one of the thousands he seemed to own. This one was gray with a Jolly Rogers pirate flag and read: *Yo Ho Yo Ho. A Drunken Life for Me.*

The *Bowman's* captain assigned a seaman to drive them into town. They were told Grayson and Tara would meet up with them there. Their driver dropped them off at the Thomas J. McIntyre Federal Building on Daniel Street in downtown Portsmouth. After being directed through the metal detectors, they were met by a large, humorless man in a dark suit. A fed. He again checked their IDs before stoically nodding. "Follow me."

Bannon and McMurphy exchanged glances behind the man's back.

McMurphy leaned closer and whispered, "Is he Agent J or K?"

"Which one's the funny one?" Bannon asked.

"J."

"Then this is K. Definitely."

"Or Lurch from the Addams Family." McMurphy lowered his voice and made it very deep. "You rang?"

Bannon could barely suppress his laughter.

They were taken to a second-floor conference room. No one else was inside.

"The others will join you shortly," Lurch said.

"What others? What's going on?" Bannon asked.

The man left without answering, quietly closing the door behind him.

McMurphy made a beeline to the buffet of sandwiches, pastries, and desserts set out on the counter in the back. He grabbed two sandwiches and sucked a smear of mustard off his thumb before wrapping his mouth around a turkey, ham, lettuce, and tomato on rye. "You want something to eat? A coffee?"

"What I want are answers."

The door opened behind him. Secretary Grayson strolled into the room. "And you will have them." She sat down at the head of the long table. "I'll have a coffee, black. Thank you, Chief."

Behind her, another man wearing a dark suit and white dress shirt strolled in. As much a uniform for the FBI as the ODUs were for the Coast Guard, Bannon thought. The man carried several file folders under his arm. He shut the door and placed the files on the table to Grayson's left.

"Have a seat, Brice," Grayson said as McMurphy placed a coffee in front of her.

McMurphy took a seat next to Bannon, who had pulled out a chair to Grayson's right. McMurphy slid a hot coffee over to him and dug into a second sandwich. The man had an insatiable appetite.

The suit gave the buffet spread in the back a longing look but remained seated.

"Let's begin," Grayson said. "First, I want to introduce you both to Agent Daniel Pierce. Dan's the Special Agent in Charge of the FBI's Boston field office."

He nodded sternly. "Gentlemen."

McMurphy continued to eat, seemingly ignoring the conversation and the man.

"What's the FBI got to do with this, Madam Secretary?" Bannon asked. The Coast Guard operated under the jurisdiction of the Department of Homeland Security. The FBI was part of the Justice Department. Not that the two never cooperated…

"This situation was first brought to our attention by the FBI, so I'll let Dan fill you in on the details. But, before he does, let me just say, gentlemen, based on the Intel we've gathered and the increased chatter we're hearing, we suspect an imminent terrorist attack on U.S. soil. Something on the scale of 9/11 or worse if we don't stop it."

That got Bannon's attention. Even McMurphy put his sandwich down and listened.

Grayson went on. "Today's capture of the *MV Naeem* is a crucial step toward doing just that."

The two men gave Agent Pierce their undivided attention.

"Gentlemen, do you remember Farouk al-Kalil?"

Bannon spoke up. "That kid last year who tried to detonate an SUV full of explosives in front of the Javits Center."

"And when that didn't work, he blew himself up, killing three other people," McMurphy added.

Pierce nodded. "And wounded twelve more. Our joint task force on terrorism, working in conjunction with the NYPD, discovered al-Kalil was part of a terror organization with cells operating in New York City and Boston."

"According to the news, al-Kalil was a lone wolf. They reported he had no affiliations," Bannon said.

"A story we planted."

"More fake news." McMurphy shook his head and resumed eating.

"There was no upside to revealing that information to the public," Pierce said defensively. "By not disclosing what we knew, we hoped the cells would continue to operate with their guard down."

"I'm guessing that didn't happen," Bannon said.

"One thing terror cells have learned to do very well is to operate autonomously. These cells appear to be better at it than most," Pierce admitted. "Whenever we get close to identifying someone who might be involved with them, they leave the country, disappear, or end up dead."

"Translation," McMurphy said around a mouthful of sandwich. "You've got bupkis."

"Right," Pierce admitted. "We've continued to monitor several persons of interest. People we believe are affiliated with one cell or another without much luck. Until six months ago. We got a lead. Increased chatter about this woman." Pierce activated the room's smart board. A younger headshot of the woman Bannon had apprehended on the *Naeem* appeared on the screen behind Grayson. The woman wore a white lab coat and a smile.

"This is Safiyyah Zayd," Pierce said, "and thanks to your good efforts today, she's now in federal custody."

"Who is she?" Bannon got up and went to the coffee urn.

As Pierce spoke, Bannon filled up three cups and returned, giving one to Grayson and one to McMurphy. Pierce watched him distribute the cups like a puppy eyeing his food bowl before his owner set it down. Bannon paced the length of the room, listening. He sipped from the third cup. Grayson sat half-listening, typing messages into her phone and sipping her coffee. She'd heard all this before.

"Miss Zayd is single, thirty-two years old, and the daughter of a prominent lieutenant general in her country's Army. He's currently the commander of the southern command. Her mother was a teacher who was killed along with thirteen other men, women, and children when the school she worked at was destroyed in a bombing raid several years ago. Dozens of others were maimed and seriously injured.

"Miss Zayd is highly educated. She went to the University of Glasgow and graduated from MIT here in the States with computer science and electrical engineering degrees."

"Pretty and smart," McMurphy said. "Usually my kind of woman."

"Don't forget dangerous," Bannon said. His sensitive parts still ached.

41

"Which is why she is of interest to us," Pierce said.

"She was radicalized as a result of her mother's death," Bannon guessed. "She blames the U.S. or at least the allied coalition for killing her."

"If that's true," Pierce said, "she didn't get there by the usual means. After attending MIT, Zayd worked at the Grandville National Laboratory, a research and development center in Ohio, before returning to her country to take a position at NSEADC."

"Her government's National Space Exploration and Development Center," Grayson said without looking up from her phone.

"What did she do there?" Bannon asked.

"Specifically, we don't know," Pierce said. "Even if we did, it would probably be over all our heads. We do know she was assigned to their aerospace and avionics engineering division. In layman's terms I understand, she worked on aircraft and spaceships."

"Not your typical terrorist CV," Bannon said.

"It gets stranger from there." Pierce glanced at the coffee urn but remained seated. "Around the time al-Kalil was doing his thing in New York—badly—Zayd went missing. She left work one evening, like normal. And never made it home. Considering her father's powerful position and the work she did for NSEDC, the assumption was she'd been kidnapped, but no ransom demands were ever made. Our agents on the ground—FBI, CIA, even the NYPD Intel group—got wind of it. We suspected espionage, either politically or corporate motivated. From what little we could gather, Zayd's work involved some high-level, cutting-edge technology."

"What kind of technology?"

Pierce shrugged. "Their government wouldn't tell us, citing state secrets. We offered investigative assistance—"

"Not wanting to pass up an opportunity to peek behind the curtain," McMurphy said, "by spying on them."

"In the spirit of cooperation," Pierce countered. "They declined our offer. On our best days, the relationship between our two countries is…complicated. Even previously established cooperative channels have dried up. They clammed up tighter than usual. They assured us nothing had been stolen. That Miss Zayd's disappearance was no cause for concern. Simply an internal matter and they would treat it as such. Thanks, but no thanks.

"That changed six months ago. Surveillance photos picked her up at a meeting in Nangarhar, on the Afghan border, with a group of suspected enemy combatants. One of the people she met with was a man named Yusufi Nawab. Born and raised in Boston, an American citizen, he was a person of interest who we suspected had connections to the Boston terror cell al-Kalil also had ties to. He became aware of our interest in him and fled to Afghanistan."

Bannon asked, "Where is he now?"

"After attending the meeting with Zayd, he was killed in an airstrike." Pierce added, "According to military authorities, his body's never been identified. Since then, Zayd went to ground. Again. But we've picked up increased chatter between overseas and the cells in Boston and New York. Talk of something big in the works. We didn't know where or when, but my counterparts assigned in that part of the world have been putting pressure on their resources for any information they can get. Through those efforts, we learned an important asset from Northern Africa was coming to the States. It wasn't until the *Naeem* set sail—"

"It's not a sailboat," McMurphy said, picking through his fruit salad with a plastic fork.

"You know what I meant."

"Left port," McMurphy said, popping a cube of watermelon into his mouth and chewing.

"Fine, left port that we learned the asset was Zayd. That she was being brought here."

"For what purpose?" Bannon asked.

"We don't know." Pierce looked from Bannon to McMurphy. "But as the Madam Secretary said, whatever it is, it's going to happen here, and it's going to be big."

"And…" Grayson looked up, rejoining the conversation. "Safiyyah Zayd is an important part of it."

"Fine," Bannon said, finishing his coffee. "We have Zayd. Let's make her talk."

"We will," Grayson said, setting aside her phone. "But that's not why you two are here."

Finally, Bannon thought. "Why are we here?"

"I'm surprised you haven't figured it out yet, Brice." She glanced over her shoulder at the image on the screen. Bannon followed her glance and was still slow to put it together.

When he did, he shook his head. "No."

Without looking happy about it, Grayson said, "Yes."

McMurphy looked between the two of them. "No. Yes. What? Wanna explain it to the slow kids in the class?"

Bannon answered. "She wants Blades to go undercover. She wants her to become Safiyyah Zayd."

CHAPTER FIVE

"CAN I HAVE A word," Bannon said. "Alone?"

Grayson sighed, probably having anticipated the sidebar request. She rose. To McMurphy and Pierce, she said, "Give us the room, gentlemen."

McMurphy grabbed his coffee cup and wolfed down the last bit of his turkey and ham on rye.

Pierce glanced at the buffet set up in the back and hesitated.

"We'll only be a minute, Agent," Grayson said.

He followed McMurphy toward the door, giving the coffee urn a wistful look. When the door was closed, she said, "Brice, hear me out before you say anything."

Reluctantly, he sat down.

"There's much more to all this than what Pierce reported."

"His secrets or yours?"

"That's not fair."

He'd said the same thing to McMurphy, and they'd both been right. "You're right. But there's a lot you're not telling us. We've never operated like that before, General."

"Because there's a lot I don't know and a lot that's happening very fast."

He took in how tired she looked. The crinkly laugh lines at the corner of her eyes were etched deeper than usual. He saw the lack of sleep under her eyes. Bannon couldn't begin to imagine the sort of strain being the Secretary of Homeland Security put on a person under normal circumstances. That he usually didn't notice was a testament to how strong a woman Elizabeth Grayson was.

This was different. This weighed heavily on her. The last thing he wanted to do was add to her burden. "Okay. Tell me what you have. All of it. Let's see if we can figure it out. Together."

She sat back down and appeared to relax a little. "Everything Pierce said is accurate, as far as it goes, as far as he knows. Miss Zayd's work with NSEDC was beyond classified. Even at the highest levels, we're having trouble determining exactly what projects she worked on or what her specific expertise is. All I get from my closest contacts is the party line Pierce discussed. It's nothing to worry about. An internal matter, easily handled."

"That's what has you worried," Bannon said.

She smiled, appreciating that he read her so well. "We don't know what Safiyyah Zayd was working on, but we know it was cutting-edge, state-of-the-art stuff. We knew that before she went missing."

"You were watching her before all this?"

"Not her. Not specifically."

She didn't say it, nor did Bannon, but he knew. It was NSEDC they had on their radar. "Let's talk to her. Get some answers."

"We will, but there's a lot of moving parts, Brice, and a rapidly closing window to act on. The *Naeem* is due to dock in Boston shortly. When it does, Captain Amar is under orders to bring Zayd to an undisclosed location. Deliver her to a meeting place."

"To meet with whom?"

"We don't know. Our hope is it's with members of the Boston terrorist cell. The one Yusufi Nawab was part of before his unfortunate demise."

"How can the FBI know so little about these groups after all this time? The Javits bombing was over a year ago."

"Because they're careful, Brice. More secretive than any group we've encountered before. That we know as much as we do is a minor miracle in itself." She leaned forward. "Brice, whatever work Zayd did at NSEDC, we fear it's something she's weaponized."

Bannon leaned back heavily in his seat. "According to Pierce, she worked on airplanes or spaceships. What could she possibly have weaponized? We searched the *Naeem*. There's absolutely no contraband aboard at all. Except for her. Maybe we're making too much out of this. She could just want to do her part, strike at the Infidels in their own backyard."

"Let's hope you're right," Grayson said. But he could see in her expression she had her doubts. "What I do know is we haven't heard this much reliable chatter since the Yazidi Bombings that killed nearly eight hundred people in Qahtaniyah and Jazeera."

She took a sip of coffee. "I hope you're right, Brice, but whatever is going on, Tara's our best chance of finding out. We have no other choice."

Bannon looked up at Zayd's image still on the smartboard. There was no denying the resemblance between the two women. It was striking, almost uncanny. "How do we know arranging this meeting is really what Amar's supposed to be doing?"

"He told us. That's where I've been since the *Bowman* docked—interviewing him—and arranging his immunity deal with the U. S. Attorney General's office. It was the only way he would agree to cooperate with us."

"Of course."

"Which is why we have to act fast. We can only delay the *Naeem's* arrival in Boston for so long before we risk raising suspicions. Too long, and whoever Amar and Zayd are to meet might get scared off. We'll lose our opportunity."

Bannon grasped the urgency. "I don't like it. Tara's the most capable woman I've ever met, but she's not trained for this. Going undercover takes a certain skill." He knew. He'd worked several UC operations. Never much liked them. "It's not something you learn by leaping willy-nilly into the deep end."

"And you're too overprotective of your people."

"Damn right, I am," he shot back. "It's how I've kept them alive all these years. How they've kept me alive, too."

"Tara wants to do this."

Frustrated, he said, "Of course she does. That's who she is. She doesn't weigh the risks against the consequences like I do. And even when she does, she ignores them."

Grayson smiled. "Like you do."

"Surely the cell knows Zayd."

"Old photographs. Like us." Grayson pointed at the headshot. "That's from her access card and work ID from the Grandville National Laboratory. She's not been back to the States since she left Ohio years ago. Amar assures us none of the parties have met. He doesn't even know any of them. His contact in Alexandria gave him a burner phone. When he arrives in Boston, he's to turn it on and make a single call. He will be told what to do and where to go at that point."

"How can you know they've never met? How do we know we can trust his word? Who would trust someone they don't know?"

"It's how these cells operate, Brice. With travel bans the way they are, increased border security, and the xenophobic positions so many countries are taking, these people can't travel as freely as they used to. Communication is done through text and email, dark web comment boards, and social media chatrooms. All of it in code. As far as we know, everyone involved on this end is homegrown."

"What do you mean 'homegrown'?"

Grayson sighed. "The war on terror's been waged for so long we're dealing with a second generation of terrorists. American-born Muslims and sympathizers who've never set foot outside the United States are being radicalized, recruited to the cause through the Internet, brainwashed by zealot propaganda and radical fundamentalism."

Bannon pushed his empty coffee cup away. "So, let me get this straight. Based on the word of a sea captain who'll say anything to stay out of prison, we're going to introduce Tara as Zayd to a bunch of people who we have no idea who they are and hope no one has ever met this woman before."

"Yes."

"And Tara's supposed to impersonate an engineering genius. Pretend to be this woman to a group of terrorists who've been so careful that after a full year, the FBI still has little idea of who they are, in the hope they'll reveal their evil plan to her like a supervillain in a bad action flick. So we can come in, scoop them up, and save the day."

"In very simplistic terms, yes."

"I don't think I'm the one being simplistic here," Bannon shot back. "UC operations take time to put together. They can't be slapped together in a day. It's too risky."

"We don't have time, Brice. And we take risks every day. You do risky all the time," Grayson argued. "Why's this any different?"

"Because we're completely in the dark. We have no Intel. We know none of the players. We have zero idea what they're planning." He leaned forward. "And let's say you're right, and Zayd has developed some super-secret space weapon or something. What then? How's Tara supposed to deliver that?"

The conference room door opened. Tarakesh Sardana stepped inside.

"I'll improvise." She smiled and went straight to the back. "Coffee, anyone?"

CHAPTER SIX

AFTER GETTING KICKED OUT, McMurphy and Pierce stood in the hallway outside the conference room door. They were alone with a row of unoccupied cubicles. The floor had been cleared of personnel to keep information about the operation contained to need-to-know. McMurphy leaned casually against a filing cabinet, the top covered with leafy green potted plants.

"I got a call from my director at home last night," Pierce said.

McMurphy gave him a look. It was one of those silent, *why are you talking to me*, looks. He sipped his coffee. Pierce kept talking.

"He told me to expect a call from Grayson. Told me to fill her in on everything we knew about al-Kalil and the cells we'd connected him to."

"Must've been a short conversation."

Pierce's face got red. "Ha. Ha. He told me to cooperate fully. Give her anything she needs. Support, intel, assets."

"Let me get this right. You needed to be specifically told to cooperate with one of your own government agencies?"

"What's your problem with the Bureau, man?"

"I don't have a problem with the Bureau, specifically. My problem's with bureau-*crats* and, by extension, the agencies and the field agents that work for them. The ones who play games with people's lives by needlessly holding on to secrets like they're a stack of Atlantic City blackjack chips. Information is power, right? Whoever has the information controls the board, right? Meanwhile, good people end up dead because of it. I've been through it too many times. Buried too many friends because of it, but hey, don't take it personally."

Pierce cleared his throat, looking a little shell-shocked. "She told me I'd be working with the two of you. You and Bannon."

"Why are you telling me this?" McMurphy asked.

"Because she told me all about you two."

"Oh, I doubt that." McMurphy sipped his cup, looking bored because he was.

"Told me Bannon had fifteen years in the Coast Guard. That you'd been in even longer. She said you both spent much of that time in the sandbox." The Middle East. "Tell you the truth, I didn't even know the Guard was there."

"We were. They still are."

"What's the Coast Guard doing in the desert?"

"There's a gulf."

"The Persian Gulf?"

"You get a gold geography star, Pierce." McMurphy sucked down the last of his coffee, wishing he'd had a chance to doctor it up with some whiskey. "Did you get a chance to enjoy the hospitalities offered us by our Middle Eastern friends?"

"No. I joined the FBI straight out of college. Mostly, I've been in anti-terrorism, but stateside the whole time."

"You're not missing anything."

"Sounds like you two saw a lot of action with that Deployable Operations Group you were part of."

"We did our jobs." McMurphy wondered if this was going somewhere, but more importantly, he hoped Pierce would just shut up.

"Which brings me to what I really want to ask."

McMurphy didn't respond, but that didn't deter Pierce.

"According to what I could dig up, you both retired from active duty. Bannon runs a hole-in-the-wall bar in Hampton Beach. And you, you're…"

"Between employment opportunities."

"Okay, good way to put it. So, what are the two of you doing here, a part of this?"

"Drew the short straw, I guess."

"Seriously."

McMurphy sighed. "We're active reserve." He gave Pierce the standard weekend warrior pitch made by the reserves and National Guard. "We get to go have fun on weekends and two weeks during the summer."

But the truth was much more than that.

Bannon and McMurphy had worked for years together as part of the DOG command. They'd spent many a day carrying out operations in Iraq, Afghanistan, and Pakistan, as Pierce had said, but that was just the tip of the iceberg. They'd also carried out covert missions in places around the world, and stateside, too. The Coast Guard was the only military organization, other than the National Guard, authorized to operate on American soil. Drug cartels, pirates and smugglers, white supremacist groups, and even human traffickers kept them busy.

But all that came to an end when the Commandant of the Coast Guard decommissioned the program and disbanded the Deployable Operations Group. McMurphy, Bannon, and the others in the group were offered their choice of posts anywhere in the Pacific or Atlantic commands. And given the thanks of a grateful nation for their service.

Many of the men and women in the unit decided to stay in the Guard. They took posts in California, Alaska, Florida, the Mid-Atlantic region, and some in the Northeast. A few even returned to the Persian Gulf, where the Guard continued to maintain a presence.

Bannon resigned his commission. McMurphy gave up his Chief Warrant Officer bars.

That was until Elizabeth Grayson approached Bannon with a deal he couldn't refuse.

The former senator from Louisiana and retired four-star General had come up with a harebrained scheme a few years ago that she'd actually managed to sell the President on. She wanted to create a small team of specially trained, highly skilled operatives for unique, sensitive, and, if necessary, secret missions outside the normal channels of either Homeland Security or the Department of Defense.

"Black ops," Bannon had said when she asked him to lead it.

"Secret, but not black ops," she said. "Rather a small, efficient, and qualified team able to respond and investigate specific, targeted threats to the homeland, threats that can't be effectively handled by standard operating means or normal military response."

"Sounds a lot like black ops to me," Bannon said, wanting no part of it.

"No," she insisted. "I'm talking about a single unit that's small enough and nimble enough to get the job done. Maybe actually make a real difference in this scary world of ours."

Lizzy continued her pitch, laying out her plan, and after a lot of negotiating, including Bannon's demands that he be allowed to choose his own people without interference or influence. That any and all Homeland Security and DOD assets be made immediately available to him whenever necessary. And finally, he wanted a direct reporting line to her and no one else.

She agreed to his terms.

Then, operating from a position of strength, Bannon pressed for one more demand. He'd do it only if he and his team operated on an on-call, as-needed basis. He'd had enough of sitting around bases and on ships twiddling his thumbs with nothing to do, waiting to be called into action. He'd spent too much downtime playing cards and endlessly training, not for the purpose of staying sharp, which he believed in, but to fill up the monotonous hours between assignments when command had nothing better for his team to do.

"What did you have in mind?" Grayson asked.

Thus, the Keel Haul, a dream of his since he was a kid, became a reality. To own and run a little seaside bar in his off time. To his surprise, Grayson not only agreed, but she endorsed the idea wholeheartedly. And they had a deal.

Bannon's little group of Homeland Security troubleshooters would be known to only a few. Besides Grayson in her role as Secretary of Homeland Security, the Secretary of Defense was on board and the President of the United States. Others would be brought in or learn of their existence on an as-needed basis.

The first person Bannon talked to after coming to terms with Grayson had been McMurphy. He asked his old friend of nearly fifteen years if he wanted in.

"Fulltime pay and military benefits for a part-time gig kicking ass and taking names," McMurphy said. "Where do I sign up?"

Tarakesh Sardana became Bannon's second recruit. An ad hoc member of their DOG operation, though she wasn't Coast Guard or even an American citizen. She came stateside after that unit was decommissioned. This assignment, of course, was tailor-made for her particular skill set. She readily joined in.

When not working to save the world—or at least the homeland—Tara tended bar at the Keel Haul. The best thing about the whole arrangement for McMurphy was he got to hang out with the two of them at the Keel Haul, *and* he got to drink for free.

Of course, McMurphy told Pierce none of this.

"You're weekend warriors," Pierce said. "That's all you're going to say?"

McMurphy shrugged and dropped his empty cup into an empty wastepaper basket. It hit the bottom with a hollow metal thunk.

Tara strolled down the corridor. She'd changed into low-cut black boots, tight-fitting blue jeans, and a deep purple top. She wore her black hair loose and bouncy around her shoulders. Her dusky skin was flawless, and McMurphy thought she had the greatest cheekbones in the world. Her haladie was strapped to her left hip, where it perfectly balanced the Sig P229 9mm holstered on her right side.

"John," she said, closing the distance to the two men.

"This is Agent Pierce, FBI," McMurphy told her.

"Daniel." The agent offered her his hand. "My friends call me Dan."

She shook his hand. "Agent."

McMurphy grinned.

"Um, speaking of names," Pierce said, which nobody was. He glanced at McMurphy. "How come they call you Skyjack?"

"Tell him," Tara said.

"No."

She let out an exasperated sigh. "He doesn't like talking about it, but years ago, stationed in Hawaii, he hijacked Marine One."

"The President's helicopter?"

"He wasn't on it at the time," McMurphy said.

Pierce blinked. "Hardly the point. My God, man, why?"

McMurphy didn't answer, so Tara did. "He'd been tossed in the brig, sleeping off a drunken and disorderly from the night before. When they let him out that evening, he was late."

Pierce asked, "Late for what?"

"A date," McMurphy admitted. "She was waiting for me on the big island."

"A date? You risked arrest, a court-martial, your entire military career, for a date?"

"If you'd ever seen Arielle Dubois, you'd never ask that question." He pursed his lips and kissed his fingertips the way the French do. "Perfection."

Tara rolled her eyes. "They inside?"

"Yeah. Mom and Dad kicked us out so they could fight," McMurphy said.

"We don't have time for this." Tara crossed the space and listened for a minute. Without knocking, she opened the door and went inside.

With the door left open, McMurphy shrugged and followed her lead, hearing her say, "I'll improvise. Coffee, anyone?"

Pierce fell in step beside him. He leaned in close to McMurphy and whispered, "Someday, you've got to tell me her story."

"Her story?" McMurphy said. "Danny-boy, Blades doesn't have a story. She's the whole damn library."

CHAPTER SEVEN

NIGHT. SIX HOURS LATER.

Bannon, McMurphy, and Peirce were on the rooftop of a new warehouse facility being built overlooking a low building across an empty parking lot. Lying prone in the roof gravel behind the low parapet, they were once again in tactical gear. This time, in FBI-provided gear, their jumpsuits were urban black. McMurphy had a black wool cap pulled low over his red hair. Each man had their sidearm strapped low on their thigh. For Bannon, it was his .45. McMurphy carried a Sig P229. Pierce favored a Springfield Armory Professional Model 1911 .45. He'd also brought along a Colt M4 carbine.

All three men were looking through binoculars. The building across the way was a single-story, strip mall-style structure subdivided into several storefronts. Two were unoccupied. The others were a marine parts store, a construction rental place, and a liquor store. They were closed and the lights were out. One car was parked out front.

As soon as they'd taken up their positions, Pierce called in the license plate. The car belonged to the liquor store owner. He'd owned the business for the last seven years and was a Marine Corp vet with a spotless record. A few minutes later, they watched an older man exit the liquor store. He locked up the store and got into his car. He drove away.

With Bannon, McMurphy, and Pierce, but not seen, were nine FBI SWAT team members from the Boston field office. Men and women under the command of Daniel Pierce, who, like himself, were highly-trained SWAT agents. Bannon felt slightly less antagonistic toward the man, knowing he wasn't just a paper-pushing desk jockey.

Security spaced every fifty feet along the building's façade lights illuminated the parking lot. Across the two-lane roadway were a walking path and a low concrete wall. Beyond it, a cluster of small yachts was docked on Reserve Channel, a waterway leading out to the Harbor. The night air was humid and thick. The mosquitos were awful.

After their meeting with Grayson and Tara's adamant insistence she was doing the job and nothing Bannon said or did was going to stop her—again driving home his doubts he was really in charge in any way that mattered—she and Captain Amar and a team of Coasties piloted the *Naeem* into Boston Harbor, docking a few hours later.

Well within any ETA margin of error.

Immediately upon arrival, Amar made his call and was given the address of the building they now had under surveillance and surrounded. Amar was told to bring the woman, be there in a half-hour, and throw the phone into the harbor. Pierce told him to go ahead and dump it. Their Ops Tech guy had already gone over it and gotten anything off the burner phone they were going to.

On the roof, Bannon and the others watched through binoculars as a red Hyundai Santa Fe pulled up to the building. The car was driven by yet another FBI agent. If questioned about it, Amar was to tell them he'd hired an Uber.

"They're here," Bannon announced. With just five minutes to spare. To Pierce's credit, he had scrambled his men and had them ready and in position as soon as the location was revealed. It had been a tight timeframe, which the terrorists were counting on, but they'd made it.

Tara and Amar got out of the car.

The car pulled away.

A minute passed, then the driver's voice came through the comm unit's earpieces. "Package has been delivered."

Pierce radioed the rest of the team. "Head's up. Kestrel is on site. I repeat. Kestrel is on site."

Bannon and McMurphy exchange glances. Bannon arched an eyebrow. "Kestrel?"

"It's a bird of prey. Associated with the Egyptian Sun God Ra," Pierce explained.

McMurphy spurted laughter. "You gave Blades a code name?"

"We always do. It's protocol." Pierce returned his binoculars to his eyes.

McMurphy and Bannon continued to shake their heads.

Tara's voice whispered over the commlink. "We're inside."

AMAR OPENED THE ALUMINUM-FRAMED door to an unoccupied store. Tara stepped into the darkness beyond.

The glow of the outside security lights through the window was the only light to see by. She whispered, "We're inside."

Her wireless earpiece was directly synced to a radio transmitter sewn into the seam of her jacket. The device was virtually undetectable but strictly one-way communications. Also, the ops tech guy had installed a GPS tracker in her phone. That, she was told, would look exactly like it belonged, a piece of phone tech if they went so far as to open it up to inspect it.

Amar eased the door closed behind her.

The room was under construction and empty except for a service counter, and in the corner, several construction chests, ladders, and sawhorses were all chained together. The walls were taped and spackled but not painted yet. The floor was covered in sheetrock dust. The glass still had manufacturer stickers on them.

"What now?" Amar asked. "The person on the phone simply said to come to this building."

Tara noticed an open doorway behind the counter. It did not yet have a door and frame installed yet. The opening led into the back section of the space. She pointed. "Let's check back there."

She took the lead, pulling her cell phone from her pocket. She switched on the flashlight app and proceeded toward the dark opening. "Stay close," she whispered to Amar.

They entered into a much larger room in the center of the building. The side walls were gray cinderblock. The ceiling was corrugated steel. The grid for a suspended false ceiling was in place, but the tiles had not yet been installed. Tara swept the flashlight from left to right. Suddenly, two powerful work lights snapped on, blinding them. Tara stopped short, and Amar bumped into her. She glared at him. He stepped back.

"Turn the flashlight off," a male voice commanded from the darkness behind the work lamps.

She did as she was told, returning the phone to her jacket pocket. For a second, nothing happened. Tara held an arm up to shade her eyes and strained to see past the lights. With her night vision compromised, she could see nothing—which was the point. She avoided looking directly into the glare of the lights. Her vision would adjust, but it would take time. In the meantime, her nerves were like piano wires pulled to their breaking point.

"Is that quite necessary?" she asked.

No one answered.

"I did not travel all this way to be toyed with. We have a job to do."

"Tell us your names," a second voice commanded, also male.

"I am—"

"The man first."

"I am Captain Karim Amar of the *MV Naeem*. I was contacted in Alexandria by a man named Ebadaah Syed. He told me to allow this woman to book passage on my ship." He stepped forward. "I was given a phone. Told to call the one number stored in it when we arrived."

Amar nervously wrung his trembling hands in the silence that followed. "I did as I was told."

He looked back at Tara.

"What of you, woman?" The disembodied voice asked. "What is your name?"

"Safiyyah Zayd. You know this, and I tire of these games. Show yourselves."

Three young men stepped out from behind the light. Two were in their early twenties, babies, Tara thought. Middle Eastern with dark skin and black hair, their facial hair scraggy and poorly trimmed. One wore a dark *taqiyah*, a prayer cap, otherwise, all three wore Western clothes. The third one was large and clean-shaven, bald. He appeared to be at least ten years older than the other two.

All three were armed. The two children, as Tara thought of them, carried small Davis .380s. Dirt cheap handguns one could purchase on the streets for less than a hundred dollars. The large man carried a Mossberg 12-gauge shotgun. He carried it casually propped against his shoulder. The handguns were aimed at Tara and Amar.

Behind them, the sound of heeled shoes clicking on the poured concrete floor echoed in the chamber like gunshots.

A woman wearing black pumps, skinny-leg blue jeans, and a red leather jacket emerged from behind the light. She held her hands in the side pockets of her jacket. Her red hair was big, loose, and bouncy. Her skin tone was fair. No question, she was American-born.

She stepped up to Tara and held her hand out. Her fingernails were manicured, long, and painted red. She snapped them. "Passport."

Tara handed her Zayd's passport, having taken it off the woman immediately after her capture. She wasn't worried. The document had been issued nearly ten years earlier. The picture could easily have been plucked from her photo album. Their likeness was that close.

The American redhead held it up next to Tara's cheek. She grunted. "Huh."

She turned to Amar. "You vouch for this woman's identity?"

At first, Amar looked confused. Then he said, "This woman arrived and boarded my ship in Alexandria when Ebadaah Syed said she would. With that as proof, she was who she claimed to be." He nodded toward the passport and shrugged. "Beyond that, I do not know."

The woman stared at him while she chewed the inside of her cheek. "You're sure?"

"Of course. Why would I lie?"

Tara wanted to kick him. *Shut up.*

Finally, the woman nodded. "The agreed upon amount has been deposited into your account, Captain. You may check it now if you wish. Otherwise, you're free to go. With our gratitude."

Amar bowed and took two steps backward. "Yes, ma'am. Thank you."

As he turned to leave, the woman called out, "And Captain?"

He stopped, and half turned.

"Not a word of this to anyone. Do you understand?"

"Yes. Of course." He bowed again. "As if it never occurred."

"Very good, Captain." She waved him away like a debutante would dismiss the help. Amar practically ran for the exit. "Now, as for you..."

"Are you not satisfied I am who I say I am?" Tara asked.

The woman scrutinized her, gazing at her like she was a laboratory rat. She paced a semi-circle around Tara. In quiet contemplation, the woman rubbed her thumb and forefinger over her brightly painted mouth. She pinched her lower lip. "Do you know who I am? My name?"

Was this a test?

Tara followed the woman with her eyes. Then she looked at the three men. They'd lowered their guns, but stern expressions remained on their faces. Tara's heart beat fast, racing in her chest.

"Do you?" the woman prompted.

"Of course, I do not." Tara folded her arms over her chest.

"Tell me about yourself, Ms. Safiyyah Zayd."

The two women faced each other, combatants locking horns. The woman wore a lilac-scented perfume. Her breath smelled of minty mouthwash. Tara held her gaze for a moment, then said, "I will not."

Tara turned and started to walk away.

"Where the hell do you think you're going?" The woman grabbed Tara's arm and twisted her back around. It took every ounce of willpower Tara had to fight down her instinct to grab the woman's hand and twist it back until she snapped her wrist.

"I am leaving," Tara said, weakly shaking her arm but failing to loosen the woman's tight grip. "I will be subject to these stupid games no more. Nor will I be humiliated by your paranoid antics. I am Safiyyah Zayd. I am here to strike a blow against the American Infidels. Believe me or not. You can explain to those you serve why I have gone."

"You've got spirit. I'll give you that." The woman let go. "You can call me Bridget."

"Is that your real name?"

"Does it matter?" She marched back toward the shining lights and disappeared into the darkness. The three men remained, stoically staring at Tara. From the darkness, Bridget called out. "Remove your clothes."

Tara looked at the men. "You cannot be serious."

Bridget returned carrying folded clothes and sandals. "Yasra."

The young man wearing the *taqiyah* pocketed his handgun and crossed the room, going to a large oil drum. From where she stood, Tara could see the top had been cut out of it. The young man struck a match. He touched it to a book of matches and tossed it into the drum. Whatever was inside had been presoaked. The contents ignited with a whoosh. Flames climbed a foot over the rim of the drum. Bright orange light flickered off the walls of the facility.

Bridget reached Tara and shoved the clothes at her. "I said, take off your clothes."

Tara refused to accept the clothes. "For what purpose?"

"So we can burn them. Even if you are who you say you are. We still do not take chances. A fact you will come to appreciate, Safi."

Tara stripped off her jacket, fishing the cell phone from the pocket.

"Don't bother," Bridget said. She gestured for her to hand the jacket and cell phone over. Tara did so, and Bridget immediately dropped them into the fire. Tara did her best not to react as the garment with its wireless mic and the cell phone that contained the FBI GPS tracking device crackled and burned.

"Quickly," Bridget urged. "We need to move."

Tara hesitated for a moment, looking at the three men now leering expectantly at her. "With them watching?"

"Get over yourself, woman." Still, Bridget made a spinning motion with her finger. "Yasra. Ahmad. Reza. Turn away. All of you."

The men did, reluctantly.

Tara quickly stripped down to her bra and panties. She handed the clothes over to Bridget, including her shoes. The woman dumped them all into the fire without fanfare. Tara reached behind her back to unsnap her bra hook.

"That won't be necessary." Bridget tossed the clothes she held at her. "Get dressed. We need to move."

CHAPTER EIGHT

BANNON HAD HIS EYES glued to his binoculars. He noticed Amar exiting the building first. The captain was alone. Bannon tapped Pierce on the shoulder.

"Pigeon has left the building," Pierce said into his commlink.

McMurphy smirked. "Code names."

Bannon shook his head.

"We've got him, team leader," a reply came back.

The plan was for two team members to follow Amar back to the *Naeem* to ensure he contacted no one along the way before taking him back into custody. Back at FBI headquarters, he'd be debriefed and dealt with in accordance with whatever sweetheart deal he'd worked out with the Attorney General.

Bannon didn't care about him any longer. His attention remained solely on the audio they were receiving from the transmitter woven into Tara's jacket. The device was working perfectly. The sound clarity was studio quality. He had to hand it to the tech wizards working for the FBI. They knew their stuff. The entire SWAT team was dialed into the audio. Nobody would miss anything.

But Bannon furrowed his brow.

Take off your clothes.

"No. No, no, no."

"Easy, Bannon," Pierce said.

"Easy, my foot. You know what comes next."

Grayson had said this group was cautious. Bannon was beginning to understand how they'd stayed under the radar for so long. He shook his head as he listened, growing more uneasy by the minute.

Quickly, the woman self-identified as Bridget said. *We need to move.*

More to himself than anyone else, Bannon said, "Where are they going?"

Yasra. Ahmad. Reza. Turn away. All of you.

Pierce wrote the names down in a notebook he had in front of him. A second passed, then another. There was a loud pop. Bannon pressed his finger against his earbud. The audio was dead.

"God damn it." Bannon pounded his fist into the gravel-covered rooftop.

"Settle down, Bannon," Pierce warned. "They can't go anywhere. We've got the building surrounded. And even if they did manage to slip away…" Bannon shot him a look. "And they won't. We've still got the GPS tracker in her phone. That was the point. To follow them when they left, take us to their headquarters, to others. Remember?"

Pierce clasped Bannon on the shoulder. "We've got this."

From his position on the other side of Pierce, McMurphy said, "You know, every time someone tells us that, we find out they don't."

Pierce opened his mouth to respond but got cut off by a voice coming in over their comms. "Team leader. We've got a problem."

"Who's that?" Bannon asked.

Pierce shushed him. "Go for team leader. What's going on?"

The request was answered with dead air for a second. "Um, we lost pigeon for a moment."

"A moment?"

"But we found him."

"Is this still a problem or not?"

"Yes, sir, it is. He's… um… dead, sir. His throat's been cut, and…he's dead."

McMurphy said, "You got this, huh?"

"It's screwed, Pierce. We need to get in there." Bannon made a move to get up.

Pierce grabbed his arm. "No. It changes nothing. We stick with the plan. Tara's made contact. She's past the worst of it. Now, she can lead us to the rest of the cell. We stay the course."

Bannon didn't like it, but he settled back down and lifted his binoculars to his eyes. "If anything happens to her, Peirce, you and me will have a problem."

TARA QUICKLY DRESSED IN the most unflattering set of gray, baggy, oversized mechanic's coveralls she'd ever worn in her life. She zipped up the front and began to roll the sleeves up so her hands would be visible.

Bridget tossed her a pair of old brown sandals to put on. "Get moving."

Tara gave the burning drum a final wistful glance. Her lifelines to the FBI SWAT team and, by extension, Bannon and McMurphy were burning to a crisp. "Where are we going?"

"You'll find out."

"Yasra. Ahmad. You two remain behind," Bridget instructed. "Make sure no one follows us."

"Who is there to follow us?" Yasra asked. "No one knows we are here."

"We don't know that, do we? You stay."

"For how long?" Ahmad asked.

"Until you know it's safe." Bridget grabbed Tara by the arm. "Come on."

Tara shook off her grasp. "Unhand me."

Bridget released her arm but moved in close, crowding her. "Settle down, Safi, and do what you're told. Now, go. Follow Reza and do not lag."

Reza was the big bald one carrying the shotgun. He walked briskly toward the back corner of the large room. He had long legs, a wide, V-shaped torso, and thick, gym-produced, dark arms. Bridget walked fast to keep up with him, as did Tara.

In the back corner, there was a fire door, propped open. Rather than leading outside and right into the arms of the waiting SWAT team she knew had the building surrounded, it led down a hallway along the back of the building. At the far end, they reached a stairwell that went down into the basement of the building.

Tara felt the first hot twinge of panic. There hadn't been time to examine the building or get building plans from the city. They did not even know there was a basement in the place.

At the bottom of the stairs, Reza opened a metal fire door. It didn't lead to a basement after all. It led to a dirt-walled tunnel. The walls were braced with wooden timbers, and bare 40-watt lightbulbs were strung along the ceiling. The walls were damp. The tunnel was cool, with an earthen smell to it. Old wooden pallets were laid one after the other, forming a sidewalk of sorts over puddles of muddy water and the unevenly dug dirt and rocks.

Reza stepped to the side and let Bridget and Tara pass.

Bridget went first. The floor sloped downward, and the tunnel narrowed. They had to proceed single file. Reza slammed the door shut with a heavy metal thud and brought up the rear.

"What is this? Where does it go?"

"You'll see," Bridget said.

Reza snapped on a penlight and held it over Tara's head. The added illumination helped her avoid tripping over the unevenly placed pallets. He pushed her shoulder and grunted. Even without words, his message was clear: *move it.*

Tara walked, counting the tunnel's crude timber bracing to figure out how far they were going, but she soon learned the braces were spaced at such irregular intervals as to be useless as a gauge for how far they'd gone.

Twelve minutes later, the tunnel came to an abrupt dead end. A flat, black wall greeted them.

Reza handed his light to Bridget and appeared to dig his fingertips into the wall. He strained, pulling back, until what turned out to be a rolling steel fire door opened. Beyond the opening was a small room with gray cinderblock walls. A domed, caged light fixture hung from the ceiling. The room smelled sharply of chemicals. Once inside, Tara saw why. They were in a custodian's closet. Mops, brooms, buckets, and other cleaning supplies crowded a slop sink against the back wall. Metal shelves were bolted to one wall and filled with rolls of industrial-style paper towels, bathroom tissue, and cartons of toilet bowl fresheners.

Reza closed the sliding door behind them.

The room had a standard metal door with a brushed chrome knob and a louvered venting panel in the bottom half. Bridget snapped the deadbolt switch and opened the door. She peeked out before signaling the coast was clear.

She went out. Tara followed. They were in a narrow, tiled hallway that dead-ended at the closet. Tara looked past Bridget but could only see that the hallway went on for a good length.

Reza signed Bridget, causing Tara to realize the big, bald guy wasn't just the quiet type. He was mute. Tara didn't know sign language, so she had no idea what he'd said to Bridget.

He ducked back inside the closet for several minutes before coming out again. He locked the closet door with a key.

"What was he doing in there?" Tara asked Bridget

"Not your concern."

Tara grabbed her arm. "I am not your enemy. Tell me."

Bridget sighed. "He rigged the door with explosives. Anyone comes after us will be in for a very big surprise." She animated an explosion with her hands. "Ka-boom."

"What about Yasra and Ahmad?"

Again, the animated *ka-boom.*

They were eliminating loose ends along the way. A chill ran down Tara's back. Not only because of the sheer brutality of their actions—that was bad enough—but it was an indication of just how big the operation was. The scale must be enormous to warrant such secrecy, such sacrifice.

Bridget pushed her along the narrow hallway. "Go."

When they reached the end, Tara blinked.

They were at the underground Broadway station for the Boston T. Several people were waiting for the next train to arrive on the island platform. None of them looked up from their newspapers, smartphones, or tablets. Oblivious to their surroundings, they noticed nothing.

The three of them remained at one end of the platform, trying to look inconspicuous. Each time Tara tried to engage Bridget in conversation, the woman shut her down. "Stop with the questions. All will be explained to you. Soon."

A train slipped into the station and slowed. The brakes squealed, drowning out the automated loudspeaker announcements. The train doors sprang open and passengers rushed out. Bridget took Tara by the arm and held her back until the passengers were off the train and streaming toward the exits. Then she pushed her into the last car. Reza stepped in behind them. He remained by the doors, his shotgun left back at the custodian's closet, replaced by a handgun stuck in his belt, concealed by a jacket but visible to Tara.

The train signaled the doors were closing.

A few seconds passed, the train lurched forward, and they were off, whisked southbound on the red line, traveling ultimately to who knew where.

CHAPTER NINE

BANNON REFUSED TO WAIT any longer. "Something's wrong."

He hurried back from the parapet and stood up.

Pierce chased after him. "Stand down, Bannon."

He grabbed Bannon's arm, but McMurphy's meaty hand clamped down on his wrist. He pulled Pierce's hand away. "Didn't your mother teach you anything? Good agents keep their hands to themselves, Danny-boy?"

Pierce tried to shake his arm loose and couldn't.

"Bannon, orders from high up the food chain have ordered me to bring you two along, but this is my operation. I'll arrest you both for obstruction if I have to."

Bannon leveled him with a stare. "Try it."

Pierce tried a different tactic. "If you go in there, guns blazing, you're as likely to get Sardana killed as rescue her."

"You don't know what you're talking about. How have you not put this together?" Bannon asked. "The op's blown. That's why they killed Amar."

"They're eliminating loose ends," Pierce argued. "It's how these animals operate."

"What if you're wrong?"

Pierce held up a device that looked like a smartphone. "She's still in there. See? Her tracker hasn't moved."

"Means nothing. It's a phone. Phones get left behind. They could already be gone."

"What are you talking about?"

"Think about it, Pierce. Where are their cars?" Bannon waited. Pierce didn't answer. "There was only one car when we got here. The liquor shop owner. He's gone. How did they get here? How do they plan on leaving? They knocked out her audio. Something's wrong, Pierce."

Pierce hesitated.

"I can feel it, Pierce. We need to get in there," Bannon said. "Before it's too late."

"When he feels something, Danny-boy," McMurphy added, "I've learned it's best to listen."

Still not convinced, Pierce activated his commlink. "We're going in. Let's move!"

The three of them charged for the exit door of the building they were on. They ran down the stairwell in the northeast corner. One day, it would be a fire exit stairwell. They hit the ground floor and sprinted across the parking lot as several SWAT team members converged on the nearest side door.

Pierce shouted to them. "Go! Go!"

One of them carried a fireman's Halligan bar. He jammed it between the metal fire door and jamb while a second agent slammed a thirty-pound, steel-encased, concrete battering ram into the forced entry tool. The door bent. Then creaked. After three more attempts, it finally popped open.

Three agents rushed through the open door. Pierce, Bannon, and McMurphy quickly followed. They were in a dark service hallway that went around the back of the building, lit by the faint hue of red exit lights. On the left were overhead bay doors, one for each of the four sub-lease spaces. To the right were doors into the other storefronts.

Bannon counted down two doors and stopped.

The forced entry team jammed, hammered, and pried their way through the metal door.

The team entered a vast space. Two agents split to the left, and two others headed to the right.

Bannon slowed. His palms were sweaty. His heart raced as he thought about all the terrible things that might have already gone wrong. He forced the dark thoughts from his mind.

The space was pitch black except for the faint bluish light from the parking lot security lights out front streaming through a single door-size opening in the facing wall. He smelled smoke. "Something's burning."

Bannon spotted an oil drum, the glow of a dying fire still visible inside it. He moved toward it. The ping of a single bullet caught his attention. Two agents had gone through the opening. One of them fell forward while the other one ducked back. More shots rang out.

Over the commlink, someone shouted, "We're taking fire."

Pierce shouted. "Take cover! Take cover!"

The shots were coming from the front section of the store.

"Team two," Pierce called out. "We've got hostiles in the front of the store. They've got us pinned down in the back."

Bannon grabbed Pierce's shoulder. "Tara. Don't turn this into a hostage situation."

"Stand down, Bannon," Pierce snapped back. "My people know what they're doing."

The other two agents with them had joined the third one by the door opening. It was the only way into the front section beside the front door. They pulled their downed agent back through the opening. He wasn't moving. It was impossible to tell if he was wounded or dead.

There was a horrific shatter of glass. Bannon grit his teeth. He heard the hiss of gas grenades. Then, a pop-pop-pop of gunfire. Small to medium caliber. A flashbang went off, followed by the sound of several carbines firing. The barrage of gunfire neutralized the threat, ending it with a sharp cry of pain and the clatter of a dropped gun.

Then, the disturbing quiet that always followed a firefight.

Bannon waited a heartbeat before he rushed for the open doorway.

Pierce called out. "Wait for the all-clear." He threw his arms up in the air. "Why do I bother?"

The other three agents poured into the room. Bannon heard the sound of boots stomping through glass. He charged into the front space, his eyes watering from the still-present gas and smoke.

"Tara. Where's Tara?"

An agent pulled his gas mask off. "Not here, Commander. Just these two."

There were two bodies on the floor. Both men. Young and dark-skinned.

The agent kicked a handgun from one of their hands even though his chest was bloody and riddled with bullet holes. Both young men were dead.

"No one came out?" Bannon asked.

"Nope. Had it under surveillance the whole time. No one came out. Just us coming in."

Bannon looked around. "How?"

There had been a woman here. He'd heard her voice over the wire. Where could they have gone? He returned to the back room. McMurphy was by the oil drum.

The downed agent sat with his back against the wall. He rubbed his chest where his vest caught the slug, saving his life. "I'm fine, Pierce." He winced. "But you might need to find another pitcher for tomorrow's softball game against the BPD."

McMurphy kicked over the oil drum. It landed with a hollow, resounding crash, spilling ash and still-burning material. Everyone jumped, and two agents swung their weapons in his direction. Over the still-burning embers, McMurphy smiled sheepishly. "Sorry."

He used his toe to kick Tara's cell phone free.

Pierce and Bannon joined him.

"That explains why the signal didn't move," Bannon said. "The fire hadn't breached the casing yet." He crouched down and picked up the smoldering remains of Tara's jacket. "And why we lost audio."

He leveled Pierce with a hard stare. "They're gone. We've lost them."

"They can't be gone. We had the place surrounded," Pierce insisted.

"Yeah? Tell me where they are, then."

Pierce waved his arms and raised his voice. "Search the place. Top to bottom. They have to be here somewhere. They have to be."

His men moved out in teams of two to the four corners of the building.

Bannon and McMurphy moved out of earshot from Pierce and the others. "We've got a building with every exit covered," Bannon said. "They didn't get out through any of those, that leaves—"

"Up, down," McMurphy said, "or they beamed out."

"Let's assume *Star Trek* tech wasn't used for the time being."

"We had full visual of the roof."

Bannon dismissed that. "No good anyway, they'd need a way off the roof."

"They could be inside, hiding. Waiting for a chance to steal away," McMurphy said, working through the problem. "Or..."

Together, they said, "Underground."

They turned toward Pierce as an agent called out from across the room. "Guys, you need to see this." They joined him in the back corner. A small, wooden wedge was jammed under the open fire exit door. "This doesn't lead outside."

Instead, it led down a hallway along the back of the building, apparently alongside the service hallway they'd used to come in. They found a stairwell with a yellow metal handrail leading downstairs at the far end. At the bottom of the stairs, they found a second metal fire door.

"What's this?" Pierce asked.

The breach team had it open in seconds, and they found out.

"A tunnel," Bannon said. He snatched his .45 from his thigh holster. McMurphy did the same.

"We'll deal with this," Pierce said.

Bannon pushed past him and entered the tunnel. McMurphy shouldered past Pierce and his agents, too.

Pierce shook his head. "Son of a—Come on," he said to the two agents with them.

Bannon and McMurphy opened up the flashlight apps on their phones.

The tunnel was dirt-walled and braced with wooden timbers. They followed the bare 40-watt lightbulbs strung in a line from the ceiling. The walls were damp. The tunnel was cool and dank, with an earthen smell to it. Old wooden pallets were laid one after the other over puddles of muddy water and dirt and rocks.

Bannon led the way with his gun out, following his cell phone light over the rough boards laid down like a makeshift sidewalk. The boards were soiled and covered in dry, dirty boot prints. The tunnel grew cooler the deeper they went. Bannon felt the others behind him but didn't look back or slow to make sure they were with him. His focus was on Tara.

"Join the Coast Guard," McMurphy groused. "Go to interesting places. Meet interesting people. Be annoyed by them."

"That's not our motto," Bannon said. "It's always ready, remember?"

He brushed at his shoulders. "And, ugh, spiders."

"Looks like the end of the road," McMurphy said about ten minutes later when they reached the tunnel's apparent dead end.

Bannon stopped and panned his light along the edges. "It's a fire door."

Pierce impatiently pushed his way past Bannon and McMurphy. "Then let's find out where the hell it leads."

As he reached for the door, Bannon's stomach soured. He knew it. That sickening feeling he got whenever his instincts told him something was wrong. He grabbed Pierce by the shoulder and pulled him away from the door.

"No!"

Too late. Pierce slid the door back. There was a bright white flash of light. Bannon heard the click as the booby-trapped switch made contact. With his hand still on Pierce's arm, he held on as McMurphy grabbed him in a bear hug and threw him to the ground.

Bannon, Pierce, and McMurphy crashed to the pallet-laden floor. Filthy, muddy water splashed up around them.

The IED wired to the door exploded, unleashing a thick, hot, roaring fireball that barreled through the tunnel, incinerating everything in its path.

CHAPTER TEN

"**THE EXPLOSION EARLIER TONIGHT** that shook the Broadway Station of the T has been attributed to a ruptured natural gas line. According to authorities, the blast was caused by a welder conducting routine repair work in the subway's tunnel when a welding spark ignited the leaking gas."

The report came from the widescreen TV mounted on the wall in the small lounge area where Bannon sat. The pretty blonde reporter continued, "Luckily, the worker escaped injury, and disruption to service was kept to a minimum. OSHA and other safety inspectors on the scene are expected to deliver their final findings within a few days."

She smiled at the screen. "We're so thankful no one was hurt. Jim, how'd the Red Sox do against the Yankees this afternoon?"

Bannon aimed the remote at the TV, shutting the sound off.

Back in Portsmouth, back in the McIntyre Federal building, he checked his watch. Eleven-twenty at night. He crossed to the windows and pulled the Venetian blinds open. He looked past his ghost-like reflection in the glass at the lights of Daniels Street below, reminded of how close he'd come to being a ghost.

He'd changed into his civilian clothes—a black Polo shirt, light brown khakis, and Sperry dock siders, without socks. The collar of his shirt irritated the back of his neck. He tenderly touched his cheek and the side of his neck. The skin was still hot, as was the back of his hands, but no worse than a really bad case of sunburn. He'd been damned lucky.

When he'd called out and grabbed Pierce, McMurphy had been close enough—and strong enough—to pull them both back, yanking them to the ground. He'd slammed into the pallet walkway, face up, and Bannon and Pierce fell on top of him, face down. The fireball had rolled over them. The two agents accompanying them weren't so lucky. With no time and nowhere to go, the fireball slammed into them, knocking them off their feet.

Bannon would never forget the roar of the explosion in his ears, the sounds of the two men's final screams, the smell of flesh as it burned or the sight of their faces, blackened and charred, after being hit by the full force of the roaring fire. The skin seared off their skulls, their hands turned into blackened skeletal digits, still clutching their rifles. Their corpses, barely looking human, lay smoldering.

He hadn't even known their names. He knew them now. Acosta and Trejo. One was single, and the other left behind a wife and two children.

Bannon fisted his hand. Whoever had done this, he would track them down and make them pay. With their lives if he had to.

The door opened behind him and then quietly clicked closed.

In the reflection of the glass, he saw that it was Grayson. He turned.

"I'm sorry about what happened," she said.

Bannon grabbed the plastic water bottle he'd left on the arm of a chair. He took a slug of warm water. Then he fired the bottle across the room like a missile. It hit the TV. Water splashed across the screen, diffusing the colorful weather map calling for a beautiful day tomorrow.

"I told you!" he shouted. "I warned you. Now, two men are dead, and Tara's gone. She's in danger, and we have no idea where. With no way to help her."

"I know," Grayson said quietly.

MCMURPHY AND PIERCE STOOD in the corridor outside the small lounge. They'd been told to wait there by Grayson. She wanted a chance to speak with Bannon alone. From the muffled shouting going on in the other room, the conversation wasn't going well.

Pierce stood with an arm looped over the corner of a filing cabinet. Like Bannon, he and McMurphy were back in civilian clothes. For McMurphy, that meant his work boots, baggy white painter pants, and under an open flannel shirt, a T-shirt with a picture of a fist holding a wrench that read: *I'm a Mechanic but Even I Can't Fix Stupid.* Pierce wore slacks from another suit, a white dress shirt with the sleeves rolled up, but no tie. He wore his Springfield .45 on his hip.

He cleared his throat. "I, um, guess I should thank you. For saving my life back there."

McMurphy sipped coffee from a Styrofoam cup. It was heavily doctored with whiskey. He grunted.

"No. I mean it. Thank you."

"What'd they teach you at Quantico? Nothing. What were you thinking?"

Pierce opened his mouth to respond, then snapped it shut. He tried again, this time getting the words out. "You're right. I rushed ahead. Ms. Sardana's in danger because I didn't listen to you. To Bannon. Acosta and Trejo are dead because of me."

He was mistaken if he expected McMurphy to let him off the hook.

Men had died under McMurphy's watch, too. He lived with that guilt every day. And would for the rest of his life. Pierce didn't get a free pass from that. None of them did. "Damn right, they are."

Pierce didn't argue the point. He lowered his head. Accepting it. Owning it.

"They your first?" McMurphy asked, breaking the morbid silence that followed.

Pierce looked up. "Dead because of me? Yeah. Yes."

"It doesn't get any easier. I wish it did." McMurphy hoisted his cup. "It's why I drink."

"Coffee?"

McMurphy handed him the cup.

Pierce threw back a big gulp and gasped, his eyes blinking as he tried not to sputter. "Jesus, that's like straight whiskey."

McMurphy swirled what was left in the cup. "No," he protested. "There's some coffee in there. Keeps it warm." He drank the rest down.

"Warm? It's burning my esophagus," Pierce gasped.

"Toughen up, Danny-boy. You're playing with the big boys now."

"Big boys? You're a couple of part-time Coasties," Pierce said.

"Who work directly for the Secretary of Homeland Security. If that doesn't tell you something, you're a bigger dummy than I took you for."

Bannon and Grayson continued to argue. Their voices were indecipherable, but the emotion behind them was unmistakable. Figuring this could take a while, McMurphy thought about getting more coffee.

Before he could make his move, Pierce said, "What's the story between Bannon and Sardana?"

"How do you mean?"

"It's clear he cares about her. What? Are they lovers or something?"

"Careful, Pierce."

"I don't mean anything by it, and I don't care. I just need to know who I'm dealing with." He shrugged. "The man's just a tad more protective than he should be, is all I'm saying."

"So what?" McMurphy said. "He should just not care? Let his people go and get killed and not do anything about it?"

Pierce turned red. "No. I just meant from what I saw, the woman's more than capable of taking care of herself." He put his hands up in defense. "All I'm saying."

McMurphy thought about it for a minute. Before he spoke, he chose his words carefully. "She's important to him. Yeah, Brice loves her, but not in the way you're thinking.

Not romantically. They've got a connection. It comes from a deep, deep respect for each other. Think brother and sister, but stronger than that. Much stronger. They would die for each other.

"*Al-jamā'ah al-islāmīyah* killed Blades' parents. They're a—"

"Pro-Sunni terror group active in Egypt and Croatia back in the day. The name basically means Islamic Group. I'm aware of who they are," Pierce said. "I work anti-terrorism, remember?"

McMurphy ignored his verbal jab. "Her parents' deaths had a profound impact on Tara's life, as you can imagine. She joined the Algerian National Navy and trained in the Indian Navy's MARCOS program in Nahan."

"That's crap," Pierce said. "No way she trained as an Indian Marine Commando. Women aren't allowed in their Special Forces program."

"True, except when they host exchange programs with other countries. She was part of one such program." Pierce remained visibly skeptical. McMurphy shrugged. "You're the one who asked."

"Okay, whatever. Where she trained doesn't matter."

"Not long after completing the MARCOS training, she went AWOL."

"Why?"

McMurphy shrugged. "No idea. She won't talk about it." He looked at his empty cup, wishing he had more coffee—and whiskey. "All I know is she dropped off the grid for a while and then turned up a few years later in Afghanistan, teamed up with a badass group of mercenaries."

"Tarakesh Sardana's not her real name then."

"As made up as a porn star's stage name."

"How'd she hook up with you and Bannon?" At McMurphy's expression, he added, "You know what I mean."

"Long story short. Bannon got himself captured by a group of Taliban knuckleheads. Blades and her group of mercs raided the compound where he was being held, purely by happenchance. They pulled his butt from the fire. Afterward, Bannon talked her into joining our DOG posse."

"But she's not Coast Guard?"

"Nope," McMurphy admitted. "More like a private security contractor."

The lounge door opened. Grayson said, "If you gentlemen would please join us."

She stepped back, and McMurphy and Pierce filed in. Bannon stood looking out the window onto the street below. Grayson closed the door behind them. McMurphy and Pierce shuffled around, not sure where to stand or if they should sit. The tension in the room could be cut with a Ka-bar knife.

Grayson cleared her throat. "Agent Pierce, first, let me extend my condolences to you on the loss of your men. A terrible tragedy. I am so, so sorry."

McMurphy noticed Bannon fist his hands.

Pierce said, "Thank you, ma'am."

"The question now is where do we go from here?" Grayson folded her arms over her chest and began to pace. Her heels clicked across the tile floor. Neither McMurphy nor Pierce offered a suggestion, but Bannon turned from the window.

"We have the crew of the *Naeem*. We have Zayd. We interrogate them. Water-board them, tear their fingernails out with pliers if we have to."

"You're not serious?" Pierce asked.

"They know more than they've told us so far," Bannon said. "Damn right, I'm serious. I'll do whatever it takes to get Tara back unharmed."

"We'll talk to them. Of course," Grayson said.

"The FBI already has two profilers assigned," Pierce said. "They're working with her. They specialize in interrogation and interview techniques. They've been handpicked because of their familiarity with the Middle East."

"Working with her?" Bannon said. "What is she, a hired consultant? What are you doing, offering her some sweetheart deal, like you did Amar? Giving her a get-out-of-jail-free card? Tara's missing. She's in the hands of people willing to kill, even their own people."

Pierce took a step toward Bannon. His face was red with anger. "You think I don't know that? It was my men that were killed down in that hole. Remember?"

Bannon took a step closer. "Yeah, killed because of you. Because you hesitated when you should have acted. Because you rushed in when you should have waited. This entire operation went sideways because of you. So, yeah, I remember."

"You son of a—"

McMurphy caught Pierce by the arm, arresting his charge toward Bannon. "Easy, Danny-boy."

Grayson stepped in front of Bannon. She put her hands on his chest, gently pushing him back. "Knock it off, Brice."

Reluctantly, each man backed up a step.

"I want five minutes with her," Bannon said. "With Zayd."

"That's not going to happen," Pierce said. "Leave it to the professionals."

"Dial it down," McMurphy warned the agent.

"Brice, I'm sorry, but Agent Pierce is right," Grayson said. "It's out of your hands."

"What the hell are you talking about?"

"Orders. From Washington. I tried to fight it, but this whole thing's been taken over by Justice. The FBI specifically. A team of Federal Marshals has been dispatched. The prisoners are to be transported to an undisclosed location first thing in the morning."

"Are you kidding? That happens," Bannon pointed at Pierce. "They won't let us anywhere near them. They're the only leads we've got."

"They'll be properly interrogated," Pierce insisted. "Not tortured. Any intel we get, we'll use it to get your friend back. Unharmed."

"You're delusional. You treat them with kids' gloves. That'll take weeks. By then, Tara will be dead. You'll end up getting her killed just like you did Acosta and Trejo." Bannon stomped toward the door. He slammed his shoulder into Pierce along the way.

Pierce pushed back.

"Brice," Grayson called out.

He paused only long enough to turn on her. "And you." He glared. "I expected better from you, but you just signed her death warrant."

Bannon flung the door open so hard it banged against the wall. Then he stormed out.

McMurphy stared at Pierce and then Grayson. "Well, that went just swell."

With a sad shake of his head, he followed his friend out.

CHAPTER **ELEVEN**

THE SUBWAY TRAIN ROLLED into the North Quincy station, an outside station south of Boston, and screeched to a stop.

Bridget, Reza, and Tara exited the train from the last car. The passengers surged across the center platform then to the stairs that would take them to the commuter parking lot, still mostly filled with cars at that hour of the night. Bridget and Reza held Tara back until the platform emptied. Then, they urged her forward.

"Where are we going? I demand to know."

Bridget and Reza kept walking. Over her shoulder, Bridget said, "Damn, you're full of questions. Why don't you chill out, Safi?"

Tara gasped. "How dare you speak to me in such a tone?"

On the *Naeem*, Tara had spent only a few hours with Safiyyah Zayd. The woman hadn't said much, but Tara knew as a prominent general's daughter, and from their minuscule interactions, she was not a woman who'd tolerate being talked to in that manner.

"We're taking you where you need to go. End of discussion."

Tara wanted to argue further, but she had to tread carefully. She didn't know how much Zayd had been told about these people or what information she might have been given before her arrival. If she overplayed her hand, she risked raising their suspicions, which were already at paranoid levels.

As they stepped from the curb of the parking lot, a silver midsize SUV pulled up to them. Bridget and Reza approached it. Tara noticed the make and model. A Subaru Forester. It was not new, nor was it old. Its lights were all functioning, including the one over the rear license plate. She committed the number to memory. Nothing about the vehicle's appearance would raise suspicions. Smart.

Bridget opened the rear door and told her to get in. Tara didn't argue. Reza rode shotgun. And Bridget climbed into the back with Tara. A young Middle Eastern man sat in the driver's seat. The engine idled. He glanced into the back, a stern expression on his face. When everyone was settled, he pulled out of the parking lot and onto Hancock Street. He used his turn signal to pull into traffic. They traveled south.

"Put this on."

Tara looked down at the black cloth in Bridget's hand. It was a black hood. "This is a joke?"

"Put it on, or I'll put it on you." The woman sneered. "You won't like that."

Don't be so sure, Tara thought. She snatched the hood from her and pulled it over her head. The material was thick and impossible to see through. Not even the bright street lights and passing headlights could penetrate the tightly woven fabric. And it was stifling hot to wear.

"This is completely unacceptable. I demand to know where it is we are going."

"That would defeat the purpose of the hood, wouldn't it?" Bridget snapped her gum.

Tara settled back and did her best to pick up sounds, stops and starts, to keep track of turns, to get a sense of where they were going. Quincy was a neighboring city bordering Boston to the north. They drove through what felt like winding downtown streets for a while, then onto a highway. As time went on, they eventually slowed and continued to drive through what felt like stop-and-go city traffic again. Tara heard sounds she thought she'd heard before. Had they simply driven around in obscure ways to make her lose track of where they were? If so, they'd succeeded.

When they finally came to a stop, one that lasted longer than the length of a traffic light, she heard the engine shut off. Bridget said, "Sit tight." Car doors opened and closed. A second passed before Tara felt her door open. A hand grabbed her arm. Bridget said, "Come on. Get out."

Bridget held her arm like she was a blind person. She was led in a single straight direction and then directed to step up to avoid a curb.

"This is no way for me to be treated," Tara complained.

"Tell somebody who cares." Bridget led her up a steep incline. From the hollow, metallic sound of their footsteps, Tara deduced the ramp was metal and ribbed.

They were near water. Tara smelled the thick, moist, salty air. She heard the caw of gulls, probably circling overhead. They were at or near docks or a marina. The air was tainted with the smell of oil. She heard the gentle lapping of waves. And she heard traffic, not real close, but close enough to be heard, so they weren't at some rural dock, but one near an urban setting.

She was directed to step over a threshold.

"We're almost there, Safi." Bridget yanked Tara's arm to turn her left. They walked a dozen more steps. She was turned right. Then, three more steps. "Stop."

Bridget's grip fell away. Then Tara heard a door click shut. The sound reverberated. The hood was snatched off her head.

They stood in a windowless, dimly lit room. Tara blinked. She brushed her messy hair from her face, finger-combing it away. She quickly looked around.

Above her was a suspended, false ceiling. The grid remained in place, but many of the tiles were broken or missing. Old, stained tiles were haphazardly tossed into a pile in the corner. Above the grid was the raw, encapsulated ceiling. A single bare bulb hung from the end of an orange cord. The cord ran the length of the ceiling and plugged directly into the junction box above the closed door. The room had a second door, also closed. A square grill filled the lower half of that door. Tara could see a tile floor through the louvers. If she had to guess, she'd say that was a bathroom.

Bridget leaned casually against the wall next to the exit door. She's the important one, Tara thought. They were alone. Reza and their driver either hadn't accompanied them this far or had left once they'd entered the room.

"Now what?" Tara asked.

"Now you meet the boss," Bridget said.

"Finally. And he shall get an earful from me about the disrespectful way I have been treated."

The door behind them opened. A man stepped inside. He was tall and thin, as close as one could come to being emaciated without being sickly. He had a scraggly dark beard and wore dark, baggy pants, a dark button-down shirt, similarly shapeless, and a maroon taqiyah. She couldn't make out his features in the dim light other than to notice his dark Middle Eastern skin.

"Ah," he said, spreading his hands like a minister conveying his sermon. "Our guest has arrived. Excellent."

"Treated more like an enemy than a guest," Tara complained. "This has been inexcusable."

"I apologize, my dear," the man said, approaching her. He reached out to clasp her upper arms in greeting. "But these are dangerous times. Our enemies are everywhere. And our work is too important for us not to be overly cautious. I'm sure you appreciate that."

"What I'd appreciate would be—"

Tara froze as the man came into the light of the single dangling bulb. Face-to-face with him, her blood ran cold in her veins. No. It was impossible.

The man reacted in the same way. He turned to Bridget. "What have you done? You stupid, stupid girl!"

"What?" Bridget straightened up, reacting to the man's vehement outburst.

"It can't be?" Tara shook off his grasp. Stunned.

The man turned back. Anger and delight blazed in his dark eyes. "So, the she-devil recognizes me, as well."

His was the face of a ghost.

Tara shook her head. Of course, she recognized him, though he did not look exactly as she remembered him. The right side of his face was now horribly disfigured under the pathetic attempt he'd made at growing a beard. Burned and poorly skin-grafted, the skin was gnarly and uneven.

"Of course, I recognize you. I saw you die."

He smiled. His mouth was full of stained, crooked teeth. "You thought you saw me die. You should have remained to ensure you finished the job."

"What's going on?" the redhead asked.

"This," he said, turning to Bridget as he ran the back of his fingers over his rough, scarred cheek. "I have her to thank for this." He shook with barely contained anger. "And I have you to thank, Ms. Barnes, for bringing this she-devil into our mist. I sent you to complete one simple task. And instead, you return to me with one of the most dangerous, most treacherous American infidels I have ever had the misfortune to encounter."

"What are you talking about?" Bridget asked.

Tara cut her off. "Tell me how your filthy, flesh-stripped bones aren't lying at the bottom of the Atlantic Ocean? How did you survive, Aziza Faaid?" Tara demanded. "Tell me!"

CHAPTER TWELVE

THREE HOURS AFTER BANNON stormed from the FBI offices and a quick drive to Hampton Beach, Bannon and McMurphy were once more back in Portsmouth. This time, under cover of the early morning darkness and dressed all in black, they walked across the rooftop of a seven-story apartment building on Congress Street, south of Daniel Street. Gravel crunched under their feet as they made their way to the middle of the roof. There, they set down the large, heavy boxes they carried. They were the size of small steamer trunks.

Inside each box was a power glider.

Power gliding, an extreme sporting craze Bannon had been anxious to try, used a combined hang glider and a personal, twenty-five-pound backpack engine and propeller system. It looked like an industrial-grade exhaust fan with a diameter of three feet. Pictured on the box was a grassy field bordered by blue sky and tall evergreen trees. In the foreground stood a smiling man wearing a white flight suit, a brown canvas harness, and a white crash helmet. Beside him sat a red power glider.

Bannon had bought the gliders months ago, intending to try them out on a sunny weekend afternoon on the sandy shore of Hampton Beach. This wasn't how he envisioned his first power gliding trip, but it would have to do.

Quickly, he and McMurphy extracted the contents from the boxes, replaced the wrappings and other packing material inside, and wedged the boxes behind a ventilation shaft.

Ten minutes later, they had the engine components assembled along with the lightweight aluminum harnesses. They fit the aluminum skeletons of the gliders together, then unfurled the blue and white nylon sails. Unlike traditional hang gliders, power gliders were configured so the pilot could sit in a harness with the control bar in front of them, the engine and propeller system in the back.

They quickly filled the fuel tanks with gasoline they'd brought with them. Enough fuel for two hours' flight time, according to the manuals. They would only need a fraction of that.

They made the final connections between the backpacks and the sails, double-checked the other's work, and then lifted the contraptions onto their shoulders. As they threaded their arms through the canvas straps and adjusted them across their chests, McMurphy said, "You're sure about this?"

"We don't have a choice," Bannon said, settling the harness seat against the back of his legs and adjusting the steering arm in front of him.

"You any idea how many crimes we're about to commit? Federal and otherwise?"

"I find it best not to think about it."

"Or how many years we'll spend in the hoosegow if we get caught?"

"None if we don't get caught."

The triangular sails snapped in the gentle night breeze coming off the nearby harbor. Bannon push-started his engine. McMurphy did the same. Giving themselves a good running start, they jogged across the roof, the sails flapping behind them.

First Bannon, then McMurphy, jumped.

They landed on the building's parapet, pushed off, and leaped from the roof, plunging toward the ground eighty-five feet below. Wind in his hair, Bannon's heart raced as the propeller strapped to his back sputtered, bit the night air, and then finally caught.

He shoved at the steering bar to catch the updraft. The kite-like sail billowed.

A sudden blast of wind reversed his descent and jerked him up and over the tumble of lower buildings below. The propeller roared in his ears. Beside him, McMurphy whooped like a kid riding a roller coaster for the first time. He glanced over to see his friend grinning from ear to ear. Wind whipped in his face, warm and tasting of the ocean. He shifted position and pushed the triangular control bar to the right, toward the port and Daniel Street.

Five minutes later, like eagles circling a nest, they flew over the rooftop of the lower federal building—only four stories tall—in wide, sweeping arcs. Bannon brought the power glider down in a perfect, three-step landing.

McMurphy did the same three seconds later.

"Okay, so that was very cool," McMurphy said as they unsnapped harnesses and collapsed the sails, setting the engine and disassembled frames on top to keep them from blowing away.

With the power gliders stowed, they crossed to the metal door that would gain them access to the building. As he'd hoped, the door had a glass window.

Bannon rubbed a spot clean in the soot-smeared glass. He extracted a black case from a utility pocket the size of an e-reader tablet, his Swiss Army knife of burglar tools. From it, he selected a small, green-handled tool with a slim metal shaft. He thumbed the switch on the side. The metal tip glowed orange. He touched the glass-cutting tool to the glass and quickly cut out a circle large enough to reach his hand through.

The cut circle fell inward before he could stop it. It shattered on the floor inside the stairwell.

"If they have glass break detection alarms, we're screwed," McMurphy whispered.

"Old building. They don't," Bannon assured him.

"You can't know that."

He didn't. He just hoped and had faith in lady luck.

From his tool kit, he extracted a magnet. He reached through the hole in the glass and placed it against the magnetic contact to maintain the circuit while McMurphy used his own set of lock picks to pick the lock. They heard a click. He pulled the door open. They held their breath and waited. No alarms went off. There was no rush of well-armed FBI agents waiting for them in the stairwell as they stepped through the doorway. Bannon pulled the door shut behind them.

"I forget how adept you are at breaking into places," McMurphy whispered.

"Blame it on my misspent youth," Bannon said with a grin. "Besides, you're pretty handy with a set of lock picks yourself."

"Because of the company I keep." He slapped Bannon on the shoulder with a smile. "We better keep moving."

At the base of the first set of stairs, Bannon said, "Let Kayla know we're inside."

Lieutenant Kayla Clarke worked for the Judge Advocate General of the Coast Guard, what other branches might call a JAG officer, though the Guard did it a little differently. She was assigned to First Division, stationed in Boston, Mass. She'd also worked with Bannon and his Deployable Operations Group back in the day. Because he trusted her, he often called upon her to help them on his escapades, as she called them since he began working for Grayson.

McMurphy shot her a text. She replied by return text. She was in the van, in position a block away.

"Good," Bannon said.

McMurphy pocketed the phone. "Where do you suppose they hold prisoners in a building not designed to hold prisoners?"

With a shrug, Bannon guessed, "The basement?"

THIRTEEN

BANNON PULLED A BLACK wool ski mask over his face. McMurphy did the same. His face began to sweat immediately. Bannon checked his watch. It was a little after three in the morning. He assumed the building—primarily an office building for various federal agencies, including the FBI—would be empty except for those agents assigned to guard the prisoners.

How many there were and what level of training they'd have was anybody's guess. Bannon hoped they weren't all SWAT-trained agents like the ones that'd accompanied them to the bungled storefront meet. Despite how that fiasco turned out, he had no desire to go head-to-head with that level of trained agent.

They reached the bottom of the stairwell. Five flights, which put them one story below the ground floor. The door was solid gray metal. No window to peek through.

Bannon had debated whether or not to bring firearms. The last thing he wanted to do was shoot a federal agent. They were men and women just doing their jobs. In the end, he and McMurphy decided to come armed with their Coast Guard-issued sidearms. Sig Sauer nine-millimeters. They would only fire in self-defense and hopefully do so without killing anyone.

He nodded to McMurphy, who pulled the door open.

He slipped into a deserted service hallway.

Together, they made their way down to an intersecting hallway. They heard voices.

Bannon dropped to one knee at the corner and leaned out past the wall. There were two men in dark suits, without ties, and their white shirt collars unbuttoned. Behind them was a closed door. One sat in a folding metal chair, tilted back against the wall. The other stood in front of him, smoking a cigarette. Bannon saw no weapons but assumed they were armed.

He held up two fingers to McMurphy.

"How do you want to play it?" his old friend asked.

He wanted to get in and get out, not waste time looking for ways to sneak up on them or wait for one of them to leave, which might never happen.

"We go straight at 'em," Bannon whispered back.

They had the element of surprise and, so, the advantage. He hoped.

"Come on." He waved to McMurphy and charged down the hallway.

The standing agent snapped his head around to see the two masked men running at them. He stepped back, crouched and reached under his suit jacket, drawing his weapon. Bannon fired a shot over his head. The bullet chewed into the cinderblock wall behind the agents. "Don't!"

The sitting agent slammed his chair down on all fours and drew something from under his jacket. Not a gun, but a walkie-talkie. He shouted into it. "Intruders! We've got intruders down here!"

McMurphy fired a shot so wide it pinged off the metal pipes running along the ceiling. We must look like the gang that couldn't shoot straight, Bannon figured, but that was fine. The last thing he wanted was for anyone to get hurt.

Both men raised their hands without drawing their weapons.

Bannon swung a fist and connected with the standing agent's jaw. He spit blood and spun away from the blow, but Bannon was relentless. He backhanded the man's face with the butt of his Sig. That raked a cut across the agent's chin.

He hated to do it, but the stakes were too high to give in to his compassions. Reinforcements were on their way. Time wasn't a luxury they had.

McMurphy reached the sitting agent, but not before the man dropped his raised hands and drew his weapon, a .40 caliber Glock 23. He squeezed off a shot. In the enclosed space, the noise was deafening. McMurphy closed in on the man. He ducked under the gun, slapped it away, and spun the startled agent around. He snaked his big arms around the man's throat and head, putting him into a sleeper chokehold. Softly, he said, "Relax. Go to sleep now. Nightie-night."

The agent went limp. McMurphy gently laid him down on the floor.

Meanwhile, Bannon was still duking it out with his guy. The agent swung a punch but missed. Bannon slammed the butt of his gun down on the back of the man's skull. With a grunt, the agent collapsed to the ground.

"Sorry," Bannon said, stepping over his prone body. He collected the agents' dropped firearms while McMurphy tried to open the door they'd been guarding. Locked.

Bannon heard the sound of racing footsteps coming closer. The Calvary.

McMurphy stepped back and kicked his boot through the door. The frame splintered and the door flew open, crashing into the wall. Bannon stepped inside.

The room was a cafeteria. A chrome service counter and a closed roll-down gate extended along the back wall. Large tables with built-in seats were folded up and lined along one wall. Carts of staked metal folding chairs were pushed up against the opposite wall. Around them were workplace posters reminding employees of safe food handling practices and to not throw utensils out in the trash when scraping plates and trays.

Fifteen cots filled the otherwise empty space.

The slumbering crew of the *Naeem* was startled awake. Some began to rise while others had already jumped to their feet. Thin, green Army blankets were wrapped around their shoulders, bunched up on the empty cots, or piled on the floor where they'd fallen. They all stared at Bannon and McMurphy, still shrouded beneath their ski masks, as they rubbed sleep from their eyes, trying to figure out what was happening.

Bannon scanned the room and found Safiyyah Zayd sitting on a cot with her legs still curled under a blanket. Her full dark hair was mussed from sleep. She wore a gray FBI Academy sweatshirt and unflattering baggy navy-blue sweatpants.

"We've got company," McMurphy shouted.

Several agents appeared at the door McMurphy had kicked in. He fired his Sig wildly in that general direction, hitting everything but human flesh. It was enough to keep the responding agents at bay.

Bannon grabbed Zayd by the arm and pulled her off her cot.

"Unhand me." She shook her arm loose. A crewmember attempted to come to her rescue. Bannon pointed his Sig at him. The would-be hero shrunk back. To Zayd, he said, "Don't you recognize a rescue when you see one?"

To McMurphy, he said, "We need another way out."

"Coming right up."

McMurphy grabbed a cart of metal folding chairs and charged across the room. He slammed the heavy cart into a set of double doors beside the service counter. It made a horrific crash. Chairs went flying, McMurphy slipped and fell to the floor, but the doors burst open.

Bannon popped off a couple more shots at the agents crowding around the door they'd come through. He ran to McMurphy with Zayd in tow. She was barefooted. He didn't care. He got McMurphy to his feet. They climbed over the spilled chairs and reached the service corridor behind the kitchen.

"If you want to escape," Bannon shouted to the *Naeem* crew, "Stop them."

He waved at the agents peeking into the cafeteria.

Bannon pushed McMurphy and Zayd through the back door. "Keep going."

In the lead, McMurphy tossed his gun to Bannon and pulled Zayd along by the hand.

"Who are you people? Where are you taking me?"

"Shut up," Bannon said, keeping an eye out behind them for any sign of pursuit.

They went around a corner and ran to a large service elevator.

"Yes?" McMurphy asked.

They needed to get upstairs, reach the lobby level. Bannon looked around quickly for a stairwell. He didn't see one. "We don't have a choice."

Bannon pushed them inside the elevator and started to pull the steel doors and gate down.

"With every agent in the building on our tails, you think locking ourselves in a steel container's a good idea?"

"No. But we're out of time and options." The elevator only serviced two floors. It reeked of oil and grease. Bannon hit the up button. The elevator jerked, then started its slow crawl up. Bannon's face was sweaty, and the ski mask itched, but he couldn't risk taking it off until they made good their escape. If they made good their escape.

"You think this thing could go any slower?" McMurphy asked.

"Who are you people?" Zayd demanded again. "Where are you taking me?"

Both men ignored her, remaining silent until the elevator shuddered to a stop.

"I'll open," Bannon said, handing McMurphy his gun. "You cover."

His old friend nodded and knelt on one knee so he could see between the steel doors as Bannon threw up the inner safety gate. He waited for a second. The outer steel doors remained closed. They didn't hear anything.

McMurphy nodded.

Bannon grabbed the handle and pulled the upper steel door up, shoving the lower half down with his foot. His breath held.

"Clear," McMurphy announced, standing up. He sounded as surprised as Bannon felt.

"Come on then." He grinned at McMurphy. "It looks like you've still got a wee bit of that Irish luck in ya, after all." His attempt at a brogue was atrocious.

"That or God looks out for fools and drunks. Either way, I've covered both bases."

They raced down the corridor. This one was wider than the one downstairs. They came to what looked like a loading dock and a closed overhead bay door. The pull chain was locked off with a padlock. They didn't have time to pick it. Bannon knew Hollywood was full of crap when it came to shooting off padlocks. Doing so would more than likely result in someone losing an eye from a fragmented, ricocheted bullet than the lock popping open.

"Find me something to pry it open," Bannon said.

The two men looked around. Even Zayd joined in the search. Smart enough to figure out the two men trying to break her out was a better option than whatever the feds had in store for her. She was wrong, but for now, Bannon thought, it worked.

She found a pair of small bolt cutters inside a rolling metal podium. "These help?"

Bannon worried they were too small for the job but took them and fit the cutting blades around the padlock shackle.

"Hurry it up," McMurphy said. "We've got company coming."

The sound of people running echoed down the corridor.

Bannon squeezed the short orange handles together, feeling the blades bite into the silver metal shackle. He grunted.

"Let me." McMurphy pushed him out of the way. He grabbed the bolt cutters and squeezed, gritting his teeth until his face turned bright red from the strain.

Bannon glanced nervously down the corridor. The posse was getting close.

He pulled his cell phone out and speed-dialed Kayla. When she answered, he said, "We're at a loading bay. It's probably at the back of the building."

"On my way."

"Hurry, we've got a gaggle of really pissed-off agents closing in on our tail."

"I'll be there."

McMurphy let out a loud groan. The shackle snapped in two. The lock fell to the floor. In pieces. He pulled out what was left of the shackle and freed the chain. Zayd reached around him, grabbed the door chain, and yanked. He pulled the chain hand over hand like there was no tomorrow, raising the door as fast as she could.

A bullet pinged off the metal.

Someone yelled, "Freeze!"

Three men appeared at the far end of the corridor, men in suits, looking very unhappy. They rushed toward them, guns out.

Bannon shot wildly down the hall. Bullets pinged off metal pipes and chewed chunks of concrete from the walls.

The agents ducked and scattered.

Bannon shouted, "Go! Go! Go!"

McMurphy and Zayd dove under the door they'd only managed to lift about two feet off the ground. They rolled across the pavement outside. Bannon dove after them.

Outside, they got to their feet as a black van barreled down the narrow alley toward them, driving in reverse. It slammed to a stop. Red brake lights flared. It had no markings and no license plate. Zayd tried to dart away, making a run in the opposite direction, but Bannon grabbed her arm and pulled her back. McMurphy slid open the van's side panel door. Bannon shoved Zayd into the empty cargo space. He wasn't gentle about it.

From the light streaming under the partially open door, he saw a jumble of shadows. The posse was at the door.

McMurphy shot his gun in the air as rapidly as he could while shouting, "Allahu Akbar! Allahu Akbar!"

He pushed Bannon toward the open van. They hopped inside. Bannon slammed the door shut as several agents braved the gunfire, rolled out under the door, and opened fire. Bullets pinged off the bumper and metal skin of the van.

Kayla jammed the gas pedal down and drove on smoking tires out of the alley. Bannon, McMurphy, and Zayd tumbled around in the back like bingo balls spinning inside a cage. At the intersecting street, the pretty brunette wrenched the steering wheel to the right and bounded down the apron and around the corner on what felt like only two tires.

Her three passengers were thrown first in one direction and then the next, slamming into the sides of the van, muffling curses. Only then did she call out with a grin, "Hang on."

CHAPTER FOURTEEN

AZIZA FAAID DID NOT tell Tara how he survived. Not at first. He backhanded her across the face with a closed fist instead.

For such a skinny man, he packed a powerful punch. The blow sent her reeling across the room. She staggered back and placed her hand on her hot cheek. She tasted blood. It came from a cut to her lip. She touched her fingertips to it and looked at the dollop of blood. She swept her hair back and glared at him.

"You'll pay for that."

"What? Going to blow me up again?"

She took a step forward but stopped when Bridget raised her pistol. "Someone needs to tell me what's going on. You're saying this is not Safiyyah Zayd?"

"It is not," Faaid said. "You were duped. Tricked. Easily fooled."

"Impossible," Bridget shouted.

"This woman's name is Tarakesh Sardana. Her friends charmingly call her Blades." He stared hard at Tara. The hatred in his eyes was easy to read. "She tried to kill me. And she failed."

"I'll just have to make sure the second time's the charm," Tara said.

To Bridget, Faaid said, "I never told you the story of how I came to America, did I?"

From her expression, the woman didn't seem all that interested in hearing about it now, either. She kept her eyes—and her gun—squarely on Tara.

"A small group of us had successfully stowed a stolen shipment of man-portable SA-18 Russian surface-to-air missile launchers on an unsuspecting cargo vessel, the *MV Caleb*, leaving Morocco to make the trip to America. To make a short story shorter, Ms. Sardana and her teammates intercepted the *Caleb* before we could get aboard and retrieve our weapons.

"The plan had been to board the ship posing as pirates. We were going to steal several crates. It didn't matter which ones. Rough up the crew a little and escape with the launchers without the Captain or crew ever learning they'd aided in the smuggling of surface-to-air weapons into the United States.

"Imagine my surprise upon finding Ms. Sardana and her friends aboard. Still, I thought, incorrectly as it turned out, I had the situation well in hand. We left the *Caleb* with our missile launchers loaded on our boat. What we did not know as we prepared to make our escape was that Ms. Sardana had placed an IED of her own making inside one of the crates."

Tara had outdone herself that day, she thought. Now she shrugged, feigning innocence. "A going-away present."

Faaid wasn't amused. "The device was remotely activated. She blew up my ship. Killed my crew. She sent our missiles to the bottom of the Atlantic Ocean."

"And you, too, or so we thought," Tara said. "How did you survive?"

"The call of nature," Faaid said, amused.

"Excuse me?"

"I had to go the bathroom," he explained. "My men were securing the weapons to the stern deck. I went below to use the—what do your American sailors call it—the head when the ship exploded. What a sound it made. Bulkheads blew apart, trapping me below deck. The stairs were blocked by debris. The entire space was engulfed in flames and smoke." He stroked the savage burns on the right side of his face with the back of his fingers again. "Water rushed in at me with the force of a tsunami. The ship split in half. I clawed through the deluge of water and managed to swim out, escaping from the boat as it broke into pieces and sank. Debris was all around me. Something struck me in the head. Dazed, half-conscious, I had no idea how far underwater I was. I held my breath and swam, using the glowing light of the burning wreckage on the surface to guide me. Like a light from above."

He paused for dramatic effect, Tara supposed. "It was Allah's decree that I survive. That I live on to fight his fight. I broke the surface before my lungs gave out. Debris floated and burned around me. The air hot with smoke, searing my lungs and throat with every gasp I took. But I survived, floating, hiding among the wreckage. I watched as the *Caleb* sped away."

"You left a little surprise package for us on our ship, too, as I recall."

"I did. But when your ship did not explode, I knew my attempt to scuttle the *Caleb* had failed. I clung to a piece of driftwood until your ship was out of sight. Then, I managed to steer myself to one of the lifeboats we'd set adrift when we boarded the *Caleb*. Ironic that the means by which I meant to seal your fates turned out to be my salvation."

"I call it dumb luck."

He ignored her. "It took me most of the day and into that night, but I reached it. I climbed inside. Exhausted, I slept. And felt the agony of my hot, burned skin. For days, I drifted, thirsty and tired, covered with only a tarp to protect me from the relentless sun during the day and the cold at night. Then, blessedly, it rained. Long enough and hard enough, I did not die from thirst and dehydration."

"How did you make land? The *Caleb* was three days out from Boston, traveling at twenty-four knots. You couldn't have survived until you drifted into port."

"I did not. I had the great fortune of crossing paths with a fishing trawler. They saw the lifeboat and came to investigate. They found me near death from starvation and my burns. They brought me aboard their boat. The kindness of strangers, yes. It almost made me wish I didn't have to kill them all. But I did. It was Allah's will."

"That's your justification for slaughtering a ship full of fishermen? God made me do it."

"As I have admitted, it gave me pause."

"You're a psychopath."

"Allah sent those fishermen to rescue me, to pull me from the brink of death and provide me the means, the sustenance, and shelter so that I might rally from my bleakest hour victorious. That was all the proof I needed that my path is a righteous one. One guided by Allah."

"You killed a bunch of people who did nothing but try and save you."

"I could not allow those men to radio your Coast Guard. I am but the tool. I had no choice in the matter."

"It was all Allah's doing. Wow," Tara said. "That's the worst excuse I've heard since 'I was just following orders.'"

"I am a man with a purpose. I have been tested and survived. I have been shown the way. Now I'm stronger and more committed than ever to the cause, to his cause, because of it."

"This cause of yours, of his, what is it, exactly?"

"To bring our enemies to their knees. Finally, and completely. To end this ever-lasting conflict by ushering in a new and lasting caliphate." He clenched his fist and gritted his teeth.

"Let me guess. With you as the chosen caliph." Tara raised an eyebrow. "I stand corrected. You're not just a psychopath. You're a delusional psychopath."

He ignored her insults. "You—and your friends—are to bear witness to my most glorious revenge upon the American infidel. And then, upon you and your two friends."

"Yeah. Certifiable nut job," Tara said.

He raised his hand to strike her again, but she was ready for it this time. She caught his wrist, arresting his swing. "I gave you that first one." He tried to pull away, but she tightened her grip on his wrist. "I will end you, Faaid. You have my word."

"Says the woman who is my prisoner," he said with confidence that did not reach his eyes. There, she saw uncertainty.

She released his arm with a shove. "Like you say, I've got friends. Friends who'll come for me. Who will stop at nothing until they've found me and rescued me. Or avenged me." She flashed a grim smile. He took an unsteady step back. She enjoyed the unnerved expression on his face. "Whatever happens to me," she said. "I'll have the satisfaction knowing this ends only one way for you."

CHAPTER FIFTEEN

BANNON CREATED A QUICK sign on his laptop computer, printed it out, and tacked it on the front door of the Keel Haul. It read: BAR CLOSED. WATER MAIN BREAK. COME BACK TOMORROW. It wasn't yet dawn, and the bar wasn't due to open until eleven, but he knew they wouldn't be done with what they had to do by then.

He made sure the door was locked. All the heavy curtains and shutters were in place over the windows. McMurphy had locked up the back. He was now behind the bar drinking a beer while coffee gurgled hot and black in the coffee maker.

Bannon pushed the square wooden tables and chairs out of the way, clearing a space around their guest. In the center of the room, Kayla finished zip-tying Safiyyah Zayd to a chair.

The Keel Haul was designed to look like the interior of the sailing ships of old. The walls were polished knotty pine. The ceiling had thick timber ribs running along the width of the room. Lighted lanterns hung from the beams. Candle-like sconces glowed over the booths. Scattered throughout the place were wooden barrels and sea chests. Ropes, anchors, pulleys, fishing nets, and period-appropriate coastal maps were hung on the walls. The smell of teak oil filled the air.

Bannon loved that smell.

McMurphy poured a cup of coffee and slid it across the bar to him. They were still dressed in their black raiding clothes but without the hot, itchy ski masks.

"We've got her. Now, what do we do with her?" McMurphy asked.

Bannon sipped his coffee and glanced over his shoulder at their prisoner. She glared back at him. He shrugged. "Talk to her."

"I can't get over how much she looks like Tara," Kayla said, accepting a coffee from McMurphy. "It's uncanny."

"Downright spooky," McMurphy agreed.

Bannon couldn't argue. But he also knew he couldn't let her physical resemblance to his friend distract him from what he had to do next. Not with Tara's life hanging in the balance. He grabbed a chair from a nearby table and spun it around backward. He sat down facing her, his arms folded over the back.

"My name is Brice Bannon."

"I do not care who you are. You will pay for how you have treated me. My country—"

"Your country what?" Bannon asked. "Before you try to run some line on me, let's get something straight. I know exactly who you are, Miss Zayd. You work for NSEDC, your country's answer to NASA. Or you did until you disappeared several years ago with, I'm guessing, whatever secret or proprietary information you stole regarding their space program. Whatever it was, it's made them very nervous. Trust me, since you joined your little terror cult, they're as happy to have you off the board as we are."

Zayd pressed her lips together in a firm line.

"So we're on the same page. I don't care two whiffs about that. I care about just one thing. My friend. She's been taken by the people you came here to meet, and now you're going to tell me everything you know about them." In response to her defiant stare, he said, "Because if you don't, things will get very unpleasant for you."

"There is nothing you can do to me. You will not hurt me. Your government is too timid to do what it really takes to win. That is why you do not scare me."

"You're a smart woman, a scientist, so try and follow along." Bannon pointed at McMurphy and Kayla. "My friends and I broke you out of a federal building. We took you from the FBI. Exchanged gunfire with them." To McMurphy, he said, "How many federal and state crimes did we commit tonight?"

"Too many to count."

Bannon returned his attention to Zayd. "Do you think we'd do all that if we simply wanted to talk to you?"

Before she could answer, Bannon kept going. "If we wanted to talk, to just interrogate you, we would have done that while you were in custody," Bannon lied. He had her nervous. Good. He needed her to believe if they were willing to go to such lengths to grab her, to break the rules the way they did, that would mean the rules didn't apply to them. Once the rules were tossed out, she wouldn't know what they were capable of. Rogue agents were unpredictable. For someone in her position, that was a terrifying proposition.

"What do you want?" she asked, licking her dry lips.

"I told you. Everything about the people you came here to meet. Who are they? Where would they take…you? How do we find them?"

"I do not know," Zayd said. "That is the truth. It was Captain Amar who coordinated everything. Through his contact in Alexandria. Speak with him."

"I sure would like to," Bannon said. "Except your people killed him. Eliminated him as soon as he delivered who they thought was you. Why would they do that?"

She reacted to that. Shaken by the news. "I…I'm sure I do not know."

"Guess."

"Perhaps they realized he tricked them. If they learned your imposter was not me, she too is dead."

That was what Bannon feared most. Hearing it said out loud was like a kick in the gut. He stood quickly and shoved his chair away. The legs scraped noisily across the floor. Zayd blinked and jerked back at the sudden movement.

"I cannot help you," she said. "I cannot help your friend. Please, just let me go."

"Don't be naive," Bannon said over his shoulder. He grabbed his cup of coffee and drank. It was just coffee, but he half-wished McMurphy had spiked it with some whiskey when he wasn't looking.

"Do you believe her?" Kayla asked, her voice a whisper.

"She's lying," McMurphy declared. "They all lie."

"We'll never know," Bannon said. "Not without some kind of leverage."

There was a knock at the front door.

He drank his coffee and smiled. "And there it is now."

He looked through the authentic brass porthole, complete with dog ears and nuts. The door had been salvaged from an 18th-century British frigate he'd discovered during a dive off the coast of Rye Beach. He'd restored the door to near pristine condition before fitting it to the bar's entrance, giving his ship-themed watering hole the perfect entryway.

He unlocked and opened the door, stepping back.

Secretary of Homeland Security Elizabeth Grayson strolled into the bar, all business.

Bannon looked outside, checked both ways, then relocked the door. He joined her at the bar with the others. She'd barely glanced at Zayd as she walked by.

"Coffee smells good. Got any more?"

Bannon lifted the hinged service counter and went behind the bar. He poured a cup from the pot for her and another for himself.

Grayson stared disapprovingly at McMurphy. "Certainly, you're not drinking at this hour, Chief. It's barely dawn."

He tilted his head back and drained the last of his beer, then dropped the empty bottle into a recycle bin under the bar. He wiped his mouth by dragging the back of his catcher's mitt-sized hand across his lips. "Not anymore, Lizzy."

She shook her head, more amused than annoyed. "No problems last night, I take it?"

"No. We didn't hurt anyone, did we?"

"One agent twisted an ankle. Other than that, only their pride," Grayson said. She and Bannon had hatched the scheme while "arguing" in the lounge of the McIntyre building the night before.

"And the FBI believes it was Zayd's friends who broke her out?" Bannon asked.

"Bought it hook, line, and sinker," Grayson said over the lip of her coffee cup, shooting McMurphy a look. "Though that Allahu Akbar bit was a little over the top."

He shrugged with a wide grin on his face. "I needed to sell it."

"Still," she said, unable to contain a smile, "the Boston field office will be busy looking for a mole that doesn't exist and searching for a terrorist they let slip through their fingers. They'll be doing whatever they can to redeem their damaged reputation."

"In other words, kept busy so they'll leave us the hell alone."

"Yes." Grayson hadn't lied when she told Bannon the DoJ was trying to yank the case out from under her. The Attorney General had made the case to the President that domestic kidnapping and terrorism were their wheelhouse. Grayson argued a massive manhunt would put her agent in danger. A more surgical approach was needed. Ultimately, Grayson would've won the battle against the Attorney General and DoJ, but bureaucracy takes time, the sort of time they didn't have. Staging the breakout forced the FBI's attention elsewhere, putting them in serious CYA mode, while giving Bannon what he wanted most: unobstructed access to Safiyyah Zayd.

"You were a little rough on Agent Pierce back there," Grayson said, demonstrating a large dose of her usual compassion. "The poor man did just lose two men."

"That he wouldn't have," Bannon said, not being smug but angry. "If he'd listened to us."

"And me?" Grayson raised her eyebrow. "'I just signed her death warrant.' A little harsh, don't you think?"

"Like Skyjack said, had to sell it. Did you get what I requested?" Bannon asked.

She withdrew a computer tablet from her oversized briefcase bag and handed it to Bannon. "You want to show her, or shall I?"

"Better together," he said.

Bannon and Grayson returned to where Safiyyah Zayd remained zip-tied. She had been watching them at the bar, but they were too far away and spoke too low for her to hear anything. Suspicion filled her eyes as they sat down. Grayson had met with her on the *Bowman* when she was first captured. Zayd knew who she was. At that time, Grayson had tried the carrot approach. She'd tried to appeal to the woman's humanity. She hadn't gotten very far. Now, it was time for the stick.

"You remember who I am, don't you?"

"You are the Secretary of Homeland Security. An American spymaster."

"That's right. Then you also know I report directly to the President of the United States. That makes me a very important person. A person who can get things done."

"I told him," Zayd glared at Bannon. "I do not know where your friend is."

"And," Grayson said. "We believe you. I know how secretive the cells can be. How they operate. It's no surprise to me you don't know the identities of any of the members here. Except for Captain Amar, of course. Still, we think you can help us."

"Even if I could, why would I?"

Bannon answered. "There is a simple secret to getting someone to do something they don't want to, to make them act against their own self-interest. It works every time. Want to know what it is?"

"Torture me if you must. I cannot tell you what I do not know."

"We're not going to torture you."

Zayd visibly relaxed upon hearing that.

"The thing to remember," he said, "is physical torture isn't the only way to get what you want from a prisoner. The secret is to have the right leverage against a person. For some, that's torture, sure. They'd do or say anything to make the pain stop. But there are other ways."

"Why are you telling me these things?"

"Because," Bannon said, "while you don't know who your friends are or where they might be, you do have other information we want. Things we believe will be of use to us, not only in finding our friend but also in stopping whatever horrific event you were brought here to cause."

"Again, why would I help you?"

"Well, we could offer you a deal," Grayson said. "Immunity from prosecution for crimes committed here or abroad. We do that a lot with criminals. Make deals with small fish to get the larger fish. But we're not going to do that. The United States has a long-standing policy, one which I believe in, to not negotiate with terrorists."

"Then I suppose we have nothing more to say to each other," Zayd said, trying to sound brave.

"Oh, but we do," Grayson assured her. To Bannon, she said, "Show her."

He clicked a button on the tablet. The screen lit up. He turned it around to show Zayd.

It was a frozen video image. Bannon hit play. The screen glowed. On it were bright and dark shades of green with occasional bright flashes of white light. The image jumped around, chaotic, and difficult to follow. The war on terror had raged on for so long, everyone instantly recognized a military night-vision helmet cam video. The tip of an M16 could be seen as the wearer, a soldier, ran through what looked like the living space of a residential home.

From the microphone came heavy breathing. Off-screen, people called out, "Clear. Clear."

"Recognize that living room?" Grayson asked.

Zayd leaned forward and squinted.

The jumbled image rushed through a hallway. "This way," a soldier called out.

Ahead, a door burst open. The night vision technology made the dark room visible. The soldier had entered a bedroom.

Zayd gasped.

A figure in the bed sat up. Shocked at what was happening, the heavy-set man tossed the covers back. He swung his feet onto the floor. "Don't move!" The soldier shouted. "Don't you move!"

The images on the screen were hard to see. Jumpy and jumbled. The camera view swung away and then came back again. The man on the bed, visible only from the neck down, raised his hands. A hand reached out and grabbed him by the shoulder. He was pulled forward and slammed down to the floor.

"Don't move!" the soldier commanded.

"Do you recognize that man?" Grayson asked.

Zayd's mouth hung open. She closed it. Tears filled her eyes. "Father."

Bannon pulled the tablet away and switched the image off.

"That's right," Grayson said. "Your father, the general, was apprehended today. Last night, actually."

"Why? Who were those men?"

"A covert SEAL team. I sent them to your father's estate and had him arrested. He's currently in our custody as an enemy combatant."

"My government will protest."

"Oh, they already have," Grayson said. "And while our Secretary of State wasn't too happy about it, he is explaining to your government that your father is wanted on suspicion of committing terrorist acts against the United States."

"You cannot do this."

"I told you, Ms. Zayd, I am a very powerful woman who gets things done. Sometimes not very pleasant things." she pointed at the tablet in Bannon's hand. "Like that."

"It is not true! My father's done nothing wrong."

"But you have, Safiyyah, and he will answer for your crimes."

"Answer, how?"

"First, he'll be taken from your country under cover of night. He'll be interrogated. He'll be labeled an enemy combatant. Stripped of all legal rights, he'll be dumped in Guantanamo Bay. Gitmo."

"I'm sure you've heard of it," Bannon said. From the fear in her eyes, she was quite familiar with its reputation. "Nasty place," Bannon confirmed.

"Where he'll remain," Grayson added. "Indefinitely."

"You cannot do this."

"It's already done," Grayson said. "As Commander Bannon said, it's all about having the right leverage."

A long silence followed.

Zayd lowered her head and stared at the floor. Tears fell from her eyes. When she finally looked up again, she said, "What do you want to know? I will tell you everything."

CHAPTER **SIXTEEN**

AN HOUR LATER, BANNON stood outside at the retaining wall separating Hampton Beach from the parking lot on Ocean Boulevard. Across the street from the Keel Haul and near the bandshell, where performances were scheduled throughout the summer. It was a favorite spot of his. The sun was coming up, creating another magnificent sunrise over the Atlantic Ocean.

One for the record books, he thought, having watched hundreds of them from here. Low, ribbon-like clouds were strung out near the horizon. They were painted in brilliant orange and red as yellow-white rays of sunlight shot through breaks in the clouds like biblical laser beams. One could almost hear the sound of a choir singing.

The gentle waves of a low tide washed up on the sand. Quiet and calm. A young couple in shorts and sleeveless T-shirts ran by. Their bare feet slapped the wet sand at the water's foamy edge. Her ponytail swished behind her head. Two gulls chased each other across the dry sand near a metal trash can.

Bannon held a bottle of Coors Light beer and drank the last of it down.

A hand reached out, holding another.

Bannon looked to his right.

Grayson offered him a weary smile along with the beer. She took a sip from a second beer she kept for herself as she took a moment to watch the sunrise.

A sight to behold. At once, it was both inspiring and humbling. Bannon thought everyone on Earth should start their day this way. He was convinced if every person experienced that kind of peace and beauty, just for a little while each morning, maybe then, there'd be a lot less ugliness in the world.

"I haven't done something like this since I was in college," Grayson said, breaking the quiet with her soft voice.

"Take the time to watch a sunrise or drink a beer before dawn?"

"Both, actually." She pinched her eyes. "Makes me wonder why I don't just retire and do things like this more often."

"Because the world needs people like you at the wheel." Be pointed toward the jogging couple. "So they can go on enjoying doing that carefree."

"Needs people like you, too, Brice."

She'd spent the last hour talking with Zayd, draining the woman of every last drop of information she had to give. He could tell the interrogation had taken its toll on her.

"Who'd you get to shoot the video?" he asked.

"Your friend Chief Petty Officer Johnson and his men, Reyes and O'Neil. We got permission to use the police academy kill house facility. From pictures Kayla dug up, we decorated it to look like the general staff house in Quetta. A half-assed job, but good enough to pass muster with all the jiggling and night vision filters."

"And the guy who played Zayd's dad?"

"There, we got lucky. Found a standup comic from one of the local comedy shops. Turns out he's an aspiring actor."

"Aren't they all?"

She smiled. "The resemblance wasn't great, but it worked for the few seconds of screen time we gave him."

"It convinced me, and I'm the one who asked you to put it together," Bannon said, impressed. "What'd she give you?"

"She started off claiming the bombing raid that destroyed the school where her mother was killed was carried out by American and British forces."

"Any truth to it?"

"I'm familiar with the incident, but it's the first I've heard allied coalition forces were behind it. We'll dig deeper into it. In the meantime, not to sound callus, it doesn't change what we're dealing with now. Justified or not, Zayd became our enemy that day, vowing retribution against the West. What's troubling is how she intends to carry out her revenge."

Bannon sipped his beer and listened.

"Zayd's work at NSEDC involved electromagnetic propulsion and the development of a magnetohydrodynamic drive or MHD accelerator."

Bannon shook his head. "I cheated off Betsy Wharton to pass my AP Science final in high school. You'll need to explain that."

"Put in simple terms, an MHD accelerator uses electric and magnetic fields, thus no moving parts, to propel—in the case of NSEDC—a rocket into space. If a payload could achieve escape velocity without using traditional fuels, it would be a game-changer for space exploration. Zayd worked on a specific system to launch a scramjet to high altitude. Other applications are maglev trains and propulsion systems for maritime ships and submarines. As is, MHD accelerators have proven to be impractical because of cost, the size and weight of the electromagnets needed, and other technical limitations. As such, the programs are largely considered theoretical and experimental."

"Sounds rather benign and space exploration-y then," Bannon said, failing to see a cause for concern.

"Except alternative propulsion methods aren't the only applications." She finished her beer. "Have you ever heard of a railgun?"

Bannon started to make a Flash Gordon joke but, reading Grayson's somber expression, decided against it. "Something DARPA's working on, right?"

The Defense Advanced Research Projects Agency, sounding like a nefarious evil science organization, is the agency that developed new, cutting-edge, future technologies for the Department of Defense.

"The weapon uses the same technology Miss Zayd is an expert in. They are capable of firing a projectile with a muzzle velocity of more than twice that of similar conventional weapons. One defense contractor in California has developed and tested a working prototype, claiming they can have the weapon ready for production in two to three years."

"Meaning other than this prototype, they don't exist."

"Oh, they exist, Brice. We know India has one. Russia, China, the UK, and Turkey aren't far behind. Our Navy has been field testing one for the last two years. It has plans to install them on their next-generation destroyers. It will be a game-changer when it comes to intercepting ballistic and supersonic missiles, stealth air, and swarming surface threats."

"We're talking about a ship-based weapon. Something big? Like battleship big?"

"What's been developed so far," Grayson said.

And here came the uh oh.

"DARPA and our contractors, and others around the world, are also working on a more compact version."

Bannon hated to have to ask. "How compact are we talking?"

"We have one designed for use with the XM2118, the armored mounted combat vehicle meant to replace our aging Abrams battle tanks in the next decade."

"You think someone is ahead of us in developing such a scaled-down version."

"Miss Zayd confirmed it. She developed the thing after leaving NSEDC, using the stolen Intel she took with her."

"The intel her government refused to admit she had."

"Beside the point. For now. According to Zayd, this terror cell has such a weapon. Zayd was brought here to make it operational."

"A vehicle-portable electromagnetic railgun. On U.S. soil."

"Yes."

"What's the capability of such a weapon?"

"Hard to say, a lot of factors to consider. But a large-scale railgun can accelerate a seven-pound projectile to Mach 7—seven times the speed of sound—and generate nearly fifty megajoules of muzzle energies. To put that in perspective," Grayson said, "the kinetic energy equal to the impact of a five-ton bus traveling at over three hundred miles per hour."

Bannon whistled. "Jesus."

"And a potential range of over one hundred miles."

"If they have it, they'll want to use it." Bannon marveled at, and was disgusted by, the level of atrocity people were willing to commit. "A mobile weapon that size could go anywhere. Be hidden anywhere. Does she know what the target is?"

"She says no. I believe her. She thinks we have her father. As long as she believes that, I think she'd do anything to protect him."

Bannon agreed. Her Intel was solid. Scary as hell, but valid all the same.

The sun was full up now. A few more people jogged past them on their morning runs. He watched a few beachcombers walking along the shoreline, regulars he recognized by sight. He focused on a young couple walking hand in hand kicking at the lapping water, talking amiably. They had their long pants rolled up past their ankles, their shoes dangling from their hands. They seemed at peace, completely oblivious to the dangers in the world.

Ignorance was indeed bliss.

Another thought struck Bannon. "As soon as they put Tara in front of that weapon, expecting her to activate it or whatever she's supposed to do, she's toast."

"I know," Grayson said. "I am so sorry I put her in that position."

Bannon didn't let her off the hook, nor did he come down hard on her. The op had been ill-advised from the start. They'd moved too fast, with insufficient intel. But she'd been right, too. He hated to admit it. They'd never have learned what danger was lurking out there if they hadn't acted. Maybe not until the terrorists had struck. Not until it was too late.

At least now they had a chance to stop it.

He just needed to figure out how.

"Hey, guys." In unison, Bannon and Grayson turned to face Kayla. She offered them two steaming hot coffee cups. "I think I might have something."

Bannon tossed the empty beer bottles in a nearby trash can.

"Trying to think of a way to help find Tara, I started going through the background data we have on Captain Amar and his crewmembers. By we, I mean the FBI files I hacked—oops, did I say that out loud—not an easy task when you don't know what you're looking for. Fishing more than anything else, hoping something would pop up."

"And something did?" Grayson asked.

"Yes. I think. None of the crew has any connection to the United States. No friends. No family. Whenever they came to port, as near as I could tell, they hung around together, visiting the same harbor bars and…. other even less savory places, except for one person. Captain Amar. He's got several transatlantic trips under his belt."

"Not surprising, considering his occupation," Bannon said. "It was probably why they chose him. No reason to suddenly suspect another voyage."

"Anyway, I discovered he has a sister. She lives in Dorchester," Kayla said.

"The FBI missed this?" Grayson asked.

"It took some, okay, a lot of digging," she said with a barely concealed sense of pride. Bannon was sure it was more than justified. "She's married. Humaira Tumandar."

"How did you…" Grayson asked.

Bannon smiled. He'd come to rely on Kayla Clarke's amazing cyber-tech skills. Nothing she came up with surprised him anymore.

"I found a student visa for a Humaira Amar. I followed that breadcrumb to the school she attended. That led me to a graduation announcement, a citizenship application, a wedding announcement, and to her social media. It was purely by chance, luck, really. I spotted Karim Amar in a group picture posted on Instagram. Or at least someone that looked like him. I went back to Custom and TSA records detailing his various arrivals and departures over the last ten years. The wedding date lined up with a period when he was here. I dug deeper into family records and found that Captain Amar does—did—have a sister named Humaira. She came to school as an exchange student first, then received a student visa…"

She made a circling gesture with her finger. "Completing the loop."

Kayla looked at a piece of paper in her hand. It was Keel Haul stationery from a pad with the bar's logo and contact information on it. Bannon kept it by the register to jot notes on. Apparently, she'd done the same.

"She met and married Behram Tumandar. He goes by Ben. And according to a real property search I did, they own a small house in Dorchester." She handed him the paper. "This is the address."

Bannon planted a big kiss on her forehead. "Lieutenant, you're amazing."

She beamed, agreeing. "Yeah. I am."

SEVENTEEN

AZIZA FAAID CALLED FOR Reza. The large mute came into the room immediately, carrying a length of thick, five-sixteenths inch anchor chain, a cuff attached to one end. With him, he also brought in a metal folding chair. He stood on the chair and looped the chain around one of several large pipes running along the length of the ceiling. He cinched the chain tight and snapped the cuff around Tara's right wrist.

It reminded her of how the Puritans secured their prisoners in the 17th Century. Old school.

"A leash," Faaid said. "For the dog."

"I need to go to the bathroom."

Bridget brought in a bucket and set it down in the corner.

Reza carried the chair with him as he left the room. Bridget and Faaid turned to follow him.

"Don't I even get the chair to sit in?" Tara called out.

"Sit on the floor. We gave you enough chain for that." Faaid paused to consider. "I think."

He slammed the door shut. Then he locked it.

Reza put a chair down next to the door and sat down. Putting himself on guard duty.

Faaid patted his shoulder. "You are a good man, Reza. A good man."

He and Bridget walked away.

They entered a large room that looked like a lobby in an old-fashioned movie theater or opera house but with everything stripped from the walls. Blue indoor-outdoor carpet covered the floor in three sections broken up by two tiled aisles that led from one end of the space to the other.

"Why did you not kill her?" Bridget asked. "If she's as dangerous as you claim—"

He stopped and turned. "If! If! Do you doubt what I have told you?" He pointed at his scarred face. "Do you doubt the injuries I have sustained for the cause?"

"No. Of course not. What I'm saying is that's all the more reason we should kill her. Why run the risk of keeping her alive?"

"Because she has information we need." They reached a doorway. He paused. "The Coast Guard must have intercepted the *Naeem*. Boarded her."

"The Coast Guard?"

"I told you that *kuratana* operates with a team. Two men. One claimed to be a commander in the United States Coast Guard when I encountered him. His name was Bannon. Brice Bannon. With them was another man, a most disagreeable individual called McMurphy. Large. With red hair. I have to assume they are working with her again."

"They cannot know where we are. We were careful. We followed your instructions to the letter. They can't be of concern to us."

"Oh, but they can, Ms. Barnes. They most assuredly can." He thought about them, about his brief encounter with the two men on the *Caleb*. "Don't you see? It had to be them. They boarded the *Naeem,* took Zayd—the real Zayd—prisoner. Then, in the devious way they operate, they turned Captain Amar against us. Turned him into a traitor to his people. A traitor to Allah. How prophetic of me to have had the man eliminated." He smiled. "To think, my reasoning was simply financial and to ensure his silence. But Allah, he has a greater plan. He knows all."

Bridget rolled her eyes. "I say all the more reason to kill her."

He turned on her, tired of her constantly second-guessing his decisions. "Then what of Zayd? How do we complete our mission without her? Do you possess the expertise to make our weapon operational?" He sneered. "A woman like you?"

"Careful how you speak to me, Faaid. With one phone call, I'll—"

He held up a hand. "Of course, Ms. Barnes. My apologies. Let me explain." He didn't add, in simple terms, even you can understand. "Ms. Sardana will tell us where the Americans have taken Safiyyah Zayd. Once she has done so, then, perhaps, I'll allow you to kill her."

"You'll allow me?" Bridget asked with a raised eyebrow.

Faaid held up a warning finger. Arrogant woman. "Get the information first. We cannot move forward without Safiyyah Zayd's assistance."

TARA HAD BEEN LEFT alone for hours before someone returned.

She used that time to examine every inch of her captive space. A simple, barren room. The walls were wood veneer. The floor was covered in old, natty, green indoor-outdoor carpet. It was torn in places and smelled of mildew. She'd picked at a section and peeled it back. The floor was tile underneath, which told her nothing. She suspected windows were concealed behind the large sheets of plywood screwed to the one wall.

The overhead pipes to which she was chained ran the length of the room, close to the back wall. She tested the length of her chain. She could reach one side wall but not the other, the one with the door she believed led to a bathroom. She was stopped by the metal straps that attached the pipe to the ceiling. Nor could she reach the door out of the room. Even stretching as far as she could, her fingertips fell short of the doorknob by nearly two feet.

Tara turned the bucket over she'd been given to do her business in. Still, she wasn't tall enough to reach the pipes near the ceiling. "Damn it."

She wrapped her hands around the chain and yanked, pulled as hard as she could, but the pipe was thick cast iron, too thick to break. Still, she kept trying, testing various spots, searching for a weakness. But she found none. Out of ideas, she sat on the floor to rest and think. The length of chain required she hold her arm in the air like a marionette puppet.

She fiddled with the iron cuff. It was wide, nine inches, and clasped with a welded iron loop. A thick padlock secured it tightly to her wrist. Even if she were to dislocate her thumb—as she had once before to slip from a pair of handcuffs—this cuff was too tightly squeezed around her wrist to slip out of it.

There was a way out of this. She knew it. She just had to find it.

When the door finally opened again, it was Bridget Barnes who walked in. Her red hair was tied in a frizzy, sloppy ponytail. She carried a chair in and, after shutting the door, sat down. She kept her distance from Tara. Smart. Because Tara already wanted to tear the woman's throat out.

"We need to talk."

"Do we?" Tara said. Her shoulder began to ache from having her arm held over her head by the chain.

"When did you intercept the *Naeem*?"

Tara remained silent.

"How did you know Safiyyah Zayd would be on that ship?"

Tara countered with her own question. "What's a pale, white inbred like you doing mixed up with Faaid and his pack of religious zealots?"

"Oh, you want to trade life stories. Maybe over croissants and lattes at Starbucks."

"I'm more the happy hour and whiskey type, thanks. Moonshine for you, I suppose." If she could get the woman rattled, get her to make a mistake...

Bridget sized her up, tilting her head one way and then another. "When I learned who you really were, I realized we have a mutual acquaintance. We know some of the same people."

"I doubt that. Can't see us having the same circle of friends."

"Don't be so sure."

Tara wanted to keep the woman talking. "Tell me who you are. Why are you here, taking orders from Faaid?" Strange bedfellows, for sure.

"Let's just say my interests and friends of mine align with Faaid's. For now," Bridget said.

"Really? Let me guess. Anti-government militia group. Timothy McVeigh types. Still, getting in bed with this bunch is pretty radical."

"It's not that straightforward."

"Never is."

"That's true." Bridget leaned forward, but too far away for Tara to get her hands on the woman. "What do you say we avoid a lot of unpleasantness, and you tell me how much you know about Zayd's mission?"

"I know it will fail."

Bridget smiled. "And how do you know that?"

Tara returned the smile. "Because we have her, and you do not."

"Tell us where she is."

"Why would I do that?"

"Because we will kill you if you don't."

"You're going to kill me either way. I prefer to die knowing I took my secrets to the grave, thanks."

"We'll torture you. Tell us now, and I promise your death will be quick and painless."

Tara shook her head, pitying the woman. "Bravo. Straight out of the Villains for Dummies handbook. But I guess that's the best I can expect from a redneck in over her head."

Bridget jumped to her feet and pushed the chair away. Angry, just the way Tara wanted her. She stormed over to Tara and backhanded her across the mouth. The blow reopened the cut in her lip. It began to bleed again.

"Tell me where Zayd is!" Bridget shouted, jumping out of Tara's reach.

Tara spit blood at her. "Suck it."

Bridget moved in to strike her again.

No one gets two shots, Tara thought. With one hand around her chain, she kicked her legs out, scissoring them between Bridget's ankles. With a twist, she dropped the woman to the floor. Bridget tried to crawl away, but Tara twisted around and grabbed her foot with her free hand. She pulled Bridget back, grabbing first her ankle, then a fistful of her jeans, then her belt, pulling the struggling woman toward her.

Desperate to break free, Bridget kicked out. Her heel landed squarely in Tara's stomach, knocking the wind from her lungs. She grunted but managed to hold on to her. She kept pulling her closer.

But with only one hand and her other arm stretched out toward the ceiling, the cuff biting into her flesh, there was little more she could do. The chain rattled and pulled. The cuff broke the skin. Blood slicked her wrist. Tara let go of Bridget's belt and grabbed for the woman's face. Her fingernails tore through Bridget's milky-white cheek. The woman screamed.

The commotion caught Reza's attention. Still posted outside the door, he rushed in. With a powerful grasp, he took hold of Tara under her unshackled armpit and hauled her to her feet.

Bridget scrambled away, breathless. Fear in her green eyes.

Tara struggled against Reza's grasp. She couldn't break free against his strength.

Reza drove a fist into her gut, expelling what little air was left in her lungs with an explosive grunt. Tara doubled over. The chain rattled. The cuff cut deeper into her flesh, drawing more blood. Reza pushed her roughly against the back wall. Tara hit the back wall hard.

She stood up, leaning over, her backside against the wall behind her for support. She fought the urge to vomit. Her black hair hung over her face in sweaty ringlets. She stared through them, stared hard at Reza, who had now stepped back. Bridget had hauled herself to her feet. She stood leaning against the far wall, steps away from the door, panting. Blood dripped from the scratch marks dug into her cheek.

"I'm going to kill you for that," Tara said between great gasps of air. "I'm going to kill you both."

Bridget shouted, "Tell us where Zayd is!"

"Screw you," Tara said, sinking back down to the floor. "Screw you all to hell."

CHAPTER EIGHTEEN

THE TUMANDAR FAMILY LIVED in a rundown, working-class neighborhood in Dorchester, Massachusetts. The house was a narrow, two-story structure with an attic window facing the street that was covered over with old newspapers. The house had beige vinyl siding and black plastic shutters. The small front porch had a roof on the verge of collapse. A low, sagging, chain link fence rimmed the postage-stamp-size yard, a riot of overgrown, neglected, waist-high weeds. There was no garage.

The early morning sun was already bright and hot, the air sticky and thick.

Bannon pulled his black F-350 pickup to the curb out front. The truck had a red and white dive sticker in the back window and a steel tool chest in the bed. Getting out, he and McMurphy surveyed the house and the neighborhood from behind dark Ray-Ban sunglasses. "You think everything's okay back at the Keel Haul?"

"Sure," Bannon said.

Grayson and Kayla needed to return to their jobs. Bannon put in a call to Chief Johnson, taking him up on his offer to help out. Asked him to come down to the Keel Haul with a few men to babysit Safiyyah Zayd. He sweetened the deal by offering the MSST team free rein of the kitchen and, once the mission was complete, drinks on the house.

Johnson said that last part wasn't necessary. They'd love to help out. He laughed, "But since you so generously offered, we'll happily take you up on the free food and booze."

"Wouldn't have it any other way," Bannon said.

McMurphy opened the low half-gate. It swung outward on squeaky hinges. He jumped back.

Two large black pit bulls with spiked collars rushed the fence in the neighboring yard. They leaped at the fence, rattling the chains and barking relentlessly.

"Jesus."

Bannon laughed, patting him on the shoulder. "Relax, tough guy. They're in the other yard."

"Dogs can jump, you know. You ever see a dog jump? They can. And they can rip your face off, too."

They walked up the short, cracked walkway and climbed the sagging front porch steps. Bannon rang the doorbell while McMurphy kept a wary eye on the berserk animals as they showed no sign of letting up.

Bannon reached for the doorbell again but stopped short when the door suddenly opened.

"Yes?" A woman in her early thirties appeared in the doorway wearing a nursing uniform. She looked tired as she attached a clip-on earring to her earlobe. Her dark hair was pulled back into a short ponytail. Her bangs and wisps of hair too short to pull back framed her narrow, dark face.

"Mrs. Tumandar?"

"Yes," she said again.

"I'm Commander Brice Bannon. This is Chief Warrant Officer McMurphy. We're with the United States Coast Guard." He held out his identification. In the leather case, along with his Coast Guard ID, was his private investigator's license.

She noticed it. "That says you're a private investigator."

"I am that, too. A sideline of mine. Has nothing to do with this."

"What is this exactly?"

"We'd like to ask you some questions. Might we step inside?"

"No." She stepped outside and pulled the door closed behind her. "I'm on my way to work. Please tell me what this is about."

Bannon and McMurphy stepped back, not wanting to crowd the woman. "It's about your brother. Captain Amar."

At the mention of her brother's name, her face clouded. "Karim. Is he okay? Has something happened?"

Bannon dodged the question. "When was the last time you spoke to your brother?"

"It has been a while. We are not close. He lives very far away."

"Morocco."

"Yes," she said. "Though he spends most of his time at sea."

"What can you tell me about him?" Bannon asked.

"Not a thing until you tell me what is going on. Is he in trouble? Is he hurt?"

Bannon exchanged a glance with McMurphy. The dogs had settled down. They paced, sniffing around the dead flower beds in their yard. McMurphy kept a wary eye on them. Bannon said, "We believe your brother's involved with some bad people, with a terrorist organization."

Dropping a bomb such as that, Bannon expected a lot of different reactions. As far as he knew, Humaira Tumandar could be as deeply embedded in the terror cell as her brother had been.

She sighed. "I am not surprised by this news." She looked Bannon in the eye. "I knew this day would come. Is he dead?"

"Yes. I'm afraid he is. We're sorry for your loss."

"Did he hurt anyone?"

Interesting she'd ask that. "Not that we are aware of," McMurphy said. "Not yet."

Her tired eyes now looked sad. "My brother and I were not close. The last time I saw Karim was on my wedding day. He and I, we see…saw the world each in a different way."

"How so?"

"Karim was swayed by extreme radical ideology early on. Always an angry man, even when we were children. Since he was a very young man, he believed in their cause. I did not. To me, the world, the people in it, our differences, are what make it beautiful. Not something to fear. That is why I came to America. Why I wanted to stay. I heard such wonderful stories growing up, and so I wanted to see it, to experience it for myself. Karim called me a traitor to my people."

"You became a nurse."

"Yes. To help people and to give back. I reject violence in all its forms. I have seen the pain, the hurt such hatred creates. It is not much, but I help where I can."

"Then I'm hoping you can help us."

"I don't see how. As I have said, I have not seen Karim in many years. We have exchanged a few letters and emails if only to assure the other we are well. I am sorry."

"Your brother came to America a few times a year. He was a cargo ship's captain."

"Yes, of that I knew. He loved the water, the life of a sea captain. It was truly the only place I saw him happy."

"He did not contact you? Stay here with you and your husband when he visited?"

"No, as I have said, the last time I saw Karim was at my wedding."

"Do you have any idea who he knew here? Did he have any friends? Do you know where he stayed while he was in port? Anything at all could be helpful."

"You believe he was part of some terror operation here in America?"

"Yes. We do."

"I am sorry, gentleman, I am. But I do not know."

"Thank you for your time." Disappointed, Bannon started to turn away. Then he thought of something. "Would we be able to speak to your husband? Is he here?"

Humaira lowered her eyes to the floor. "My husband and I. We are no longer together."

"I'm sorry." Bannon paused, unwilling to release the thread he was tugging. "Can you tell us where we can find Behram,

Ben? Perhaps he's spoken with your brother. He might know something."

"My husband and Karim did hold similar views."

Bannon felt a twinge of excitement. "It's important we speak with him."

"Ben and I are...we met in college. We fell in love. We were very happy for a time, but recently, things have gone very badly for Ben."

"How so?"

"My husband is an accountant, a CPA, by trade. He is very good with numbers and worked for a very fine company. In their accountant department."

"Worked?" Bannon asked. "He's not with them any longer?"

"No. They let him go."

"He was fired," Bannon surmised. "May I ask why?"

She cast her eyes down and away, overwhelmed with shame. "Ben was always one to speak his mind. Outspoken, you would say. Things can be...difficult for Muslims here. As much as I love being here, even I must admit that. Most of us are good, hard-working people. We mean no one any harm."

"Of course," Bannon said. He gave her arm a squeeze. "And many people can be ignorant. And hurtful. Luckily, they are in the minority, even though it doesn't always seem to be the case."

"Yes. That is with people everywhere. I have met, I am friends with people of many faiths, that are simply wonderful. It is why I became a citizen. Ben was born here. He grew up in Brooklyn before moving to Boston. He does not see people in that way. Even before 9/11, he says being Muslim in America was difficult."

"You say you and Ben are no longer together. Did you divorce?"

"Yes."

"Because of his views?"

"Partially, yes. After he was terminated, he found it difficult to find another job. He searched for many months without success. At that time, he grew sullen and angry. Distant. He became…difficult to be with."

"I understand."

"We agreed it would be for the best if we were no longer married."

"May I ask why he was fired?"

"When we met, Ben was fascinated by where and how I grew up. He became obsessed. He would ask endless questions about my parents, about how I grew up in my country. What were the people like? Our history. He studied the Quran and Islam. It was sweet. His parents were not religious at all. I suspect they became that way to fit in. To assimilate. To not draw attention to themselves, to the fact they were different. When Ben met me, I think it sparked his curiosity, yes, but also a bitter resentment as well. He spoke often of being angry at his parents for not embracing their religion and culture. For pretending they were something they were not.

"Over time, his anger grew. He became increasingly outraged by the wars raging in the Middle East. He began to believe in the terrorist causes, sympathizing with them."

"He became radicalized."

"Yes."

Bannon heard the shame in her voice.

"As I said, he was always outspoken. He would lecture people at work. Fight with them when they disagreed with his views. Call them names. The other employees complained to management. Clients put in complaints as well. Soon his bosses could no longer put up with his behavior. They fired him. I do not blame them. He left them no choice. Even I began to find Ben's behavior insufferable. He demanded I stop calling him Ben. 'My name is Behram,' he would say."

"And you think he might know something about your brother?"

"He and Karim met at the wedding. He was fascinated with Karim." She laughed. "He spent more time with him than with me at the ceremony. He and Karim remained in contact on Facebook and through Skype. I was not aware of this until recently."

"How recently?" McMurphy asked, one eye still on the roaming pit bulls.

"After we separated, Ben moved out. While trying to find a new job, he took part-time menial labor work—at construction sites, as a busboy, driving the Uber car. But he made little money at it. And, of course, he made the same mistakes as he did at the accounting firm. His views, which he continued to share, became more radicalized and less welcomed by those he interacted with.

"Before long, he was unable to pay his rent. Even the minimal amount charged to stay at the halfway shelter he'd found downtown. I felt sorry for him. So when he asked, I allowed him to return home." She cast her eyes upward. "We have a furnished room in the attic space. It has its own facilities, a bathroom, a stove, a cooktop, and a sink. He has his mini-refrigerator from college."

"He lives here? Upstairs?" Bannon pointed up. "Is he home?"

"No. He went out early this morning."

"His room. Would you mind showing us?"

She glanced at her watch.

"We wouldn't ask if it wasn't extremely important," Bannon said.

Humaira hesitated but then nodded and took them inside. She led them directly to the attic apartment, not allowing them to detour. They clumped up old wooden stairs painted battleship gray. On the wall of the stairwell to the attic was an old, tattered, and yellowed poster of Phil Simms, the New York Giants quarterback from '79 to '93.

"Your husband's a football fan?" McMurphy asked, passing the poster.

"No. That was there when we moved in. He never bothered to remove it."

The attic had a low ceiling that sloped downward on both sides. McMurphy and Bannon had to remain in the center of the room to not hit their heads. Even then, they had to duck to avoid striking the light fixture, a single bulb with no cover. The room was stifling hot. There was a window air-conditioning unit in one window, currently off. Bannon doubted it had the BTUs to combat the heat that would rise in that tiny space in the summer.

McMurphy went to check the bathroom.

Bannon stood in the center of the room, very concerned.

The place smelled strongly of gasoline. The room's furnishings consisted of a twin-size bed, an old door placed across two paint-splattered sawhorses forming a makeshift table, and a single metal folding chair, similarly paint-splattered. On the table was a battered old laptop.

But it was the rest of the material on the table that alarmed Bannon.

"Nothing of interest in the bathroom," McMurphy reported. He stepped up beside Bannon and looked at the table. "Oh, hell."

On the table were the remains of a very large bomb-making operation. Wire, electrical and duct tape, batteries, gunpowder residue, and the unrolled wrappers of hundreds, maybe thousands, of firecrackers—Bannon had read where gangs and terrorists paid kids upward of fifty dollars an hour to strip the gunpowder from the fireworks—pliers, wire strippers, and hundreds of empty boxes of nails bought or stolen from hardware stores. On the floor were leftover fuel cans, fertilizer bags, several glass jars, a car battery, and one propane tank.

Humaira gasped. "This is not—"

"What you think it is? It's exactly that," Bannon said. "A bomb-making factory."

CHAPTER NINETEEN

HUMAIRA TUMANDAR SWORE SHE had no idea what her husband had been up to in the tiny, overheated attic. She worked days, often double shifts, because money was tight. Often, Tumandar was home alone. All day long. She could not possibly have known, she insisted, visibly shaken.

"I never come up here," she said. "I would have no reason to."

Bannon believed her, but that would be up to the police to sort out. He contacted them and then put a call into Grayson. While they waited for arriving officers, Bannon questioned Humaira further. "Did he say anything about where he was going? Did he have plans?"

"No. No. As I have said, we barely spoke. I have not even seen him in days," she said.

"Are you saying he hasn't been here?"

"No. I hear him through the floor, walking, pacing, all hours of the night. My bedroom is directly below. He was here last night. All night. But he must have left early. While I was in the shower."

"How does he travel? Does he have a car?"

"Yes. It is an old vehicle. White. With one blue door."

"One blue door," McMurphy said, "Why?"

"He was in an accident. He could not afford to fix it properly, so he bought the door at a junkyard and had a friend install it. It does not open easily."

"Do you know the make, the model of the vehicle?" Bannon asked. He and McMurphy continued searching the room as they peppered the woman with questions.

"Old. I do not know. Scout. Does that mean anything?"

"A truck?" McMurphy asked. "It looks like a small truck?"

"Yes. I am sorry I do not know cars. I do not drive. It has a big cargo space. An SUV."

McMurphy pulled out his phone and scrolled through it. He showed her a picture.

Excited, she said, "Yes! That is it. But white."

He showed the picture to Bannon, explaining, "It's a vehicle called a Scout. They were manufactured by International Harvester back in the '60s and '70s. It was their answer to the Jeep, a precursor to today's SUVs. My brother had one."

Bannon called Grayson and gave her an update, giving her the information he had about Tumandar and the vehicle. She assured him she'd contact the Boston P.D. and the State Police, have them put a BOLO out.

McMurphy grabbed an empty cardboard box from the floor under the table. In it was a few loose firecrackers rattled around in a gritty dust Bannon knew was gunpowder residue.

Bannon noticed a stack of papers underneath. He picked them up and rifled through them. They were printed pages and glossy magazine articles of public venues in and around Boston. The Garden. Fenway Park. Events at the harbor.

163

Information about the Freedom Trail and other upcoming summertime activities in and around Boston.

Bannon stopped. One brochure caught his attention. It was for an annual art exhibition and festival being held at the docks near the Boston Aquarium. Vendor booths, carnival rides, educational lectures sponsored by the aquarium, and various wildlife and sea life preservation organizations. The dates were circled in heavy red felt marker. Today was the third and final day of the event.

Bannon fisted the brochure. "I know where he's planning to attack."

They raced downstairs, grateful to be out of the oppressive attic enclosure.

They reached the front door as two Boston squad cars pulled up behind Bannon's truck. The neighbor's dogs went nuts.

Bannon turned to Humaira. He clasped her hands in his. "Thank you for your help. I'm sorry you have to go through this, but these officers will be very kind to you."

Three uniformed officers crowded around them on the porch, one of them a woman. She wore sergeant stripes. Bannon handed his Coast Guard business card to the female officer. "This woman is a cooperating material witness, working directly with the Secretary of Homeland Security. She's a witness, not a suspect."

The female cop looked annoyed. "That'll be for the detectives to decide. Either way, she'll be treated respectfully, Commander."

Bannon felt a little embarrassed being so heavy-handed. Or maybe it was because he'd been called out on it, rightfully so. "She's had a rough time of it, is all."

"Understood," the cop said. "She'll be fine. You have my word, Commander."

Bannon smiled. "Brice. Also let your command know, I believe Tumandar is planning an attack at the Arts Festival taking place at the Aquarium Harbor."

"How do you know that?" the cop asked.

McMurphy was already in the truck. He banged the side of the door to get Bannon's attention. "Let's go."

Bannon shoved the crumpled brochure into her hand. "Just let 'em know."

He jumped into his truck and sped north to South Boston and the harbor. As they drove, McMurphy was on the phone with Grayson and Kayla Clarke, giving and getting updates. The festival was in full swing, and according to police and city authorities, the crowd was expected to reach several thousand throughout the fast approaching midday hour.

"The perfect time to strike," Bannon said.

While Bannon didn't have sirens installed on his truck, he did have blue flashing emergency lights in the grill and over the sun visors. As the massive black truck barreled up the highway, motorists assumed they were cops or a legitimate emergency vehicle of some sort and moved aside to let Bannon speed past them.

They reached the harbor in record time but were stopped by two police officers at a roadblock on Atlantic Avenue and India Row. Bannon pulled the truck to the curb in front of

Harbor Towers apartments. They got out. Grayson had called the Police Commissioner, the Mayor, and probably even the governor's office to clear the way for Bannon and McMurphy. They'd receive VIP cooperation up and down the rank and file.

"Any sign of the suspect vehicle?" Bannon asked after introducing themselves.

"Not here," the one cop said.

"Nothing over the radio either," the other one added. "We've got the area cordoned off to a mile out. Uniforms are searching for anything suspicious and moving civilians out as quickly and quietly as possible."

That was good news, Bannon thought. Unless Tumandar had another target in mind and Bannon's assumptions were wrong. What if he'd mistakenly diverted the BPD's attention and resources in error? He couldn't think that way. There was no time for recriminations.

Trust your instincts, he told himself.

"Come on." He led McMurphy past the roadblock on foot. They walked the block and a half to the docks. At Milk Street, they hooked a right. There, they were met by a steady stream of people coming away from the harbor, many grumbling about how their plans were ruined, as the police quietly evacuated the area, trying to do so without creating a panic.

Milk Street turned into Old Atlantic Avenue. A paved roadway that looped around the large parking garage, a Legal Seafood Restaurant, and the hotel across the way. On the opposite side of the street, the Duck Boat Tours picked up and dropped off tourists, and Boston Long Warf was where the harbor cruises and whale-watching tours departed.

The area was still a sea of people, despite the authorities' efforts to clear them. Somewhere, a band still played. A jazz piece. White vendor tents were set up along the harbor walk. From them, vendors and artists were selling framed artwork, clothes, and culture-specific handmade jewelry. There were various conservation awareness booths and a crapload of carnival-style food vendors. Some were closing shop as police and security personnel moved from tent to tent, urging them to leave.

Bannon and McMurphy stood in the middle of it all and looked around.

"If you wanted to plant an IED to inflict maximum damage," Bannon asked, "where would you put it?"

"Look around," McMurphy said. "Anywhere. Everywhere."

"Good point."

Even with the police and security thinning the crowd, there were still hundreds of people about, many of them ignoring the calls to leave. "Maybe the better question is, how do you do it?"

"If it's me, I put it somewhere it won't be found, where there's a lot of people. Then I get the hell out. But that's not how these whack-a-doos think," McMurphy said.

"No, they're willing to die for their cause. They don't care about getting out. Inflicting the most damage and death as possible is all that matters."

"The cops have the streets locked up tight. There's no getting through the roadblocks," McMurphy said.

"Humaira mentioned he left early this morning," Bannon said absently, mulling over the problem.

McMurphy followed Bannon's train of thought. "He's already here."

Bannon nodded. "Waiting."

"Waiting for what?"

"The right time."

"That would be right now," McMurphy said, his voice tight with frustration. "The crowd's thinning out as we speak. If he waits much longer, he'll miss his opportunity completely."

They looked around. There were very few cars about. The road was kept clear for the duck boats and other tour vehicles. The valets handled hotel traffic at the other end of the harbor. There was a drop-off loop for guests to drive up and check-in.

"Maybe he chickened out," McMurphy suggested. "Lost his nerve."

Bannon felt a band of panic tighten around his chest. "Doesn't feel right."

He noticed a line of cars parked along the front of the hotel, wondering where the valet lot was. He put his hand on his friend's shoulder.

"Check the hotel," he said, turning behind them. "I'll grab some cops and start on the parking garage. If he's here, he's gotta be at one or the other."

"Roger that," McMurphy said, heading off toward the hotel.

Neither of them had moved far when a loud screeching of tires came from the parking garage. The sound echoed in the enclosed structure. Bannon looked toward the seven-level garage. A young man and woman were pushing a stroller with a little girl in it. They looked with panicked expressions at the exit-only side of the garage entrance, where the screeching was coming from.

With a crash, the white and orange mechanical arm exploded outward into the street in pieces. The man grabbed the woman by the arm and picked up the stroller. They ran, narrowly avoiding getting run down by a white vehicle racing out of the garage.

On squealing tires, it turned toward the harbor.

An old Scout. Like the picture McMurphy had shown him on his phone, only white. But with a blue driver's side door. The window was rolled down. The driver was a dark-skinned man with a beard. He wore a dark *taqiyah*.

People screamed and ran.

Bannon drew his .45 and shouted to McMurphy, "Get the people out of here."

As the car raced toward them, Bannon fired several shots. His bullets pinged off the grill and one fender. A third bullet struck and cracked the windshield, but none of it slowed Tumandar down. The car continued to race forward, aimed at the panicked crowd.

Bannon had only seconds to act. He ran toward the car.

"Brice!" McMurphy yelled. "What the hell are you doing?"

He didn't answer. He had to time this just right.

The car swerved toward him.

Bannon dropped his gun, leaped, and dived at the open window as the Scout rocketed past. He grabbed Tumandar through the window and seized the black and red plaid work shirt and the gray T-shirt the man wore. Tumandar tried to shake him off, swerving the vehicle sharply left, then right. Bannon hung on. His leg dangled. He picked his feet up off the ground. The car raced forward, picking up speed, taking his breath away.

"No!" Tumandar shouted. He yanked the wheel to the right, another attempt to shake Bannon off. "You cannot stop me! Death to America! Allahu Akbar!"

Bannon threw a punch at his head and grabbed the wheel. He tugged the vehicle away from the sidewalk, away from a blue and yellow refreshment stand where several people were hunkered down behind, trying to hide.

The Scout jumped the curb and swerved between a lamppost and a metal bollard.

Bannon's legs slammed into the bollard. He cried out.

They headed directly at the crowd outside the Aquarium and IMAX Theater. They raced across the brick pavilion, sending people scurrying left and right amid shouts of anger and outrage. Tumandar slapped at Bannon's arms. Bannon shoved the steering wheel to the right. The SUV turned, squealing on bad tires down a wide pathway between the theater and the parking garage. The vehicle's tail end swerved and crashed into a cluster of metal and rubber garbage cans. The cans went flying, spewing refuse into the air.

People continued to scream and run for cover.

Bannon looked into the cargo area of the vehicle and caught sight of metal gas cans, plastic milk jugs full of nails and other shrapnel, and a couple of propane tanks, all taped together with duct tape. Tumandar's intentions couldn't have been any clearer. Mow down as many people as he could before crashing the explosive-filled vehicle for maximum damage and mass casualties.

Bannon half hung out the window. Tumandar floored the gas. The old Scout accelerated. Bannon pounded on the horn and wrestled for control of the wheel.

The vehicle raced along the pathway, zigzagging. It bumped down a step and came to an open area, a concrete platform at the base of a dock alongside one of the two Harbor Towers. Several wide concrete steps led to a picnic area where tables and attached benches lined the platform. In a panic, people had fled the area. The platform was edged with concrete bollards with black looped chains between them. Beyond the platform lay Boston Harbor. The green water below gently lapped against the thick support pylons.

Bannon yanked hard on the wheel, twisting the vehicle to the left, aiming it for the bollards and, ultimately, the Harbor beyond.

Tumandar howled, "No!"

The vehicle bounded down the steps. The back end bottomed out. The bumper struck concrete and sent a firework's display of sparks into the air. Bannon bashed his head against the roof. He bit his tongue as his teeth snapped shut. Still clutching the steering wheel as if his life depended upon it—because it did—he kept Tumandar from twisting it back toward anywhere people were.

The Scout crashed through a bollard. The concrete post exploded in a cloud of dust.

The side of the vehicle caught the edge of a metal gangplank that crossed to the wharf alongside the Harbor Tower apartments. Its tires caught. The Scout rode up at an angle, half on, half off the ramp. Green foamy water lay below.

Bannon released the wheel and kicked against the door, propelling himself as far from the vehicle as possible. The Scout continued its angled trajectory upward.

Bannon hit the water and dove deep.

Above him, the vehicle ran out of gangway and slammed into the aft deck of a docked yacht. The gasoline, propane tanks, and shrapnel-filled jugs exploded on impact. The twin inboard yacht engines and full fuel tanks exploded.

Bannon felt the concussion and the loud thump of the explosions underwater.

He kicked hard and swam until the water over him grew dark. He surfaced and drew a deep breath. He was under the picnic platform. He'd surfaced in time to see the yacht erupt into a rolling, black, oily fireball. The blast shattered windows over a block away. Secondary explosions followed. Projectiles slammed into the surrounding buildings, boats, and docks, pelting down in the water like metallic rain. Blackened and burning metal and fiberglass fell from the sky like fiery hail. The fire alarm in Harbor Tower tripped and began to blare.

What was left of the Scout—which wasn't much—a blackened husk stuck out from the boat's aft deck. The gunwale was destroyed. A roaring inferno consumed the yacht. The vessel took on water, listed to port, and began to sink.

Bannon swam out from under the platform once the largest chunks of debris had finished falling. He grabbed the concrete edge where the platform had married up with the gangplank, which had fallen into the harbor and was sinking, too.

A hand seized his wrist and hauled him out of the water.

Breathing heavily, as if he'd just run the Boston Marathon, McMurphy threw his arm around Bannon and pounded his water-soaked back.

"I thought you were a goner that time," McMurphy said, "You crazy, stupid, son of a—"

"Tell me no one was on board that yacht?"

McMurphy hooked a thumb at Harbor Towers. "Owner ducked inside to have a cocktail. Good thing for him."

Bannon smiled, relieved. "He's gonna need a few more when he comes out and sees that."

The burning yacht listed farther to port. Flames flared and roared, consuming the rich teak trim of the once handsome bridge. They crackled and licked high into the sky, chasing the thick, roiling plume of black smoke, even as the fire department pulled up with pumpers and quickly started the hopeless task of hosing down the ship as it slipped further into the water.

Bannon and McMurphy stared down into the harbor water. It was McMurphy who asked, "Now what?"

CHAPTER TWENTY

AZIZA FAAID WAITED IN the large open room for Bridget Barnes to emerge from her talk with Tarakesh Sardana. He smiled, having listened to Tara get the better of the American woman, even though the she-devil remained chained up, before allowing Reza to go in and rescue her. Should bring the little *alkaliba* down a peg or two, he thought. Seeing the deep bloody scratches raked down her cheek. He could barely contain his smile of satisfaction.

"Please, tell me what you learned for our prisoner, Ms. Barnes."

"Screw you, Faaid."

"I warned you. Ms. Sardana is quite formidable."

Bridget glared at him, wiping blood from her cheek. "All the more reason to kill her now and be done with it."

"As things stand, you might be correct."

She eyed him with suspicion. "I thought she was our only lead to Zayd?"

"She was. But circumstances have…shifted."

"Shifted, how?"

Faaid explained. "We know the federal authorities took Ms. Zayd. The Coast Guard being part of America's exalted

Department of Homeland Security, it makes sense they would be involved with her abduction before arriving on these shores. But from there, what?"

"She'd either be designated an enemy combatant and turned over to the military," Bridget said, "or law enforcement would take custody of her. Local cops, maybe, but more likely the FBI."

"Exactly. Which leaves me to ponder, what would they do with her?"

"Question her."

"Ah, but where?"

"There's a large FBI field office in Boston. I'm not sure if they'd have the proper facilities to hold and interrogate prisoners there, though." Bridget rubbed her bloody fingers down the thigh of her jeans. She turned back toward the room where Tara was held. Hatred filled her green eyes. Reza had dutifully returned to his chair beside the door. "You can be sure she knows. I'll take another crack at her."

"As amusing as that might prove to be, it will not be necessary. My needs require you to be in one piece, Ms. Barnes. A condition I fear you might not be in after a second encounter with Ms. Sardana."

"Up yours, Faaid. Why won't it be necessary?" she asked, mimicking his condescending tone.

"Because I know exactly where Safiyyah Zayd is."

"What? You knew, and you sent me in there—with her—anyway?"

He smiled. "While that is something I might consider doing, but alas, no. As I said, things have changed. This is new information that has come to my attention."

"From where?"

"The televised evening news. There was an incident last night," Faaid said. "In Portsmouth, New Hampshire."

"What's Portsmouth got to do with anything?"

"Follow along if you can, Ms. Barnes."

"Careful, Faaid." She waved her cell phone in his face. "We both work for the same person. And he likes me better. A single call from me and I end you. Remember that."

He bowed slightly. "Threats are unnecessary, Ms. Barnes. We are, as they say, on the same team. The *Naeem* was boarded by the Coast Guard while en route to Boston," he explained. "If it were you, where would you divert the vessel to buy yourself the time you needed to substitute Ms. Sardana for Ms. Zayd?"

"Fine. Portsmouth. What happened there last night?"

"At around three in the morning, there were reports of an exchange of gunfire in the downtown area. And of a van with no plates speeding through the deserted nighttime streets."

"Speeding away from where?"

"The McIntyre Federal Building on Daniel Street. Soon after, a number of our people reported increased attention being paid to them by the FBI. People we know to be on their various watch lists were called in. Some were apprehended. Rather aggressively, I might add. Discretely, we've learned a VIP prisoner was being held at the facility, awaiting transportation with several others to an undisclosed—"

"You think that was Zayd…" Bridget hesitated, speaking slowly as she worked through the problem, putting the pieces together. "You think she was broken out. But by whom?"

"Well, certainly not by us." Faaid sighed. *Simpletons.* "It had to be Ms. Sardana's old teammates, Bannon and McMurphy."

"Why would they kidnap her from their own people?"

"Because, my dear Ms. Barnes. The two of them, the three of them actually, operate outside normal parameters. Since being maimed and nearly killed by them, I've made it a point to learn all I could about Brice Bannon and his merry band of infidels. While I have not figured everything out just yet, I've learned enough to know they operate as some sort of small, clandestine ops group."

"Terrific. Good to know. What's all that do for us?"

"It tells us exactly where Safiyyah Zayd is."

"Okay. How? Where?"

"Brice Bannon owns a small, rundown seaside bar called the Keel Haul in Hampton Beach."

Bridget rolled her eyes. "Again with New Hampshire."

"I don't understand why he owns it—or runs it—or how it fits in. He's a spy for his government." Faaid waved his hand in the air, dismissing it as unimportant. "What I am sure of, it is there you will find Safiyyah Zayd."

"Me?"

"Yes. Take some men and retrieve her," he said, asserting as much authority as their peculiar partnership would allow. "And Ms. Barnes, select as many men as you think you need, then double it. Do not underestimate these men." Faaid touched his scarred face. "That would be a grave mistake."

TARA SAT ON THE mildewed, stained green carpet. It had been many hours since Bridget Barnes had paid her a visit. Without windows or other means to mark the passage of time, she hadn't even received regular meals, she had no idea how long it had been. The stuffy, dry heat made her sleepy. She passed the time dozing and thinking about—looking forward to—their next encounter. In the meantime, she concentrated on figuring a way out of this room, but without much success.

Her arm, hung in the air from the length of chain, ached at the shoulder.

To give it relief, Tara decided it was time to stand up. She was reluctant to admit it, but the beating she took from Reza had taken a toll. She was stiff, sore, and every muscle ached. And her head throbbed.

The oversized coveralls were heavy. They made the oppressive heat all the more unbearable. Her dark skin was coated in a sweaty, wet sheen. She put her unshackled hand on the floor to push herself to her feet but stopped.

She looked at the palm of her hand. Rubbed it with her fingers. A fine, chalky white dust adhered to her sweaty skin. She looked down at the floor. More fine, white, chalky powder. She looked up at the ceiling.

Tara pushed herself to her feet. She gripped the chain with both hands and gave it a good, hard yank. The pipe clanged hollowly overhead. A small cloud of powdery dust fell from the ceiling.

One of the support straps around the pipe was working loose from the ceiling.

Excited, she tugged at the pipe again. More dust fell.

Looking like a bell ringer in a cathedral, she tugged and tugged, happily watching the white dust fall. Her shoulders burned from the effort, but she kept at it until she heard a key scraping in the door lock. She stopped yanking and turned around. The door opened.

Tara sidestepped and covered the small pile of white dust on the floor with her worn brown sandals.

Reza came in alone, carrying a tray. On it was a plate with mashed potatoes, some kind of meat, carrots in a disgustingly thick orange gel, and a red plastic cup. He approached, giving her a look that said no games.

"I'll be cool." She raised her hands, palms out.

The large man moved in closer. Cautious.

He leaned over to put the tray down on the floor. He must have thought he remained a safe distance from her, but Tara had carefully tested the limits of her chain. A little closer, she urged silently. A little closer. The tray touched the floor. Reza took his eyes off her for only a second.

It was all she needed. She sprang!

She rushed at him.

He straightened up, but as quick as the big man was, Tara was quicker.

She leaped and vaulted onto his back. She wrapped the length of chain around his neck and pulled. Reza dropped the tray, grasping for the chain. He tried to dig his fingers between the thick iron links and his throat. Tara pulled back harder, riding him like a bucking bull.

Reza staggered around, his eyes bulging.

He tried to move toward the door. That proved to be a mistake. Reaching its limit, the slack pulled the chain tighter around his throat. With a strangled gurgle, he lunged toward the opposite wall. And Tara couldn't have been happier.

When he reached the spot where she'd been standing, where she'd been diligently working the support strap loose from the ceiling, Tara climbed further up his broad back until her knees dug into his shoulders. She yanked the chain, pulling it tighter around his neck.

His dark face began to turn purple.

Tara reached out with her unshackled arm and grabbed the cast iron pipe overhead. Hanging like a trapeze artist by one hand, she pulled her cuffed arm up, like she was doing a dumbbell curl in the gym, only with Reza as the dead weight.

She didn't need to lift him very far. Just enough to get his weight off his feet. She ground her teeth from the strain. He gurgled and struggled under her. His efforts grew more frantic, more desperate as oxygen deprivation starved his brain, as his life ebbed from his body.

Tara groaned and pulled harder.

Concrete dust puffed downward from the effort.

Reza's tip-toe feet came off the floor. He kicked them.

"Come on," she said through gritted teeth. "Come on!"

Pull. Pull.

Then it happened. The strap gave way. The cast iron pipe bowed, unable to hold their combined weight without the strap. It creaked and sagged, and finally, at the closest coupling—near the side wall—the pipe broke open. Tara, Reza, the chain, sections of pipe, and the sudden, unexpected flow of spilled sewage fell to the floor.

She collapsed onto Reza's crumpled form. Thick, brown, smelly water spewed from the split pipe. She was breathing hard. Reza coughed. The looped end of the chain had slipped from the broken pipe. The chain around Reza's neck loosened. He dug his fingers between his throat and the thick length of chain, pulling it free.

"Uh, uh, big boy," Tara said, panting and sweaty.

She stepped on his back with both feet and pulled. The chain wound tightly around his neck again. He sputtered in surprise and frustration, but her hold was solid. She pulled. And pulled.

They splashed around in the raw sewage that soaked the ugly green carpet. Tara's wet sandals slipped, but she held on and pulled until Reza's death throes became weaker. Until, finally, they stopped altogether. Even after they did, Tara pulled, yanking hard one last time to make sure the deed was done. With grim satisfaction, she said, "One down."

With no remorse for the dead, she unwound the chain from his neck. Him or me, she told herself, simple as that.

She patted the dead man down and found the keys to the door, which hung open, but no key for the padlock securing the length of chain to her wrist.

"Fine. I'll deal with that later." She pushed him away and stood up. With her breathing labored and her face a smeary, sweaty mess, she smelled her wet coverall sleeves, sopping from the spilled waste, and frowned. "Oh, that's gross."

She coiled the length of chain up. She'd find a way to pick the lock or cut it off later. For now, she had to get out of this room and get as far away from Bridget Barnes and Aziza Faaid as possible.

Her prison room opened onto a great open space. Reza had left no weapon out there for her to claim, only his folding metal chair. What was this place? The walls were the same fake wood veneer that had been in her room. The floors were covered in blue indoor-outdoor carpeting but with two tiled aisles. She dropped down to one knee. There were metal slots in the carpeted sections of the floor. A regular pattern, as if at one time there'd been rows of seats secured to the floor, like in a movie theater or an airplane.

The seats were gone.

In the front section of the room was a U-shaped counter. Tara had worked at the Keel Haul long enough to recognize a bar when she saw one. The walls on either side were blank, except for brackets that, at some point, had held something. Tara got the sense a demolition job had been started and then interrupted, never to be finished.

She moved toward the expansive windows on the other side of the room. A light blue cloudless sky filled the window panes. She began to suspect where she was, and she did not like the idea at all.

Behind her, the heavy metal clang of a door opening caught her attention. She darted back to the wall beside the door. It opened. A young Middle Eastern man in his early twenties stepped through. He had a rifle slung over his shoulder.

Tara took a deep breath and rushed at him.

Caught by surprise, he yelped. He tried to slip the rifle from his shoulder. Before he could get his hands around it, Tara snapped the length of her chain out. The knotted end hit the young man in the chin like a punch. He staggered back. Tara pounced. Her knees slammed into the man's chest. He fell to the ground. She pummeled his face with punches, left, right, one after the other, without letting up. The chain rattled and snapped, hitting the wall and floor with wild abandon with each thrown punch.

By the time she finished venting some of her pent-up rage on the unfortunate man, his face looked like a bloody, deflated speed bag. Not taking any chances, she pulled the knife he carried and, with two hands, drove it through his chest cavity.

She stood, breathing hard and achy, and staggered back, doing her best to rein in her rage and her fear. When she felt in control of herself again, she relieved the dead man of his rifle. He wouldn't need it anymore. She wiped the blood from the five-inch blade and dropped it into the smelly pocket of her coveralls.

Armed with the rifle at the ready and the stolen knife in her pocket, she pushed through the door the man had come through. She hoped her instincts were wrong. She pushed through the door, confirming her worst suspicions.

She frowned. "I hate being right all the time."

A bracing early morning wind caressed her cheek. The sky was a cloudless robin's egg blue. The clean smell of the ocean couldn't be mistaken. She gripped the handrail and looked left and then right.

She saw nothing but ocean.

She turned around and looked up and down the outside passageway upon which she stood. The ship was white and pristine with clean, sharp lines. She guessed it to be about three hundred feet long. She turned back and faced the sea.

How far out in the Atlantic Ocean were they?

That was anyone's guess.

CHAPTER TWENTY-ONE

BY THE TIME BANNON and McMurphy were done getting grilled and giving statements to the local police, the FBI—Pierce was none too happy to see them there—and Homeland Security, night had fallen. Once released, with promises to give written statements in a couple of days, they drove up the coastline, returning to New Hampshire.

Bannon drove. His clothes had dried but were now stiff and uncomfortable, and he smelled like smoke and diesel fuel. His ribs still hurt, his ankle ached, and his cut lip stung. He couldn't remember when he last felt this achy and sore. He sighed. He knew by tomorrow, he'd feel even worse. In the meantime, he looked forward to a long, hot shower and a few hours of sleep.

McMurphy didn't wait. He leaned against the door and was asleep before Bannon reached Atlantic Avenue. He slept the entire trip north, snoring the whole time.

An hour later, Bannon pulled to the curb in front of the Keel Haul.

As soon as he switched off the engine, McMurphy straightened up, as alert as if he'd been awake the whole time. "That was fast."

Bannon unlocked the Keel Haul's front door and entered the bar, greeted by the aroma of fresh-brewed coffee. The bar was dark except for the backsplash of light that glowed from under the bar, a neon sign for Anchor Steam beer, and a pale rectangle of light spilling in from the kitchen door where the swing door was propped open.

McMurphy locked the door behind them. They found Chief Johnson behind the bar chatting with Reyes, sitting on a barstool across from him. Both men were drinking coffee.

Bannon crossed the room, noticing O'Neil seated at one of the back booths, his back to the wall, his legs stretched out. His Sig P229 in his hand. Still dressed in the gray FBI sweatshirt and dark sweatpants, Safiyyah Zayd was curled up and presumably asleep in the opposite seat.

The TV over the bar was on. The sound muted. Images of the burning yacht and what was left of the Tumandar's Scout were on the screen. An arc of high-pressure water from a fire truck pumper was turning the roaring boat fire into a column of oily black smoke. The video was from earlier in the night. The scroll read: TERROR ATTACK AT THE HARBOR.

"Been watching the news," Johnson said, sipping coffee. "Holy crap, Commander, I'd buy you a drink if we weren't in your bar."

"Thanks, Chief, but a cup of that coffee is what would hit the spot right now."

"Coming right up." Johnson pulled the glass pot from the machine and poured it.

"I'll take that drink," McMurphy said, going behind the bar to serve himself. He rummaged through the ice before

186

coming up with a bottle of Coors Light. He twisted the top off and drank.

"Things always this exciting around here, sir?" Reyes asked as Johnson handed Bannon his coffee.

"Just another Saturday night," McMurphy said between sips of his beer.

"Everything okay here?" Bannon asked.

"Quiet," Johnson said. "Most excitement we had was chasing away some persistent old coot in a captain's hat demanding we open the place up for him."

"Repeatedly," Reyes said. "Wouldn't take 'we're closed' for an answer."

"Captain Floyd. A regular."

"I gathered," Johnson said.

Bannon took his coffee and walked over to O'Neil. The young man straightened up and started to swing his feet off the bench. "No need for that here, Troy."

"Yes, sir." Still nervous.

"Here, it's Brice."

"Yes, si—Brice. Nice place you've got."

Bannon looked around. "I like it. How's the arm?"

He wasn't wearing the sling. "Good as new." He raised it to demonstrate and winced. "Almost."

Bannon smiled and then glanced at Zayd. "Any trouble from her?"

"Not a peep. I mean it. She literally didn't say a single word all night."

"Yeah, well, with the closest thing to a lead we have burned up in the Boston Harbor, she'll be saying plenty if she knows what's good for her."

Bannon finished his coffee. He turned, intending to return the empty mug to the bar before going upstairs to his apartment. "Chief, you good to hold down the fort a little while longer? I'd like to grab a shower and some rack time."

Before Johnson could respond, a deafening explosion blasted the front door open. The door blew across the room, followed by a blast of fire and a plume of gray-black smoke.

Bannon ducked.

O'Neil jumped to his knees. Using the back of the booth as cover, he aimed his Sig at the now missing front door.

With a scream, Zayd sprung up into a sitting position, wide awake now.

"Stay with her," Bannon yelled to O'Neil. He pulled his .45 and started to move for the door.

Reyes was crouched behind a table he'd flipped onto its side, his gun out. McMurphy and Johnson remained behind the bar. The Chief had found Bannon's 12-gauge shotgun and had it aimed at the door.

A second blast came from the back.

Bannon heard the back door smash against the wall. A well-planned, two-prong attack, trapping them. Whoever it was, they were after Zayd. But how? No one knew she was there except the people in the bar, Grayson and Kayla.

McMurphy called out. "Kitchen."

Bannon shouted, "Go!"

McMurphy vaulted over the bar with surprising agility for a man his size. He cuffed Reyes' shoulder. "You're with me, seaman."

They sidled up to either side of the propped open kitchen door.

They had one advantage. The attack team had to come through the two pinch points. If they could keep them from getting through the doors, they could hold them off until the police arrived. Three minutes. That would be all they needed.

Bannon pulled his cell phone out and dialed 911 as the front windows smashed inward. Two canisters had been tossed through the glass, shattering it. They hit the floor, bounced, and spun, spewing thick gray clouds of smoke.

"They're here for her." Bannon pointed at Zayd. "They don't get her."

O'Neil pulled Zayd from the booth and pushed her to the floor.

Like Reyes had, Bannon flipped a table onto its side and ducked behind it. He kept his .45 aimed at the front door. Johnson remained behind the bar, aiming the shotgun at the front door. Smoke filled the bar. Fast.

It would be their undoing. Bannon knew it, but there was nothing they could do about it.

The seconds ticked by.

McMurphy slipped through the open door into the kitchen. Automatic gunfire echoed from the tight space back there. Bannon felt pulled in two directions. He wanted to go help his friend, but he couldn't abandon the front of the bar.

Another second passed.

The smoke reached Bannon. Not smoke. CS gas. Tear gas. His eyes began to water. The smoke burned his throat. He coughed.

Bannon heard more objects bounce on the floor. One, followed by two more.

More gas canisters?

No, Bannon realized. He shouted, "Grenades!"

He dove toward the back of the bar. The grenades exploded. First one, then quickly the next two. The table he'd crouched behind slid across the floor, clipping him in the calf. The roar of the explosions made his ears ring. Paper napkins fluttered through the air.

O'Neil shielded Zayd with his body and covered his ears. He twisted around and pointed his gun at the front door. Tears streamed down his face. Bannon's vision was blurry. His eyes burned.

"Chief," Bannon shouted. "Still with us?"

"Yeah." He coughed. "And hopping mad."

"I can't see!" O'Neil shouted.

"Don't rub your eyes," Bannon warned.

From the kitchen, there was a loud bang and more shooting. Then it happened.

The first of several dark-clad figures rushed through the front door. They wore gas masks. Through the smoke and tears, they looked like shadowy wraiths on a ghostly plane.

Bannon shot the first one. He died instantly. Johnson fired off a shotgun blast. A gasmask-muffled cry of pain followed the boom. The attackers came in low and immediately spread out. Bannon fired off two more shots. It was impossible to know if he'd hit anything or not.

Their attackers returned fire, using automatic weapons. Bullets chewed holes in the wall. Glass broke. Pictures broke and fell from the walls and crashed to the floor.

Bannon dropped low, where the smoke was only a thin veil. He saw a group of men, single-file, moving along the side wall. They were going for Zayd.

O'Neil popped off a couple of shots. On his hands and knees, he tried to shield Zayd and coughing between trigger pulls, he didn't hit much.

"O'Neil. Take Zayd through the kitchen." It was quiet back there. He hoped McMurphy and Reyes had secured an exit for them. Besides, they didn't have any tear gas to contend with back there. Bannon blinked and fired a shot at the lead man advancing along the side wall. The man was a vague, blurry, black shape. The shape cried out and collapsed to the floor.

Bannon coughed up phlegm. His nose ran, and tears rolled down his cheeks. His eyes burned so badly it felt like acid had been thrown in his face.

Suddenly, the fire alarm began to ring. Johnson had found the alarm pull handle behind the bar and tripped it. Bright white emergency lights snapped on, diffused in the smoke like headlights on a foggy morning. The sprinklers activated, showering stagnant, foul-smelling water down on them. For the second time that day, Bannon was soaked through to the skin.

One of the attackers lobbed a grenade behind the bar.

Johnson scrambled over the bar, rolled, and jumped as the grenade exploded.

The sprinklers began to dissipate the gas.

"Chief! Fall back. Fall back!"

Soaking wet, O'Neil pulled Zayd along the back wall, moving low toward the kitchen door. He passed behind as Bannon provided cover fire, and Johnson scrambled across the floor toward the kitchen, returning fire as he backed up.

Johnson reached the kitchen door at the same time O'Neil and Zayd did. He grabbed the woman and pushed her through the doorway. The Chief followed her through. Bannon did his best to hold the forward attacking force at bay.

"Commander!" O'Neil shouted. "Look out!"

Behind him, near the kitchen door, O'Neil shouted again, "Get down!"

Bannon dropped down to the floor.

The seaman squeezed off several shots over Bannon's head.

An attacker near the bar had had Bannon in his sights. Hit twice in the chest, Bannon's attacker fell back, toppling a table and several chairs. In response, others opened up with automatic fire. Hit by a hail of bullets, O'Neil cried out.

He fell back, his arms splayed out.

Bannon ran to him.

The young man hit the floor, his body riddled with bullets and wet blood. He lay facing up at the ceiling.

Bannon placed his hand on the young man's shoulder. "Troy, stay with me, son."

O'Neil coughed up blood. His face streaked with tears and snot and blood, yet he forced a smile. "Don't let them win, sir."

"I won't. You have my word." Bannon saw an approaching shape in his peripheral vision. He twisted around and fired two rounds, killing the man instantly.

"I done good, didn't I, sir?"

"Outstanding, seaman."

"You said, 'You'll do it for the next guy.'" He coughed up more blood. "I'm glad… it was…for you, sir."

He died before Bannon could respond. Determined to kill those who killed O'Neil, Bannon fired his .45 until it clicked, having run dry. He pulled his backup, but the attackers had pulled back. They provided cover fire for each other as they retreated to the wrecked door and slipped back into the darkness.

More gunfire erupted from the kitchen.

He charged for the kitchen, O'Neil's dying request firmly in his thoughts. "Don't let them win."

He swung around the doorjamb, gun first, but he was too late. Johnson and Reyes were on the tile floor. Reyes had taken a bullet in the side. None of them wore vests. None of them had expected this. Johnson had a gash under his eye, a bruise already forming.

"They were waiting for us. Got me with a rifle butt," Johnson said. "They got the woman. I'm sorry."

Bannon checked on Reyes. The young man was applying pressure to his own wound.

"Seven of them, sir. Nothing we could do."

"McMurphy?" Bannon asked, coming to his feet.

The back door had been blown open with explosives just as the front door had been. He could see the gravel parking area out back and the night sky over the side streets and parked cars. There was no sign of their attackers.

Bannon heard a groan and followed it to find McMurphy struggling to sit up on the far side of the cooking stoves. His head was covered in blood. He cradled it in his hands. "Please tell me we won."

Bannon helped him to his feet. "Far from it."

"Zayd?" McMurphy asked.

"Gone."

Johnson looked around. "Where's O'Neil?" He called out, "O'Neil!"

Bannon glanced at the door, aware of the sound of approaching sirens. He looked at the door back into the bar. "He didn't make it."

TWENTY-TWO

TARA TOOK A MOMENT to get her bearings. She wasn't an expert on boats, like Bannon and McMurphy, but over the years, she's been around them enough to know which end was which. This one appeared to have been a transport vessel of some kind, perhaps a large ferry. It was large and rode low in the water. She figured at least three decks in addition to the bridge deck.

She returned to what she'd determined to be a passenger section before it was subjected to an unfinished guy job. A quick count of the slotted rows told her the room had once held seating for three or four hundred passengers. But what the ship's function was or had been didn't matter. Her first order of business was to get a message to the outside world. Alert the Coast Guard. Get word to Bannon that she was alive, if not necessarily okay.

Also, Bannon needed to know about Faaid. The last time they'd tangled with him, surface-to-air stinger missile weaponry had been involved. She didn't know what Aziza Faaid was up to—not yet—but she knew it wasn't good. The man had proven to be dangerous. Whatever he was up to had to be stopped. He had to be stopped. Permanently.

She moved forward and stepped through a curtained archway that took her into the first-class section of the ship. The rows of seating in the forward cabin had been removed as well, but unlike the midsection, this space didn't look like a half-finished construction teardown. The walls were paneled with new paneling and teak trim. The floor was black marble tile. There were a dozen cream-colored leather sofas and glass-topped coffee tables throughout. The room came to a point, following the bow of a ship and provided a one-hundred-eight-degree view of the ocean ahead.

Tara took it all in and then dismissed it as irrelevant. Her only concern was finding the bridge or, at the very least, a radio room. She crossed the room and climbed the open staircase she found going up. She coiled the chain still attached to her right hand. With the rifle strapped across her back and the knife gripped in her left hand, ready to strike, she ascended the stairs.

At the top, she stepped quickly into a small galley kitchen. No one was there. For that, she was grateful. She'd not eaten and had had very little to drink since being held captive. Shaky from lack of food and water and achy from all she'd endured since being brought onboard—being chained up, the beatings she'd taken, and her fight to escape—all she wanted to do was slip in between her cool, Egyptian cotton sheets on her bed at home, curl up, and sleep for a week.

Since that wasn't an option, not for the time being anyway, she pulled open cabinets until she found a stack of protein power bars. She wolfed three down and pulled a bottle of water from a refrigerator. She gulped that down, too.

Two doors led out of the galley, facing forward. She smiled, reading the brass plate: Bridge. She moved toward the one door but paused, listening. She heard footsteps and voices. They came from the lower deck. At least two people. Coming upstairs. Speaking Arabic.

Tara crouched below the half-wall that enclosed the stairwell and unrolled the chain a short length. She held her breath and waited.

The stairwell was narrow. Only one person could come up at a time.

A man dressed in a brown tunic and slacks, like the man she'd already killed, stepped into the galley. His attention was down the stairs, still speaking with his companion.

Tara jumped up and snapped the chain out. It lashed around the man's neck. She stepped in behind him and pulled. He gurgled, clawing at the chain around his throat. Tara pulled harder, yanking him back and off his feet. The sense of *déjà vu* was not lost on her.

The second man, on a lower step, paused. He stared at them with his mouth agape.

"Nahuel!" The man Tara was choking squawked, slapping at the chain around his throat.

Tara kicked her foot out and drove it into the lower man's gut. He groaned and doubled over, clutching his stomach as the wind was driven from his lungs. Tara spun the man she held and shoved him face-first against the bulkhead. His nose hit the wall, breaking with an audible crack.

She pulled him back as the other one tried to straighten up and catch his breath. He balanced precariously on the edge of the lower step. Tara shoved the man she held at him. They crashed together. The lower man's foot slipped. He fell back, waving his arms. He gave out a sharp cry of surprise as he lost his balance and tumbled down the stairs.

The racket was louder than Tara would've preferred, but by the time he hit the bottom, his head rested at a peculiar angle, making it obvious his neck was broken.

No one came running, so all's well that ends well, Tara thought. For her, anyway.

She cinched the chain tighter around the first man's neck, redoubling her efforts to end him, too. It didn't take long. When he was dead, she uncoiled the chain from his throat and let his body collapse into a pile on the floor.

Breathing heavily and more tired than she'd care to admit, Tara cautiously stepped through the door into the bridge. There was a single person present. A young man dressed in the same style of brown tunic as the others, like the other Middle Eastern. He sat in the captain's chair. His feet up on the console in front of him. He listened to a pair of headphones.

He'd heard nothing of the struggle in the galley.

Tara came up behind him and placed the blade of her knife to his throat. His eyes snapped open, but otherwise, he didn't make any attempt to resist.

"Don't hurt me," he pleaded.

"You speak English."

"Of course. I'm from Brooklyn." He cast his wide eyes in her direction. "Please don't hurt me."

"Do exactly what I tell you, and you'll be fine."

He eyed her with suspicion but said nothing.

"Activate the ship's SART."

"What?"

"The search and rescue transponder."

"I know what it is. I can't."

Tara pressed the knife harder to his throat. "I've just killed three of your shipmates. Don't think I'll hesitate to kill you, too."

The young man visibly blanched, but his eyes hardened with defiance. "It's not that I don't want to. I can't. The transponder. It was disabled. And before you ask, the SAT-AIS has been destroyed, too. Captain's orders."

The IMO required all international traveling ships over three hundred gross tonnage and all passenger vessels to be equipped with a Satellite Automatic Identification System. The device transmitted a unique identifier as well as position, course, and speed at regular intervals, allowing ships to be tracked by a marine traffic controller. With it disabled, the ship was untraceable by base stations dedicated to monitoring such traffic.

"What about the satellite EPIRB?"

The Emergency Position-Indicating Radio Beacon. A tracking transmitter that could be triggered during an emergency. A humanitarian consortium of treaty-based, nonprofit, intergovernmental rescue services from forty-four nations and agencies called COSPAS-SARAT monitored for such radio beacons, ready to forward such alerts to over two hundred countries around the world.

He shook his head and swallowed hard. "Destroyed."

"What about the damn radio?"

The young man pointed at it. The mic had been removed, preventing any outward communication. "Mr. Faaid's got it," he explained.

She pressed the blade harder against his throat.

He quickly added, "There is a portable EPIRB on board."

"Where is it?" she asked, hopeful.

"Mr. Faaid's got that, too."

Frustrated, Tara spun the chair around. "So, what, you're just a pilot?"

"What? No. I don't know how to drive this thing. The ship's automatic navigational system's on."

"Then what are you doing up here?"

"They told me to look for ships and listen for incoming calls. If I hear or see anything, I'm supposed to tell the captain." The young man couldn't be over twenty years old. "No. Don't."

She tore the headphones from around his neck. She pressed one cup to her ear. She heard an Arabic voice talking. A propaganda-filled recruitment pitch. Today's terrorists were being indoctrinated via podcasts. She tossed the headphones to the console.

"How many personnel aboard?" She added, "I dare you to lie to me."

"Twenty-five, including the captain and Mr. Faaid."

Twenty-two since she killed three people getting up to the bridge. Twenty-one if one counted Reza. There had to be a way to get a message out, a distress signal, something. "What about a sat phone? Anyone aboard have one?"

"I don't know."

"A satellite phone. Connects to a satellite instead of a cell tower."

"I know what it is," he said. "If someone's got one, I haven't seen it. They took our cells and all our electronic devices before we boarded. Can't even get Netflix."

A shadow passed by the window in the galley door, catching her eye.

She took a step back and twisted the radio operator in his seat before yanking him to his feet a split second before the glass shattered. Tara ducked behind the young man.

"No! No, no, NO!"

Someone opened fire with an automatic weapon. The young man's body shuddered and jerked as he was riddled with bullets. The sound was deafening. Bullets hit the panoramic windows sending cracks racing through the glass. Bullets pinged off the metal consoles. Glass screens shattered. The console popped and sparked.

When the shooting stopped, Tara dropped the lifeless body and darted to the back of the bridge. She ran for the rear door and yanked it open. Any hopes she harbored they hadn't discovered she'd escaped were dashed.

CHAPTER TWENTY-THREE

OUTSIDE. NIGHTTIME.

Bannon stood under the overhang that extended from the Keel Haul. The bar occupied the end unit, one of dozens of seaside shops, T-shirt stores, food vendors, and arcades. He leaned against the side of the building. A beer bottle dangled from between his fingers, undrunk after the first sip. Hampton Beach police cars lined the street. Emergency lights flashed, painting the beach community with pulsating electric blue and white light. The blast of radio traffic punctuated the quiet lapping of the nearby waves and the low murmur of the gathered crowd. As many people on the street as there were during the hot summer days or when the bandshell was rocking.

The cops kept them behind barriers across the street.

Bannon thought he'd been achy, tired, and sore before. He had no words for how drained and beat up he felt now. His eyes still teared from the CS gas. It clung to his clothes like dust. Blood covered his hands, matted his hair, and stiffened his clothes as they dried. He held a cell phone in his hand. It was smeared with CS dust and blood.

A black government SUV allowed through the roadblocks pulled up in front of the Keel Haul. Elizabeth Grayson got out of the back seat.

"Brice. Are you all right?" Her concern for him was both genuine and deep. "What the hell happened?"

Dressed in jeans and a blousy white top, Bannon wondered if he'd ever seen her in anything but a pantsuit or her Army uniform before.

Bannon stared off at nothing, barely acknowledging her presence. "They came for her."

"Zayd? That's impossible."

Bannon shrugged, still kind of out of it. "A hit squad of some kind. We killed seven of them. There were at least eight or maybe more, all armed with automatic weapons, CS gas canisters, and grenades."

"Grenades?"

He nodded. "Grenades. Like a damn army. The ones we killed are Middle Eastern. All men. But there was a woman with them. She got away."

"A woman?"

"A redhead. I didn't see her. McMurphy did."

He looked at Grayson for the first time. "How'd they know Zayd was here?" If his voice sounded accusatory, he didn't care.

"They couldn't have," Grayson said. "Is everyone okay?"

Was she avoiding the question? He squared her with a look. He trusted her, but bureaucrats couldn't help but be bureaucrats. Their traits are infectious, like a disease. Grayson wouldn't have been the first leader Bannon followed, that he liked and respected, that had changed over time. For the worse.

He answered her question. "McMurphy took a blow to the head. Concussion, maybe. The EMTs are checking him out. Reyes took a bullet to the gut. He's been transported but is expected to be fine. Johnson's a little banged up, but otherwise, good, too. O'Neil..." He choked up. "O'Neil died saving my life."

"Oh, Brice." She touched his arm. He didn't react.

"How did they know she was here?" He asked again. "Pierce? I had a run-in with him at the Harbor. Could he have put it together? Any of the agents we encountered snatching her, could any of them have learned it was us?"

"No. There's no leak, Brice. Everyone's convinced it was the terror cells we're chasing." She took a moment to look over the crowd, the police moving in and out of the bar. "This didn't come from them."

Bannon pushed off the wall and walked over to a trash can. He lifted the lid and slammed his full beer into it so hard the glass bottle exploded. Grayson jumped. He stood looking down at it, his fists clenched. Then he moved toward the bar. She met him at the doorway to the Keel Haul. He handed her the cell phone.

"What's this?"

"Troy O'Neil's phone. The last call on it, an hour before he died, was to his mom." He went back into the Keel Haul.

Grayson looked at the blood-smeared phone for a moment before following him inside. Seeing the wreckage, she stopped short. Her breath caught in her throat.

Forensics people were moving through the upended tables and chairs. The gray, powdery dust coating the floor had been turned into a wet paste by the sprinkler system. Standing puddles of water were trampled through. Soggy napkins were strewn about, stuck to the floor, some with their edges burned. There were blast marks where the grenades had exploded. The splatter of mustard, ketchup, and cocktail sauce from exploded condiment bottles reminded Bannon of when they used to go and play war at the paintball park. A haze of smoke hung in the air. It stung Bannon's eyes.

Cops in uniform and detectives milled around, moving into and out of the kitchen. They spoke with Johnson, who stood with his back to the kitchen door frame. McMurphy sat on the edge of a booth, an EMT fussing over his cut forehead and trying to keep him from drinking a beer.

Bannon had draped O'Neil's body with a sheet from his upstairs apartment. Blood had soaked the white cotton red. The bodies of dead terrorists littered the front half of the Keel Haul. Two more were on the tile floor in the kitchen, killed by McMurphy before he got conked on the head and got knocked out.

Kayla Clarke had cleared a spot at the bar and was working on a laptop computer. She had been Bannon's first call after Grayson. She lived nearby and had been the first to arrive after the cops.

"Someone told them she was here," Bannon said. Like a dog with a bone, he couldn't let it go. "It had to be the FBI."

"There could be another explanation," Grayson offered gingerly.

Bannon stared at her. She recoiled at the anger he projected. "No way."

"I'm sorry, Brice. It's the only thing that makes sense," she said, not backing down.

He shook his head. "No. She'd die first. Besides, we didn't grab Zayd until after Tara was gone. She'd have no idea we did that, much less give us up. No."

"Before we could get on top of it," Grayson said, "news got out there'd been a disturbance at the federal building. If the terrorists got wind of that…if they told Tara that…she'd know it was you. She'd know you'd bring Zayd here."

"We don't know that. Maybe they still think she's Zayd."

Even before he said it, he knew that wasn't true. If Tara had successfully maintained her cover, they wouldn't have come after Zayd at all. They wouldn't know to. He was grasping at straws, any straws. No, Tara was compromised. She was their prisoner, probably tortured, possibly, maybe, already…

He couldn't finish the thought.

"What now?" Grayson asked.

"We fix this," Bannon said. "We figure out a way to win. I made a promise."

"Hey, guys," Kayla called out. "You'll want to see this."

Bannon and Grayson crossed over to where she stood at the bar. McMurphy stood up, too. When the EMT tried to sit him down again, McMurphy brushed him aside. He joined them, crowding around Kayla's laptop.

On the screen was a picture of a large, white and red passenger transport-size catamaran. The kind that ferried people and vehicles. From the image on the screen, Bannon guessed the catamaran was one hundred meters long with a thirty-meter beam and could see it had two vehicle decks, a passenger deck, and the bridge deck above the twin hulls.

"I was reviewing the evidence the police collected from Tumandar's attic apartment. Most of it was what you'd expect. Bomb-making material, receipts from places where he bought the stuff he used to make his bombs, a bunch of pro-radical propaganda nonsense." She looked at Bannon. "The brochures you found of potential targets. Except for the harbor, all of them were places he'd rejected for one reason or another, thankfully.

"The cops downloaded a ton of stuff off his computer. I cloned it and have been going through it, looking for anything that might help us. I came across this."

"Which is what?" Bannon asked. His tone was sharp with impatience and frustration.

Kayla shot him a look but then went on. "I give you the *Jean-Paul Dauphin*. It's currently docked at Boston Harbor."

"And why do we care about a French ferryboat?" McMurphy asked, sipping his beer.

"At first, I thought maybe it was a potential but ultimately rejected target. A ship capable of carrying a thousand passengers and almost five hundred vehicles, with a crew of twenty-five, makes sense as a target, right? Now I'm not so sure."

"Why not?" Grayson asked.

"Because it's not part of any regular ferry service. It's not here to pick up or drop off passengers, vehicles, or anything else I can find. I can't figure out why it's here at all."

If there were anything out there to find, Kayla would have found it. Tracks were being covered.

"Here's where it gets weird. Weirder. I researched the ship's registry. It's sailing under a Denmark flag, but the International Maritime Organization number doesn't exist. I've tracked the ship's ownership through IMO and every database I can think of. I've uncovered three shell companies so far. I'm still following the breadcrumbs down that rabbit hole…"

"To the chief's point," Grayson asked. "What's the significance of this ship?"

"I don't know, but there was a bunch of stuff about it on Tumandar's computer," Kayla said. "I figure, if the ship's important to him, it must be important—"

Bannon finished for her. "To his terrorist buddies, too."

He turned to McMurphy. "Feel up to taking a drive back to Boston?"

McMurphy pounded down the last of his beer. "Try going without me."

TWENTY-FOUR

TARA RAN THROUGH THE rear door of the bridge. It put her in the back end of the galley. A tunic-wearing crewman—the one who'd been shooting at her—backed away from the bridge door and twisted around. Still armed with the Russian AK-47 he'd already tried to kill her with, only the stairwell down to the passenger deck stood between them.

Tara swung her rifle off her back and fired two rounds. She struck the crewman with one and missed with the other. He fell against the bulkhead and grabbed his bleeding arm. Tara fired a second time, not knowing if she hit him or not, as she vaulted over the railing and dropped to the base of the stairs below.

She landed awkwardly, narrowly avoiding the broken body of the man she'd pushed down the stairs. She darted across the first-class section, which was still empty of people. It wouldn't be for long. She ducked through the curtain into the midsection. She held the rifle at the ready but didn't encounter anyone. She needed to get below deck. Find a stairwell down.

She intended to get to the engine room. From there, she could disable the ship. Keep it from going wherever the hell it was headed. After that, she had no idea. One step at a time, she told herself. Do whatever she could to not get herself killed.

As she ran along the row of cabins, past the one she'd been kept prisoner in, she tried to figure out how long it'd been since they boarded. How far had they traveled? In what direction? For what purpose? She was full of questions and had no answers.

She would disable the ship and find a lifeboat. Surely, a ship this size would have lifeboats. If she could get to one undetected, launch it without getting herself shot, she could escape. But what of Faaid and the others? Leave them here to escape?

Hell, no!

Tara found a door near the rear of the mid-ship section. She pushed through, determined. She wasn't going anywhere until she made sure Faaid and his ship were dead in the water. Or just plain dead.

On the wall of the stairwell, Tara found a framed schematic of the ship meant to outline escape routes in the event of an emergency. The ship was a passenger transport catamaran called the *Jean-Paul Dauphin*. A large ferry designed to transport both passengers and vehicles. One this large would transport upward of a thousand passengers and five hundred vehicles. Shaped like a sailing catamaran, the ship rode on two hulls resembling skis. There was an open space between them and one or more decks across the span between them. The ship would be powered by four independent marine diesel engines, two in each of the twin hulls.

A plan began to formulate, but she didn't get that far.

According to the schematics, there were two vehicle decks below the passenger deck. She passed the door to the upper vehicle deck and proceeded to the next level down. She stopped and glanced through the portal-shaped window in the door to the deck beyond. The catamaran's redesign seemed to involve more than a disrupted demo job and fancy forward passenger section. The lower vehicle deck had been completely repurposed and went a long way to explaining why the vessel rode as low as it did.

The deck had been converted into a well dock, sometimes called a well deck. Open at one end, it consisted of a channel between raised, open passageways on either side and a stern gate that could be lowered into the water, like a dock ramp at a boatyard. When down, the channel between two railed passageways would be flooded, thus allowing smaller boats to launch or dock from under the catamaran between its twin, ski-like hulls.

Tara eased the door open. Crouching low, she moved along the passageway, along the chipped yellow railings from which ropes, boat bumpers, and life rings hung. As she moved closer to the stern, she saw a vessel held in a cradle made of thick nylon netting suspended over the water sloshing around on the well deck. A metal gangplank with rails extended from the passageway to the boat's stern. The boat faced the stern as if prepared to launch.

Above the passageway was a bank of windows. Control rooms behind the angled glass. It would be from these rooms the stern gate would be raised and lowered, the flooding of the well dock supervised, and any work being done would be overseen. Inside the rooms, dark-clothed figures moved back and forth. Most wore yellow hard hats. All were Middle Eastern in appearance.

On the boat cradled in the well, two men wearing welding gear were working on the bow section of the vessel. The welding torch popped, and sparks flew. From where she was, she couldn't see what they were welding.

Tara estimated the length of the vessel to be thirty-five feet. A Bowrider, it had a deep-V hull and was similar in size and construction to the type of ships the Coast Guard used for their fleet of medium response boats. A common enough vessel, this one had no name or identifying registration numbers on the hull. She moved closer, trying to see past the bridge, to see what the men were working on. When she did, it sent a cold shiver down her spine.

It was a large gun. But not just any gun.

Tara had seen prototypes of this kind of weapon—an electromagnetic railgun. Yet she couldn't believe it. Though she was technically 'retired' from the field, like Bannon and McMurphy, she stayed current on the latest developments in cutting-edge weaponry. Not only those made by the United States but also the progress made in this area by other countries, too. As far as she knew, China was the only country other than the U.S. close to building this kind of weapon. But the size was all wrong. The railguns she'd read about would require a battleship to accommodate it, which was what the Chinese had done.

This. This was impossible.

A door opened from one of the overseeing control rooms. Aziza Faaid stepped down to the passageway on the opposite side of the deck. He spoke with a man wearing coveralls. He stopped and put a phone to his ear.

Had to be a sat phone to work out here, Tara surmised. Good to know.

She started to move away, backing into the shadows and using the various ropes and life rings to hide her presence. Stopping them wouldn't be enough. Leaving them motionless in the middle of the ocean wouldn't cut it. She knew that now. The railgun was their endgame. She needed to send the Catamaran, that boat, the railgun, and Aziza Faaid all straight to the bottom of the ocean. And this time, she was determined to get it right.

Tara continued her retreat. No alarms had sounded yet, which surprised her, and Faaid didn't appear concerned over her escape. Still, she'd left six bodies in the wake of her movements. Puzzling, but she wasn't going to waste time dwelling on it. She needed to find a quiet place to hide and regroup. A place to figure out what she needed, how to get it, and how best to carry out her plan of sending the devil and his ships to the bottom of the ocean for good.

She re-entered the stairwell, intending to head down to the engine room, but the door above her opened. Tara ducked into the back corner. She crouched low behind the open metal stairs. Booted feet came down the metal stairs. Two people, both men, talking in Arabic.

She was exposed. A simple glance to the side as the men reached the bottom of the stairs and she'd be spotted. All she could hope for would be tunnel vision from the two men.

They carried rifles but had them slung casually over their shoulders.

"I just wanted to grab a couple of bottles of water," one man complained, switching to English. "It's so hot."

Tara had her stolen rifle on the floor. She'd coiled the chain up and held it tightly around her fist. She tightened her grasp on the stolen knife as she listened to the two men yammering and watched them thump down the stair treads to the floor.

"Sawad, you heard. No time."

"A couple of seconds is all it would take, Wafi."

A radio crackled. One of the men held a bulky military walkie-talkie in his hand. Over it, a voice said, "The boat is almost here. Sawad. Wafi. Where are you two? Report to the well deck. Immediately."

"See?" one of them said. "I told you."

He pulled the door to the passageway open. Tara tensed. But the two men passed through onto the well deck without seeing her. She heard them run down the metal-grated passageway as the door swung slowly shut.

Tara breathed a sigh of relief, then decided to risk peeking out. An approaching boat. Someone arriving. Interesting. Tara needed to know who that could be.

She carried her rifle in her left hand, the chain wrapped around her right hand. She slowly pulled the door open. The coast was clear. She darted across the width of the passageway as cautiously as she had earlier. She made her way along the length of the walkway, remaining concealed behind the railing.

When she'd progressed as far as she dared, she stopped and watched as hydraulic pistons lowered the stern gate below the water level. Water rushed in and began to fill the well deck. The ship that served as a weapons platform for the railgun remained suspended over the sudden rush of water.

Beyond the mouth of the open Catamaran, a twenty-six-foot Sea Ray Sundancer pulled into the shadowy well deck. The Sundancer moved slowly under the cradled railgun boat and then turned. The pilot expertly pulled the cabin cruiser in behind the railgun ship. Wafi and Sawad were there just in time to drop a couple of rubber bumpers over the railing and catch the bow and stern lines tossed to them by two dark-clad men. They tied the Sundancer off and unrolled a Jacob's ladder down to the deck.

With the cabin cruiser properly tied off, four men climbed up the rope ladder. Two more figures emerged from the boat's cabin. Tara ground her back teeth. Bridget Barnes' red hair was like a beacon in the dimly lit well deck.

Tara put the rifle up to her shoulder and looked through the scope for verification, not that she needed it. Bridget waited by the ladder until another figure came up on deck to join her. Tara shifted the scope and sighted in. Shocked, she nearly dropped the rifle.

The second person, wearing a gray FBI sweatshirt and dark sweatpants, was Safiyyah Zayd.

How could that be?

CHAPTER TWENTY-FIVE

BANNON AND MCMURPHY SHOWERED and changed clothes. Grayson smoothed their departure over with the investigating detectives. In his F-350 parked at the curb a block from the Keep Haul, Bannon pulled out and hooked a quick U-turn as three black Chevy Suburbans with tinted windows pulled to the curb on Ocean Boulevard. In his rearview mirror, Bannon saw Agent Pierce hop out of the driver's side.

"Outta there in the nick of time, "McMurphy said, watching through the side-view mirror.

"Perfect timing," Bannon agreed.

As they drove south, Bannon had a sense of *déjà vu*. He and McMurphy didn't speak, but McMurphy didn't sleep either. They were each processing the events of the last thirty-six hours. They'd lost men before, and they would again. They would grieve later. For now, they had a mission to complete, and the mission came first. Above all else, otherwise, there would be a lot more to mourn than one dead Coastie and a couple of FBI field agents.

But these deaths couldn't be ignored. Someone would pay for them. That, Bannon vowed.

They drove down Route One. That late at night, there were no other cars on the road. When they reached Boston, they looped around onto ninety-three south, then drove north up Atlantic Avenue, past the twin Harbor Towers apartments where Tumandar, his explosive-loaded SUV, and the docked yacht now rested on the floor of the Harbor. Sections were still cordoned off. Powerful work lights still glowed as the forensic teams, the TSB, and others continued to work the scene collecting evidence.

When they reached Columbus Waterfront Park, McMurphy pointed to the right.

They circled the park and pulled into the Commercial Wharf parking loop. Bannon parked facing the Boston Yacht Haven. They got out and walked along the J-shaped wooden wharf. It extended into the harbor and then made a nearly ninety-degree turn north. Because of its size, the *Jean-Paul Dauphin* should have been berthed along the south pier.

It wasn't.

Bannon called Kayla. "The *Dauphin's* not here."

"I'll check with the dockmaster," McMurphy said, going off in search of him or her.

"I can't help you with that," Kayla said over the phone. "But I do have more information about the ship itself. Turns out it used to be the *Agros Traveler*, built in Australia. Its port of Registry was Limassol, Cyprus. According to records, it was sold for scrap and towed to Bangladesh, where it was broken up three years ago."

"Supposedly," Bannon said.

"In the legal profession, we prefer 'allegedly.' I'll keep digging through the web of ownerships and shell companies to see what I can find."

"Thanks, Kayla. About before…I was a bit testy. I'm sorry."

"No need, Brice. I get it. What are you going to do now?"

"Honestly, I don't know."

"Just be careful, and call if you need anything."

"Will do." They hung up. Fences mended.

McMurphy came back, puffing on a lit cigar. "Dockmaster said the *Dauphin* cast off near midnight the night before last."

The same night, they brought the *Naeem* into port. The night they handed Tara over to the terrorists. Bannon looked out at the harbor, past the lights of Logan Airport to the left, out through the channel leading to the open ocean. With no idea where they were heading, the ship could be anywhere.

"I'm open to suggestions."

Standing beside him, McMurphy puffed his cigar and smiled. While Bannon stared out to sea, McMurphy's gaze shifted a bit more to the left. "I've got one, but you're not gonna like it."

His old friend was right. Bannon didn't like it. But he liked the alternate—do nothing—even less.

After asking, "Are you serious?" They jumped back into the truck and took the tunnel under the harbor to Logan Airport. He parked the big Ford truck in the airport's main parking structure. They hoofed it through the terminal buildings, and at the one closest to the cargo hangers, where the major air cargo companies operated from, they went back outside. Using the nighttime darkness and shadows for cover, they darted from buildings to trees, ducked behind electrical boxes and dumpsters, and dashed from parked cars to bushes, making their way to the cluster of buildings around the Massport Fire Rescue headquarters.

Everything was locked up tight at that time of night.

They hopped a fence. Sticking to the shadows, again darted from an empty cargo container to a luggage trolley to the corner of the building McMurphy was looking for. They sidled up next to it. McMurphy looked out past the corner of the building. When he looked back, he had a big grin on his face.

"She's there," he said.

"Tell me again how you know about this?"

"Saw it on the news."

Mildly surprised, Bannon said, "You watch the news?"

McMurphy rolled his eyes. "Fine. The TV was at the OTB place I use. I happened to see the story while I was waiting in line to place my bets."

McMurphy leaned out for a second look.

"You win?"

McMurphy turned back. "What?"

"Your horse. Did it win?"

McMurphy harrumphed. "You think I'd be here, risking the rest of my life in Leavenworth, if that nag won?"

Bannon smiled. "Yeah. You would be."

McMurphy shrugged, agreeing.

"There's only one guard. You distract him. Go." He pushed Bannon out of the shadows and onto the tarmac.

"The guard's a Marine," Bannon muttered under his breath. He looked to where McMurphy had last been, but his friend was gone. Bannon pulled some papers from a nearby trash can, hoping to make them look like airline tickets. He hissed, "And he's armed to the teeth."

The marine had an M16 rifle shouldered and an M9 Beretta pistol holster on his hip.

Bannon looked down at his papers and furrowed his brow, trying for an expression of exasperated confusion as he strolled toward the Marine, eyeing him with suspicion as he approached.

The Marine sergeant was guarding the latest, most powerful, and most expensive helicopter the Marine Corps owned—a CH-53K King Stallion. On the way over, McMurphy gushed about how the chopper had a cruising speed of one hundred seventy knots and had a range of four-hundred-sixty miles. That it could accommodate thirty-seven personnel and crewed with two pilots and a combat crew of three. How it could carry a thirty-five thousand-pound payload, triple what its predecessor could handle. "That's like four Humvees," he'd rattled off excitedly.

"Sir, you can't be here," the Marine said to Bannon as he approached.

Bannon ignored him, stared at his papers, and kept walking with his head down. He muttered nonsense under his breath and even scratched his head.

"Sir," the Marine tried again. "Sir!"

When he got close, Bannon looked up. He grinned. "Oh, thank goodness. Someone I can ask. Maybe you can help me. I seem to be lost. I'm supposed to be at—"

"How did you get in here?"

Bannon looked around. He hesitated, then pointed. "Through a gate, over there. It's wide open."

"That's impossible. This is a restricted area. You must leave immediately."

"I get that. Sure. Happy to." Bannon pointed at his papers. "If you can just—"

Bannon noticed a barely discernable dark shadow race across the open tarmac between the hanger and the helicopter. Crouched and as silent as an apparition, McMurphy disappeared behind the far side of the helicopter.

"You need to leave," the Marine insisted. "Now."

"That open gate." Bannon pointed in the direction behind him, away from the chopper. "I can show you. It's just hanging open, swinging in the breeze."

"I'll deal with that. You can't be here."

Bannon looked past the Marine's shoulder. McMurphy had climbed into the cockpit of the helicopter. He put on a set of headphones and gave Bannon the thumbs up.

"If you could just tell me how to get—"

"You need to leave, sir. Now. Or I'll be forced to place you under arrest." The Marine pointed the way for Bannon to go, using his other hand to turn Bannon in the direction he'd come.

Bannon pointed at the helicopter. "But what about him? Is he supposed to be in there?"

The Marine spun around, slipping the M16 from his shoulder.

Bannon snaked his arm around the man's neck and clasped the inside of his other arm while applying forward pressure to the back of the man's neck. He knocked the man's cover—headgear—to the ground. The Marine struggled, of course, but Bannon's grip was firm. Soon, oxygen deprivation did its job. The man slumped unconscious in his arms. Bannon dragged him across the tarmac and gently sat him down against the hanger bay door.

He retrieved the man's cover and placed it on his head, making it look as if the man had gone to sleep. Bannon made a final check, ensuring the man was breathing, then ran across the tarmac.

McMurphy started the helicopter up. The motor began to whine, and the overhead and tail rotors began to spin. Bannon leaped into the co-pilot seat and slid the door shut. He watched McMurphy familiarize himself with the state-of-the-art cockpit.

"You see how sweet this thing is?" McMurphy marveled at the LCD screen instrument panel, called a glass cockpit. "Fly-by-wire electronic interface. Mechanical flight control backup. A split torque gearbox. How cool is that?"

"We'll get you two a hotel room later. For now, can you just get us in the air?"

He didn't have to ask McMurphy if he could fly the newest helicopter to come off the government's assembly line. That was the man's superpower. If it had an engine or motor of any kind and a steering device, McMurphy instinctively knew how to operate it. At an expert level.

Bannon found the skill uncanny.

As if to emphasize his confidence in the man, the helicopter rocked a little, then rose.

"You hear that?" McMurphy asked. "That's the purring of three turboshaft engines. Seventy-five hundred shaft horsepower each." He pointed overhead. "That's the sweet sound of seven composite rotor blades. There's four more on the tail rotor."

McMurphy nudged the machine nose forward. The running lights snapped on, and McMurphy banked to the left.

"Just get us out of here before the Marine Corps scramble fighter jets to blast us out of the sky."

They continued to climb and soon were out over the dark water of the harbor and heading out for the open sea. Logan airport and the twinkling lights of Boston quickly faded into the distance behind them. Ahead, dawn broke over the horizon. Thick purple clouds hung low in the sky as an angry red sun rose, reminding Bannon of the adage: red in the morning, sailors take warning.

The old superstition held little sway over McMurphy. With a face-splitting grin, he whooped at the top of his lungs. "Woohoo! Let's see what this baby can do!"

CHAPTER TWENTY-SIX

FAAID STOOD AT THE opening between the chipped yellow railings as his men climbed up the rope ladder provided them. They looked tired, beaten up. A few were bloodied up. The woman had taken twelve men with her to secure Safiyyah Zayd. He counted five as they climbed past him. He looked down at Bridget Barnes still on the deck below.

When she climbed up the ladder, he offered her no assistance. As her feet hit the metal grate, Faaid said, "Are we sure you got the right one this time?"

"It's her." Bridget's voice seethed with animosity.

"And what of the rest of my men?"

"Our men," she reminded him curtly. "They're dead."

"Seven of them? Against two men?"

"They had help. We're lucky any of us survived."

"And the Americans. Bannon and McMurphy? They are dead?"

"No. They are *not* dead. Did you not hear me? We barely got out of there with our lives."

She glared at him like she had more to say, but he turned his back to her, shifting his attention to Zayd as she labored to climb onto the deck. She'd been injured. He wondered how.

No doubt yet another criminal act the Americans would have to pay for.

"I warned you," he said. "The Americans are formidable."

Zayd stared at Faaid's scarred face. Self-conscious, he turned away.

"You must be Aziza Faaid."

He gave her a slight bow. "Yes. I am." He kissed the back of her hand. "A pleasure to finally meet the real you."

Bridget rolled her eyes. "Please."

Zayd withdrew her hand. "I wish I could say the same. Ghaazi Alvi did not warn me of the incompetence I would encounter upon coming to this horrible country."

"I assure you—"

The woman held up a hand, silencing him. "I am not interested in hearing your excuses for failure and incompetence." She leaned over and rubbed her knee.

Taken aback, Faaid said, "I disagree with your assessment of our progress. You are here." He waved a hand around the well deck and then toward the railgun. "Your weapon is here."

With a smirk, Bridget said, "I'll leave you two to it. I need a shower and a nap."

She walked away, looking tired and disgusted.

"Have you any idea what the Americans put me through?" Zayd asked once Bridget was gone. "What my capture has cost my fa...me."

"While I will admit your journey did not go as smoothly as we had planned. For that, you have Captain Amar to blame, not I. He was he who allowed the Coast Guard to board his ship, he who let them take you captive. He has paid for his ineptitude with his life, thanks to me. You are here," he insisted, "because of me."

The woman made a disgusted sound. "I assume you have managed to locate our target, at least?"

The man fisted his hand but bit back his retort. "We have. All the information you need regarding the *Oceanic Princess's* current position and heading are…"

One of the two men who'd emerged from the control room with Faaid stepped forward and handed Zayd a tablet in a heavy-duty, military-grade, green metal case. "…input and ready for your review, ma'am."

She accepted the tablet and, without glancing at it, walked to the gangway that led across from the passageway to the railgun boat, leaving Faaid to stand…alone. The two men joined her on the boat as she went about inspecting the weapon. Faaid watched her. He seethed at her contempt for him, for all he had done for her. He wanted to scream: *We rescued you. That was me. If not for me, you'd be in a dank American prison by now.*

But he remained silent. They were close to their goal. The Americans would suffer. They would pay and he would get his revenge.

But before he could bask in the glory of victories to come, his attention was taken by Bridget Barnes, who stormed back down the passageway toward him. "She's escaped!"

Faaid glanced at Zayd, but she was too distracted by her computer and inspection of the railgun to pay attention to the commotion being caused by the contemptuous redheaded female. He took her by the arm and steered her to the far end of the passageway.

"Keep your voice down. There is no need to disturb—"

"She's killed four of your men. She killed Reza." Bridget shook her arm from his grasp.

"I am aware. I have the entire crew looking for her. There is nowhere she can go."

"I don't care about where she can go. I'm worried about what she will do. Or did you forget the last time you two met? She blew you up. She scarred you for life. She left you for dead."

His face darkened with anger. He clenched his teeth in an attempt to contain it. "That will not be the case this time."

"Sure about that?" Bridget taunted.

"What more would you have me do? My men are searching the ship. They will find her."

"Before or after she blows us all to kingdom come?"

"We only need a little more time." Faaid did his best to put a positive spin on the situation. "Besides, what Ms. Sardana does to the *Dauphin* matters little. Once Zayd completes her work, we will leave here and complete our glorious mission."

Bridget remained unconvinced. Faaid read her expression.

"If you're so worried about what the woman will do, go find her yourself."

"I will." She spun on her heels and stormed off. To two loitering crewmen, she said, "You two. Follow me. Now!"

"Remember," Faaid called out as they walked away. "We only have twenty men left. Try not to get them all killed."

TARA WATCHED THE EXCHANGE through the rifle scope. She was too far away to hear their words, but body language told her all she needed to know. Bridget Barnes and Aziza Faaid were working together, but they were arguing. Vehemently. Faaid was a misogynistic pig, of that there was no question, but Tata had a feeling there was more to it than just that.

From what Tara could see, Zayd ignored the drama between Faaid and Bridget. She'd climbed down to the railgun boat along with two men. Tara assumed they were engineers or operators assigned to work with her. They took orders from her, quickly rushing about to perform tasks or give her things as she limped around the deck. Bannon had done a number on the woman's knee.

Tara smiled. Good. As she watched, she pieced together what was going on.

Zayd's work at the NSEDC must have had to do with electromagnetic propulsion. It's the same principles at work, whether one launches a rocket into the atmosphere or shoots a projectile at over five thousand miles an hour, nearly seven times the speed of sound, at an enemy target.

Faaid and Bridget had the weapon.

But they needed Zayd to make it operational.

Which left one final, terrifying question. What was the target?

Tara lowered the scope from her eye. She pinched the bridge of her nose, more determined than ever. Everything had to end up on the bottom of the ocean. If that meant she went down with it, then so be it.

Bridget stormed off.

Faaid yelled after her. "We only have twenty men left. Try not to get them all killed."

Bridget saluted him with her middle finger.

She had spunk. Tara had to give the redhead that.

"So, she's coming for me," Tara said under her breath as she backed down the passageway. "Well, game on."

She slipped back into the stairwell.

The twin hulls were directly under the wet dock, but she was too far forward. The access to the engine rooms and fuel storage tanks would be in the stern. That meant she had to return to the upper vehicle deck, go all the way aft, then take another set of stairs down behind the wet dock control rooms to the aft engine room.

She eased the door open onto the vacant upper vehicle deck. This deck remained as it had when the ship was used for its original purpose, ferrying vehicles and passengers over the water. A large open space capable of transporting nearly five hundred cars. Most of them would've been parked in rows on this level. The rest would have filled the space now repurposed into the well deck.

The space was a cavernous empty room. It ran nearly the full one-hundred-meter length of the ship and took up almost the entire thirty-meter beam. Lone pallets of supplies and other materials were randomly plopped down. Stored for future use. There were two parked forklifts.

Tara carried the rifle in her left hand and held the chain wrapped up in her right. She stayed low and ran the length of the empty space. When she was almost to the stairwell, two men came out of the opposite stairwell. Damn the timing.

"Hey, look." One of them pointed at her from across the space. "Stop!"

The second one brought his rifle up to his shoulder.

She paused, thought about reversing direction and running back the way she'd come, feeling like one of those little yellow ducks in a carnival shooting gallery. She decided to charge ahead.

She carried the rifle so that her finger was in the trigger guard. She swung the weapon around and pressed the butt of the gun to her hip. She fired one-handed, squeezing off two shots.

The two men dove in opposite directions. One slid behind a pallet of shrink-wrapped cardboard cartons. The other one rolled behind a forklift. She couldn't take the time to get into a protracted gun battle with the two men. Too many reinforcements would be on their way in too short a time. Safely behind good cover, the men began to shoot.

Tara fired back.

Bullets pinged and ricocheted around her as she ran the last third of the space without getting shot. She was only mildly surprised by that. Most people who take up arms, even professionals like police, other law enforcement officers, and the military, don't take the time to practice and become genuinely expert with the tools they're required to carry, even though such proficiency might one day save their lives.

Tara reached the door, banged through it, and slammed it shut behind her. She jammed the rifle under the door handle, angled so the gun would act as a wedge, preventing anyone from coming through the door. At least for a little while.

Long enough to give her time to do what she needed to do.

She charged down the stairs as fast as she could, past the closed door to the control rooms. At the next level, she stopped only long enough to jam the blade of her knife under the door, wedging it shut as well. At the bottom of the last set of stairs, she found herself in the aft engine room. Each hull had a forward and aft engine room, a room that housed the large propeller shafts, and a fuel tank room forward of the engines.

The first order of business was to get rid of the chain secured to her arm. She found a workbench in the corner and set to work on snapping the padlock shackle that locked the cuff to her wrist. A chisel, a heavy hammer, and a few awkward swings later—luckily without smashing her wrist or her fingers—the padlock broke open. She was finally free of the chain.

Rather than discard it, she wrapped the chain around her waist like a belt, twisting the ends like the sash of a bathrobe. It was a badass look, she thought with a smile.

Under the workbench, she found a handheld acetylene torch and flint striker. She grabbed them and moved forward, through the next engine room, and then into the room housing the port side fuel tank.

The first part was going to be a snap. She set down the torch and striker and smashed her elbow through the glass box encasing a red fire ax. With ax in hand, she went to work hacking through the thick fuel lines from the room-size tank to the forward and aft engines. Sweaty in the oppressive heat of the room and out of breath from the effort, she stood back and watched as diesel fuel gushed from the split lines, splashing across the floor like an open inner-city fire hydrant on a hot summer afternoon.

Alarm bells rang.

For Tara, that was like a starter pistol going off. "Clock's ticking, girl."

The room plunged into darkness. The only light was from a few gauges and the glowing red emergency exit light over the only door out of the room. A few seconds passed. Then, bright emergency backup spotlights flooded the room with a blinding glow. Fuel continued to pour on the floor. The smell made Tara's eyes water.

She had to move fast now.

She retrieved the ax and the striker and backed into the forward engine room. There, she traced the fire suppression system's high-pressure water lines. Metal pipes running along the ceiling, not unlike a standard sprinkler system, and the carbon dioxide chemical lines. She cut through them all with the ax.

Water poured from the pipes. Escaping carbon dioxide hissed from the lines she severed, preventing either from reaching the fuel tank room. The gushing fuel began to slosh over the lip of the door and spill into the engine room. As she'd planned, though, she hoped the splattering fuel didn't hit a hot exhaust pipe and spark a fire prematurely.

Tara backed up through the engine room. The fuel flooded the room, following her like she was some arsonist pied piper. She stopped at the door between the two engine rooms, watching the stream of fuel and oily water flow closer.

"Hey!"

She turned. A crewman carrying a flashlight came through the opposite door. Armed with a handgun, he fired. Tara ducked, keeping an eye on the sparks as the bullet pinged off the bulkhead behind her. She grabbed a wrench for the bench and flung it at her attacker.

He covered his head and twisted away, dropping the flashlight in exchange for a handheld radio. "Intruder in the port forward engine room! I repeat…"

Tara rushed at him. He fired several more shots. She felt a hot flash of pain in her upper arm. She ignored it, grabbing him by the front of his brown tunic. Must have been a sale on the uniforms at Terrorists-R-Us, she figured. She spun him around and pushed him forward. His sneakers splashed through the half-inch of diesel fuel covering the floor. Still holding onto the acetylene torch, she swung it like a baseball bat, striking him across the jaw.

He staggered back, slipped, and fell into the fuel and water mix on the floor, soaking his clothes. He splashed around. His nose wrinkled as he realized what he was swimming around in. Tara backed up to the door. He stared at the handheld torch and striker in her hand, then looked up at her.

Wide-eyed, he said, "Please."

She hesitated for a second, then sparked the torch. It flared, producing a hot, blue-white flame. She touched the flame to the liquid spreading toward her. The fuel ignited with a whoosh.

The man shouted, "No!"

The flames shot across the room and ignited the man's pants. He patted desperately at the flames. A horrified expression on his face. He screamed. "Noooooooo!

The flames engulfed his frantically writhing body.

Tara slammed the door between the two engine rooms closed. She spun the wheel and ran for the stairs as fast as she could. The silent blue flames were racing across the floor toward the fuel tank at the same time. She needed to put as much distance between herself and that tank as possible. She ran up the stairs, two at a time, holding her arm with one hand. Her sleeve was wet with warm blood.

She reached the abandoned upper vehicle deck level. She grabbed for the door. She pulled it open. Below her, the tank exploded.

TWENTY-SEVEN

THEY FLEW DUE EAST. The rising sun had burned off the low-lying clouds. Now, it hung like a large yellow ball in a flawless azure sky. Bannon and McMurphy slipped their sunglasses on to combat the glare. Outside of a few catnaps, they'd been operating without sleep for over forty-eight hours. Bannon's eyes felt grainy.

"I hate to be a pest," McMurphy said. "But you want me to fly in any particular direction?"

They had been on hundreds of search and rescue missions together over the years, doing just what they were doing now: looking for a ship on a vast, flat expanse. Bannon remembered one of his instructors describing it as looking for a basketball in the desert, from space.

In those situations, they usually had a starting point from which to launch their search, a ship's EPIRB, Emergency Position Indicating Radio Beacon, or a search and rescue transponder to give them a general location. Within fifty miles. From that, radar and visual search patterns could begin.

Bannon had contacted Coast Guard Air Station Cape Cod. The *Dauphin* had shut off its SAT-AIS: Automatic

Identification System. With the device disabled, the *Dauphin* was untraceable, except visually.

"Brice? You okay?" McMurphy asked.

"Sure. Just thinking. You've got a gun that can fire a round with the kinetic force of a bus going at three hundred miles an hour with a range of one hundred miles—"

"That sounds like one of those math word problems," McMurphy said. "I hate those."

"I hate this," Bannon said. "Where do you take it?"

"With a range like that," McMurphy said. "They can fire at anything anywhere along the coast."

"Head out fifty miles to start. Follow the shipping lanes south."

After flying for several hours, while monitoring the Coast Guard and maritime channels for any sightings, they'd heard nothing regarding the *Jean-Paul Dauphin*. Bannon had even contacted NOAA, the National Oceanic and Atmospheric Administration, and COSPAS-SARSAT, the international cooperative of maritime agencies and private companies that monitor with satellite-based assets, EPIRB, and other types of distress beacons asking them to join the search. So far, they've all come up empty.

Bannon's satellite phone rang. He answered.

"Brice, where are you?" Kayla asked, hardly heard over the thrum of the helicopter's rotors.

"Looking for Tara."

"Vague much, Commander Bannon," Kayla said. "Secretary Grayson wants to know if you and Skyjack had anything to do with a Marine helicopter being stolen from

Logan Airport a few hours ago." That she called her Secretary Grayson meant their boss was sitting right there with Kayla.

"Don't have a clue as to what you're talking about." He quickly changed the subject. "Tell me you've found something on your end regarding Tara or the *Dauphin*?"

"Maybe. I just got a call from Air Station Cape Cod. They're reporting a fishing trawler who's spotted a plume of smoke out to sea."

"We're monitoring emergency channels. We didn't pick that up."

"Ship's captain said he can't afford a proper radio. Then gave them a long-winded tirade about the state of the New England fishery industry and how fishermen can no longer make a living. He used a cell phone. Called 9-1-1. It was routed to the Coast Guard. That he even got a signal is a miracle."

"Give us the coordinates."

"I've texted them to you. And Brice…"

"Yeah?"

"Secretary Grayson says, and I'm quoting here, 'Put a single ding in the paint of that helicopter, don't bother coming home.'"

"Message received," he said, "Loud and clear."

He read off the latitude and longitude Kayla had forwarded. McMurphy entered them into the console and immediately adjusted course.

"How long?"

"An hour. Maybe less."

"Make it less."

With a determined scowl, he punched up the knots, too. "We'll get her back, Brice. She'll be fine."

Bannon nodded. "She better be, or there'll be hell to pay."

Forty-five minutes later, Bannon leaned forward with a pair of binoculars pressed to his eyes. His butt hurt from sitting, and his body was stiff from not moving. He pointed in a southeasterly direction.

"There!"

A faint column of oily black smoke rose from the horizon. Its plume drifted north with the winds. They were too far away to see what was burning, and Bannon's stomach tied in knots, concerned they were either on a wild goose chase or what they would find would be much worse.

"Wanna bet that's Blades playing Pocahontas and sending us a smoke signal."

Bannon prayed his old friend was right.

"You'll see." McMurphy adjusted course. The chopper's nose dipped, and the whine of the engines increased as he pushed the helicopter to its one-hundred-seventy-knot limit.

CHAPTER TWENTY-EIGHT

AS THEY MADE THEIR approach, the *Jean-Paul Dauphin* listed heavily to port. Oily black smoke rose from the port midsection. Flames licked upward from a hole in the hull at the waterline. That size catamaran would have four engines, two housed in each hull. Forward of that would be the fuel tanks. Water gushed into what Bannon guessed was the forward port engine and port fuel tank. Spilled diesel fuel blackened the water.

The ship continued making headway, albeit slowly, turning left.

"The port fuel tank's ruptured. By the way she's steering to the left, I'd say they've still got one port engine operational. Everything on the starboard side looks operational."

"Till Blades does her thing there, too," McMurphy said with gleeful pride.

"Let's hope that's what's happening." Bannon looked through the binoculars again. "If that railgun's onboard, we need to stop that ship dead in the water."

On approach, McMurphy scanned the open water. There wasn't anything else as far as the eye could see. "Nothing to shoot at out here."

"Remember, a railgun has target acquisition capabilities of up to one hundred miles. We're not even fifty miles from the coast. Their target could be anything."

McMurphy nodded. "We stop her. Then we destroy her."

"And we get Tara back," Bannon said. "What kind of armament does this thing have?"

McMurphy frowned. "You want the good news or the bad news?"

Bannon shot him a look without answering.

"We're equipped with two window-mounted and one ramp-mounted .50 cal. machine guns. But since this baby was on its inaugural press junket—meant only to dazzle the press, the politicians, and the public—there's no actual life munitions on board."

"Of course not."

Bannon pulled his .45 and checked the magazine. He'd reloaded after the incident at the Keel Haul. His backup Sig was strapped to his ankle. He was sure McMurphy was similarly armed. The man didn't go to the bathroom without his gun.

"It's not all bad news." McMurphy pointed his thumb toward the cabin. "Check the gun locker in the back. According to the inventory list, it should be stocked."

Bannon unsnapped his five-point harness and ducked into the wide cabin. He found the gun locker and smashed the electronic keypad with the butt of his .45. Inside the locker were five M16s and five Beretta M9 handguns and enough ammunition for an army.

He returned to the cockpit but didn't sit, looking through the windshield.

The *Jean-Paul Dauphin* continued to list and spew out smoke. Bannon admired the hundred-meter-long Catamaran. It was a sleek ship with clean lines, though it rode low in the water. A ship that size, with its four marine diesel engines, would have a top speed of thirty-seven knots and the capacity to travel six hundred nautical miles fully fueled.

What puzzled Bannon was there was no sign of the railgun or any weaponry at all on deck. Not even a downsized version. If the idea wasn't to mount the weapon on the *Dauphin*, where the hell was it? Maybe they're simply using the *Dauphin* to transport the weapon…

McMurphy interrupted his musing. "We're almost there. How do you want to play this?"

Bannon put a fully loaded M16 across the co-pilot seat for McMurphy. He slapped a magazine into the M16 he kept for himself. "The direct approach."

"Only place I can land this bird's gonna be on the bow. The way she's listing, it'll be tricky. Not to mention, if that tub tilts much more, this whirlybird's going into the drink."

"That happens. You'll want to go down with her."

"Rather than face Lizzy's wrath. No kidding."

Bannon clasped his shoulder. "Do what you can do. I'll provide cover fire from the cabin. Just do it fast."

Bannon returned to the cabin and pulled the two side doors open.

McMurphy flew along the ship's starboard flank. The *Dauphin* was traveling at less than five nautical knots and pulling left. He flew ahead of the ship and expertly banked the chopper, aiming for the bow deck. By approaching straight on, he reduced their profile to any potential attackers, making them a smaller target than exposing their flank. Bannon leaned out of the cargo door, the M16 set to his shoulder, the strap wound around his forearm.

McMurphy's precautions and Bannon's sharpshooter skills proved unnecessary.

No one fired at them as they landed. No one even came out. From inside the ship, alarms and klaxons were going off like crazy. The smoke rising off the port side was thick, oily, and hot. The wind blew the plume toward the bow.

McMurphy dropped the chopper down through the haze. The skids touched down, and Bannon leaped from the cabin door. Crouched, he covered McMurphy as he tied the chopper down. The bow continued to list at a thirty-degree pitch.

McMurphy grabbed his M16. "Let's get this done and get back here before this bird slips bye-bye into the briny blue."

"Sounds like a plan," Bannon said, and they moved out.

THE PORT SIDE FUEL tank exploded.

Tara was thrown against the stairwell wall by the force of the blast. She shook her head and pulled herself to her feet, feeling the ship right itself under her before listing to port. Fire alarms blared throughout the ship. She grabbed for the stair railing but winced at the pain she felt. Her sleeve was soaked with blood. Just a flesh wound, she assured herself. Still, it bled profusely and burned like the devil. "Terrific."

Red emergency lights cast an eerie glow in the stairwell. The alarms made her headache worse. Tired, she leaned against the wall and scrubbed her tired face with her hand. Her skin was greasy with girt and sweat.

"The ship's on fire, sinking," she said. "You're a terrorist. What do you do?"

The answer was simple. You make like the rats you are and scurry off the ship. They were launching the railgun boat and getting the hell out of there.

She needed a weapon.

She went back down one flight of stairs. The rifle she'd used to jam the door shut was gone. That was too bad. She pulled open the door. It led to one of the control rooms. Empty, the room looked like a hurricane had blown through it. Papers, clipboards, and electronic tablets littered the floor. Styrofoam coffee cups rolled. Their contents had spilled, staining papers and the console surfaces brown. A large crack ran through one observation window.

A ceiling tile had loosened and dropped to the top of a console. From the ceiling, a live electrical wire hung, sparking. The screens on the consoles flashed weird psychedelic colors and snowy static. A gray haze of smoke hung in the air.

Tara stayed low under the windows and pushed through the door to the grated passageway. No one was out there. Strange.

Cautiously, she glanced over the rail. The Sundancer Bridget and Zayd had arrived in had broken free in the explosion. It had drifted out under the *Dauphin's* stern and now bobbed gently in the calm waves of the Atlantic, a good hundred feet away.

As she suspected, Faaid, Bridget, and Zayd were on the railgun boat. Zayd had a panel open at the base of the gun's two rails. She seemed to be tinkering with the wires inside. An electronic tablet was propped up on a metal bracket next to her. The other two were on the upper bridge. They were arguing, again. The gangplank still extended to the boat's stern deck. Several of Faaid's men were carrying containers from the passageway onto the boat. They stowed them and returned to the passageway.

Tara couldn't hear what they were arguing about, nor did she care. They were getting ready to flee. She needed to stop them. To do that, she needed a weapon. To get a weapon, she needed to find a crewman and disarm him.

She ran down the length of the passageway. At the stairwell, she crashed through the door that would take her up to the passenger deck. All she needed was to find one person. Grab one gun. But she had to do it fast. There was no telling how much time she had before Faaid and the others cast off.

She reached the passenger deck and pushed through the door into the stripped-down midsection. She started toward the first-class section when a voice behind barked a single word. "Freeze!"

She did as she was told. She put her hands in the air and slowly turned around. At the far end of the room were Brice Bannon and McMurphy. A pair of M16s aimed at her.

"Brice! John! How?"

They lowered their weapons and rushed forward.

"Tara, thank God." Bannon embraced her in a hug, which she accepted enthusiastically. Words couldn't express how deeply grateful she was to see them.

McMurphy, being McMurphy, slapped her back with a great big grin on his face. "Blades. You look like hell." He wrinkled his nose and frowned. "And smell like crap."

Her hair was damp and stringy and fell in her face. Her arm was bloody and sore, her muscles ached, and yes, she still stunk like a sewer.

She touched the bandaged cut over his eye. His one eye had blackened. "I've seen you looking better, too, big guy."

"Guess we've all got stories to tell." Bannon gave her good arm a squeeze. His smile was wide and genuine.

"They'll have to wait. Brice, it's Aziza Faaid. He's back."

"That's impossible. We—"

"Blew that camel turd up," McMurphy said. "Hooked 'em up with his forty virgins."

"We didn't. It's him."

"How?" Bannon asked.

"He was in the head."

"Well, ain't that poetic." McMurphy shook his head.

"Zayd's here, too," Tara said. "They've got a state-of-the-art weapon—"

"An electromagnetic railgun," Bannon said. "We know."

"It's here," Tara said. "But not for long."

"Where?"

"It's not mounted on the deck," McMurphy said.

The logical place for such a weapon, Tara agreed silently. Clearly, Bannon and McMurphy didn't know how small they'd managed to scale the weapon down.

"Think smaller. It's mounted on a thirty-five-foot Bowrider. They're trying to escape with it right now. We need to stop them."

Bannon handed her his .45. "Show us."

CHAPTER TWENTY-NINE

FAAID STOOD IN THE copilot position of the railgun boat. The canopy had been removed. The bridge was open with a pass-through into the boat's bow section. Bridget Barnes stood beside him, talking into a walkie-talkie, coordinating the search for the she-devil loose on his ship, while she oversaw the launch of the railgun boat. The gangplank had been retracted. Only Faaid, Bridget, and Zayd were on board. Ms. Zayd busied herself working on the gun's controls and keying information into her tablet. A podium-style computer console set off to the right side of the boat.

"Forget the woman," Faaid advised. "The fate of the *Dauphin* no longer matters."

"I want her dead," Bridget told him, then spoke again into the walkie-talkie. "Lower the sling. Now."

A crewman in the control room nodded through the observation window and punched commands into his console. Four hydraulic cranes began to lower the boat into the rising water.

Faaid paced. There was nothing for him to do. He looked out to the ocean beyond the listing stern. Ghaazi Alvi had gone to great expense to acquire the *Jean-Paul Dauphin*, saving her from the scrapyard specifically for this purpose. Faaid wondered how the man would react to its loss. Badly, he hoped with a sardonic grin.

Bridget held the wheel of the boat, strumming her fingers, waiting as the boat continued its slow descent into the equally slow-rising water. "Come on. Come on. Could this go any slower?"

"Your impatience will be your undoing, Ms. Barnes."

She glared at him but remained silent. Perhaps the insolent *alkaliba* was finally coming around. He left her and climbed to the bow. "And your progress, Ms. Zayd? How does it go?"

Visibly annoyed by the disruption, she said, "I'm uploading the final calculations and inputs now."

"And the instructions to the others?"

"Done and transmitted. I have provided everyone with the information they need to replicate what we are doing here today."

Faaid smiled. "Excellent."

"Finally," Bridget called out. "Release the clamps."

The clamps released with a metallic snap. The canvas netting fell away. The boat dropped with a splash. Faaid and Zayd grabbed the railgun, holding on to keep from being thrown to the deck. They both shot annoying looks at Bridget.

She smiled. The boat bobbed and then settled. "We're ready to go."

Bridget activated the ignition. The boat's twin 430-horsepower inboard engines rumbled to life. The water behind them bubbled and churned. She eased the throttle forward. The railgun boat slipped forward, away from the dock.

Bridget steered the boat from the cold, dark shadows beneath the behemoth catamaran into the bright ocean beyond.

Faaid smiled, anxious not to miss their date with destiny.

NOW ARMED, TARA QUICKLY took Brice and McMurphy to the well deck. She raced to the far end of the passageway. Her sandals slapped the metal grates. Behind her, Bannon and McMurphy were right on her heels, their boots pounding. A thundering herd of elephants would have been quieter.

The railgun boat had slipped from its nest. The netting floated abandoned.

"No. No. No!" She ran to the stern end of the passageway. The boat was already heading out to sea. She fired Bannon's .45 at it, emptying the gun.

Bannon and McMurphy crowded around her.

She shoved the empty .45 at Bannon and pulled the M16 from his grasp. With the weapon pressed into her shoulder, she flipped the selector to full automatic and emptied the weapon at the boat in less than three seconds. A line of mini-geysers marked the bullets' path across the water. None reached the departing boat.

It was out of range.

Tara shoved the useless weapon at Bannon and slapped the railing. "Damn it." She leaned back against the wall, tired and angry. "So that's it. We're finished."

Bannon took the weapon from her. "We're a long way from done. Come on."

McMurphy grinned. "Wait until you get a load of my new ride."

"It's a rental," Bannon said, walking away from the departing boat.

They headed up to the passenger deck, where a small group of crewmen gathered in the forward area. They were clamoring around an older man. He had dark skin—they all did—and a white halo of hair around his dark scalp.

They were peppering him with anxious questions in Arabic.

Bannon handed his empty M16 to Tara, who was a step behind him. He raised his hands, not in surrender, but to demonstrate he was unarmed. Tara and McMurphy trained their weapons on the group. No one could tell hers was empty.

"Your leaders have left you," Bannon said, speaking loud and slowly. "We do not want to fight with you any longer, but if you force us, we will kill every last one of you."

They stared at him. Guns aimed, but their mouths hung open.

"Do y'all understand English?" McMurphy demanded to know. "Yes or no?"

"*Nem fielaan*," the white-haired man said. "Yes."

"Good," Bannon said. "Put down your weapons, and we'll talk about what happens next."

There was hesitation from the men. They looked to the white-haired man for guidance. He nodded, and with a collective clatter, they put their weapons down on the ground.

"Are you the captain?" Bannon asked of the white-haired man.

Clearly, he was afraid to admit it, but eventually, he nodded. "Yes."

"If you or your men don't act against us," he extended his hand to shake, "they will remain unharmed. You have my word."

The captain looked down at Bannon's offered hand. With much reservation, he took it. They shook hands.

"We'll relay your position to the Coast Guard. The *Dauphin* will stay afloat until they get here. If…"

The captain narrowed his eyes. "If what?"

"If you tell us what Faaid's target is. Where he's taking that weapon? If you don't, we'll blow your other fuel tank and you'll be nothing but an oil slick by the time the Coast Guard gets here."

"Threats are unnecessary. As you have said, they abandoned us. Left us here to die. I will tell you whatever you wish to know. Faaid is going after the *Oceanic Princess*."

"Who's the *Oceanic Princess*?" McMurphy asked.

"It is a what. One of your decadent American cruise ships. The vessel left Boston Harbor yesterday. It is on its way to Bermuda with five thousand drunken, hedonistic Americans. Aziza Faaid intends to blow the ship to pieces, sinking it and every living soul on board."

Bannon fisted his hands as he felt the blood pulse in his temples. With the railgun, Faaid could do it with a single push of a button. An ocean liner large enough to accommodate five thousand passengers would require a large crew of at least a thousand. Six thousand people in all. Nearly twice the initial death toll of 9/11.

He looked at Tara and McMurphy. "We need to move. Now!"

They left the crew of the *Dauphin* and climbed out onto the listing deck. They walked toward the ship's bow, holding on to the handrails as the catamaran continued to pitch, now beyond its earlier thirty degrees. As they shimmied along, Tara glanced back. The smoke coming from the blown-out fuel tank was now more a light gray than black and not nearly as thick. Seawater had rushed through the hole at the hull's waterline, which helped put out the fire she'd started, but it also continued to pull the hull further underwater.

The Coast Guard would arrive in time to save the crew, but the *Jean-Paul Dauphin* was a goner.

CHAPTER THIRTY

McMURPHY CLIMBED AROUND BANNON and grabbed one of the helicopter tie-downs to pull himself up the slippery incline that was the *Dauphin's* bow deck. He turned to offer Bannon a hand, but Bannon waved him on. "Go. Get that beast started. We'll get the tie-downs."

McMurphy went ahead and climbed into the pilot seat.

Bannon looked back. Tara was struggling to pull herself forward. Her wounded arm was a problem, but her forty-eight hours of captivity without food or much water had taken its toll on her, too. He could sympathize. The past two days hadn't been a picnic for any of them.

He reached out his hand.

She looked at it and then at him. Accepting help wasn't easy for her. They both knew it. She took his hand, and he pulled her up. They reached the helicopter. She grabbed a handhold next to the open cabin door to hold on. The chopper's engines whined to life. Overhead, the rotors began to turn.

"He must be in seventh heaven," she shouted over the noise, meaning McMurphy and his new toy.

"You have no idea. Get in. I'll deal with the tie-downs."

She didn't argue. He watched her scramble up through the open cabin doors. Once she was safely on board, he went to work releasing the tie-downs securing the chopper to the pitching bow. He released three of them but the tension from the deck's increased pitch pulled the last one too tight. There was no slack to get it undone.

The rotors were spinning at full speed now. Over the downdraught, McMurphy shouted, "Forget it!"

Bannon waved and jumped for the cabin door as the helicopter started to lift off. Tara grabbed him under his arm and hauled him inside.

As his fingers danced over the smooth touchscreen control panel, McMurphy called out, "Everybody in?"

Bannon shouted, "Go!"

The helicopter tilted to the right and forward, straining, the one skid still secured to the last tie-down. The chopper slipped along the deck. If it continued, they'd be heading right into the drink.

"Hold tight!" McMurphy shouted.

McMurphy goosed the throttle. There was a surge of power, a straining whine of the engines.

Bannon and Tara scrambled to a couple of jump seats. Too late to properly buckle in, they grabbed for the five-point harness straps and held on. The big engines whined. The chopper shuddered around them, feeling like it would tear itself apart as its rise off the deck was arrested by the remaining tie-down. Then, suddenly, the tie snapped free, and the chopper jerked into the air.

Over the whining engines and roar of wind and spinning rotors, Tara shouted to Bannon, "Thank you for coming to get me."

"What choice did I have?" he said, deadpan. "You've any idea how hard good bartenders are to find?"

Tara punched him in his arm. "Then what you're saying is I'm irreplaceable."

He got serious. "You have no idea."

"Does that mean you're giving me a raise?"

"Not a chance in hell." He smiled, and she laughed.

With the helicopter flying high and steady, they could move around the cabin without fear of being pitched into the ocean below. Bannon said, "Let's take a look at that arm."

Tara unbuttoned the front of her coveralls and slipped her arm from the bloody sleeve. She pushed the coarse material to her waist and stripped down to her black bra with no inhibitions. Bannon set a first aid kit on her lap and went about cleaning and wrapping the wound.

"You were right. It's not too serious," he said.

"We'll catch them, yes?"

Bannon finished wrapping the elastic bandage and closed up the first aid kit. "Done. Catching 'em isn't the problem. We've got to stop them." He pointed at the gun locker. "The only thing we've got in the weapons category is a few more M16s and a couple of Beretta peashooters."

"Get close enough we'll pick them off. One, two, three," Tara said. They were both proficient enough marksmen to do it. "Or," she said, "we can crash the chopper into the boat."

From the cockpit, McMurphy called out, "Bite your tongue. This baby's got a seven-figure price tag. Lizzy's already said, anything happens to her, it'll be my ass in a sling."

"No way you'd survive the crash anyway," she assured him.

"Well, in that case," McMurphy considered.

"Let's delegate a kamikaze mission to plan B for the time being." Bannon pulled out his sat phone. "Speaking of Grayson, I need to talk to her."

Bannon stepped into the cockpit to make his call.

Tara used his knife to cut the sleeves off her coveralls, then pulled it back up and buttoned it. Done, she opened the gun locker and inspected its offerings. Checking, then loading 30-round magazines into the M16s.

Bannon dropped into the co-pilot seat and pressed the phone to his ear, holding his hand over the other one, doing his best to block out the helicopter noise.

Kayla's voice came on the line. "Brice? Brice, is that you? Are you okay?"

"We're good. And the band's back together."

"Tara? You've got her? How is she? Is she hurt?"

Bannon glanced back into the cabin. She continued loading weapons. "We've got her. She's fine, too. Nothing a few days of R&R won't fix."

"Oh, thank God."

Kayla repeated everything he said, relaying the information to Grayson, who was there with her.

"We've located the railgun," Bannon said. "But we haven't eliminated the threat."

There was some static and background noise over the line. Then Grayson came on the line. "Brice, you're on speakerphone. It's just Kayla and me here. Update us."

Bannon gave them a quick debrief without going too deep into the details.

"The target is a cruise ship called the *Oceanic Princess*. According to the *Dauphin's* captain, it left port the day before yesterday bound for Bermuda."

He heard the tapping of keys on a keyboard. Kayla said, "I've got it." She paused, then gasped. "My God! Brice. There's nearly six thousand people on board that ship."

"I need to know exactly where that ship is right now. Faaid and Zayd are heading there as we speak in a boat capable of doing forty knots."

"Working on it," Kayla said.

Grayson spoke again. "Brice, a full-size railgun has a maximum range of one hundred miles. We can expect a scaled-down version to have maybe half that."

"I'm more concerned about firepower. If it's only capable of a fraction of what you've described, that cruise ship doesn't stand a chance. You need to contact that ship. Get the captain to alter course as soon as possible. Take whatever evasive actions he can in case we don't reach Faaid in time."

Kayla spoke up. "I've just got Air Station Cape Cod on the other line. They've pinged the *Princess's* last SAT-AIS. I've texted you their most recent position, current speed, and course."

Bannon showed the text to McMurphy. "Don't spare any of that seventy-five hundred shaft horsepower."

"Times three," McMurphy reminded him. "I'm on it."

Bannon felt the chopper respond to McMurphy's call for speed and their adjusted heading.

To Grayson and Kayla, he said, "Have the *Princess* disable their SAT-AIS. Tell them to shut down everything except engines, running as silently as possible. I don't know what technology that railgun uses for target acquisitioning, so they should reduce their profile as much as possible."

"On it," Kayla said.

"Do we have any assets in the area we can call on?" Bannon asked. "Anyone who can reach that cruise ship before us?"

"No, Brice," Grayson said. "I'm afraid it's up to you."

Under his breath, McMurphy said, "Isn't it always."

"Then dispatch search and rescue," Bannon said. "A full complement now. Don't wait to hear from us." He disconnected the call.

McMurphy looked over at him as Tara came to stand between the two seats. He asked, "Ready to rock and roll, boys and girls?" McMurphy pointed. "Cause there she blows."

Ahead of them could be seen the white triangle wake of a fast-moving boat.

"I give you three psychopath terrorists." He raised his finger toward a black line, little more than a smidgen of darkness on the horizon. "And one sitting duck."

"A sitting duck," Bannon agreed grimly. "With six thousand innocent people on board."

CHAPTER THIRTY-ONE

THE RAILGUN BOAT SKIMMED across the surface of the water at thirty-five knots. Bridget Barnes stood on the open bridge, one hand on the throttle, nudging it forward, the other on the wheel, which shimmied in her hand. The sun was high in a nearly cloudless sky. The day was warm, but the blowback of salty ocean spray was chilly. Her red hair whipped in the air.

Zayd operated the podium-style console mounted in the forward section where the seating had been stripped out. Her ponytail kept most of her thick black hair out of her face as she worked with a furrowed brow, inputting data and double-checking calculations, trajectories, and other targeting information.

With a mechanical whine, the impressive railgun pivoted thirteen degrees off-center.

Faaid stood at the break between the bridge and the bow, staring through binoculars held to his eyes. His gaze was in the same direction as the railgun. He pointed. "There! I see it."

In the distance, the long black silhouette of the *Oceanic Princess* could be seen near the horizon.

"We're close enough," Zayd said. "You don't need to see it."

Faaid lowered the binoculars. "We are about to strike the greatest blow against our enemies in over twenty years. You cannot want to miss witnessing it in person. Not this! Allah's greatest victory."

"Unlike you, Faaid, I do not want to die," Zayd said.

"Nor do I, my dear. As long as I'm alive, I can strike against our enemies again and again. And I will, thanks to you. Should this test run of yours be a success."

"I assure you, it will be."

"Then there is no reason for any of us to die this day. This day we shall cripple the hearts and the spirits and the souls of these insufferable people."

Bridget glanced over her shoulder, squinting. "You might be a little premature in that prediction, Faaid. We've got company."

Faaid twisted around. He didn't need the binoculars to see the dark military helicopter closing in on them fast. He looked once more at the *Oceanic Princess*. He frowned. He wanted to be close enough to see the ship crippled. To see the fires burn and to watch the bodies, the dead falling and the living jumping overboard, only to perish in the cruel seas as Allah's just revenge rains down on them.

"Go faster," he shouted at Bridget.

"I can't outrun a helicopter, you idiot."

"Well, do something." He dropped the binoculars to the seat beside him and faced the fast-approaching helicopter. From a compartment underneath the bridge cowl, he pulled out a magnificent weapon. One he'd been most anxious to try.

It looked like a metallic flying saucer with two pistol grips attached to its underside. He'd been told it was a centrifuge force weapon capable of firing two thousand rounds per second without gunpowder. Thus, the weapon had no kick, making it so easy to use even a small child could accurately fire it.

"Go faster," he repeated. "Get us as close as you can to the *Princess*. Ms. Zayd, fire at will."

He turned his attention back to the helicopter, already so much closer. Between the pistol grips of the weapon was a small LCD readout the size of an average cell phone screen. Faaid stepped to the back of the boat and raised the weapon, aiming it at the helicopter. He flipped a switch, activating the tracking and targeting system. The screen glowed green with a bright yellow bullseye. A small yellow dot moved on the screen. The helicopter.

When he had a target lock, he shouted, "I will have my revenge! Die, infidels, die!"

TARA SQUINTED TO SEE through the sun glare reflecting off the helicopter's curved windshield. They were close enough now to see the figures on the railgun boat. Bridget Barnes stood at the wheel of the Bowrider, doing an excellent job of piloting the boat over the water at a high rate of speed. They were rapidly closing the distance to the *Oceanic Princess*. Much faster than any of them liked. The boat was easily within range of their target.

Zayd stood at the bow, working on what looked like a computer console.

She could fire the railgun at any moment. They were too far away to stop her. Tara's stomach turned sour at the thought.

Faaid moved from where he'd been standing toward the stern of the boat. He held something large and gunmetal gray in his hands. They were too far away to make out what it was.

McMurphy asked the question out loud. "What the hell is that?"

"Whatever it is, you can bet it's not good for us."

"Thank you, Commander Obvious."

Bannon unstrapped and stood up. Tara stepped back.

"Now would be the time to strap *in*, Brice, not...Where are you going?"

Between the seats, Bannon paused. He gave the railgun boat another look. "We start firing, trying to pick 'em off, they'll fire that damn gun. There's no room to land this thing." He looked at Tara. "And I'm not ready to kamikaze it. So get us as close and as low as you can. I'm jumping out."

He squeezed past Tara who followed him into the cabin. "I'm going, too."

Without looking up, Bannon stuck a Beretta into his .45 holster. It didn't fit right, but it would hold the weapon until he hit the Bowrider's deck. "You think you're up for it?"

"I'm breathing. That's enough."

He looked up. She read his concern for her in his expression. "You've been through enough already."

"Brice. There's three of them."

They felt McMurphy alter the chopper's trajectory, banking to port and speeding up. He was approaching off their port stern. The chopper smoothly swept around in an arcing circle. Do a fly-by over the stern, the largest and deepest deck on the boat. The biggest part of the boat to jump to, even if it looked like the size of a postage stamp.

With no time to argue, Bannon handed her an M16.

But Aziza Faaid had other ideas.

Bullets stitched across the starboard flank of the chopper.

"That gizmo of Faaid's," McMurphy shouted. "It's a gun."

"Who's Commander Obvious now?" Bannon shouted, grabbing a canvas tie-down to keep from being pitched across the cabin. Tara seized a jump seat. She winced at the hot flare of pain that shot through her arm. She glanced out the open door. Faaid's gun had two pistol grips set under a disk that looked like a flying saucer. It fired rounds at a rate that rivaled the M16s on full automatic. Mixed in the volley were red tracer rounds.

Tara returned fire, but her rounds fell short of the boat.

Over the ping of rounds ricocheting off the skin of the helicopter, McMurphy called out, "There goes the deposit on this thing."

"Just get us on top of them," Bannon shouted.

He crouched beside Tara by the open port-side cabin door. She'd exchanged the M16 she'd been firing for a freshly loaded one and strapped it across her back. She had no holster, so she gripped the Beretta P9 in her hand, keeping her finger off the trigger. For now.

McMurphy zigzagged their approach, doing his best to avoid the deluge of gunfire.

"I can't get close with that camel turd shooting at us."

"On it," Tara said.

They were within range now. She swung the M16 off her back and pressed against the edge of the open door. She flipped the switch on the rifle to fully automatic and sent a barrage of bullets across the stern deck.

Faaid ducked and ran back to the bridge section. He crouched behind the co-pilot's chair.

"Bring us down!" Bannon shouted. "Now!"

The helicopter pitched forward and sped up.

They swept low over the stern section and banked to the right. With his hand over his holster and the M16 strapped to his back, Bannon leaped.

Tara swung the M16 over her shoulder, strapping it once more to her back. About to leap out, the chopper rocked violently. Unprepared for the sudden shift, Tara stumbled away from the open door.

Faaid was firing at them again. This time, his bullets hit their mark—the chopper's tail. Smoke billowed from the rotor housing. Flames engulfed the tail section. A hit rotor snapped off with a loud metallic bang. It spun away. Alarms blared from the cockpit. The chopper wobbled erratically and spun in a counterclockwise direction.

Tara scrambled back to the left side of the cabin, about to launch herself out of the chopper, but stopped short when she saw the railgun boat was no longer beneath them. She'd missed her opportunity.

"Swing us around!" she shouted. "Swing us around!"

McMurphy ignored her, concentrating all his effort on keeping them airborne.

The chopper lurched and dropped, then pulled up.

Tara's stomach roiled.

"Take us back!" she shouted. "Take us back!"

"Can't," McMurphy shouted back. "I need to put her down."

He switched on the emergency transponder.

"You can't." Tara watched the railgun grow smaller. "There's no place…"

"There's one place." The chopper banked left and climbed and then picked up speed, sputtering and trailing a column of thick, black smoke as they flew away from the railgun and away from Bannon.

"If we can make it," McMurphy said cryptically.

Tara held on and looked out the cabin door. She saw where McMurphy was taking them, realized what he was trying and do.

He was heading for the *Oceanic Princess*.

It was their only chance.

THIRTY-TWO

BANNON HIT THE STERN deck of the railgun boat flatfooted. He bent his knees, absorbing the impact before losing his balance and falling to the deck. He tumbled across the deck and banged his shoulder into the gunwale. The downdraft from the chopper's rotors buffered him, whipping at his hair and clothes. His pants snapped against his legs.

He twisted onto his back and grabbed for the Beretta he'd jammed into the ill-fitting holster. He cleared leather and popped off a round at Faaid.

The bullet chewed through the plastic padding of the co-pilot seat behind which Faaid hid. He flinched and ducked deeper behind the seat, still aiming his strange-looking weapon at the passing helicopter. The saucer-like disk spun. He held it by two pistol grips. The weapon spit out rounds faster than an M16 on full-automatic, with zero recoil.

Bannon glanced skyward.

The helicopter had taken fire. Black smoke billowed from the tail section. The tail rotor was spinning erratically. He could see one of the rotors had broken off. The back end of the chopper swished like a fish's tail as McMurphy struggled to keep control of the aircraft. Tara clung to the open cabin door. She looked desperately down at the boat, at Bannon. There was nothing she could do. They'd passed over the boat too quickly for her to make the jump. Even from that distance, Bannon could read the angst on her face.

Having adjusted course, McMurphy zoomed away from the railgun boat, doing his best to get out of range before Faaid succeeded in downing them. The chopper flew away.

The damage to the tail rotor was too extensive. The chopper was minutes from going down.

McMurphy had no choice but to land.

That meant ditching in the ocean. Or—if they could make it—reach the *Oceanic Princess* and make an emergency landing there. The ocean liner would be large enough to land on and might even have a helipad. Many of the large cruise ships did, and the *Oceanic Princess* was one of the biggest of them all.

If they could reach it in time. Bannon knew that was a big if.

Meanwhile, he had his own problems to deal with. He pushed himself to his hands and knees. The boat bounced over the waves, continuing its deadly pursuit of the *Oceanic Princess*.

Faaid had abandoned his attempts to bring down the chopper now that it was out of range. He shouted at Zayd, crouched behind a jury-rigged podium in the boat's bow.

"Fire the railgun!" Faaid shouted. "Fire it now!"

At the wheel, the redheaded woman named Bridget twisted around. She sent the boat into a hard, starboard turn. In her hand, she held a compact silver automatic. She took a shot at Bannon, who dived across the enclosed space behind the bridge. The bullet pinged off the gunwale behind him.

"Powering up the rails," Zayd called out. "Current at seventy percent. Eighty."

Bannon fired at Bridget, but she wrenched the wheel in the opposite direction, sending Bannon tumbling back across the deck. His shot went wild. Zayd clutched her podium stand, holding onto it for dear life. "Hey!"

She pulled herself upright, brushing her long black hair from her face. "Ninety percent. Ninety-five. We're ready!"

Bannon's stomach knotted.

He'd rolled into the corner. He jumped up to his knees and aimed his gun at Zayd's back.

Her fingers danced over the LCD screen in front of her.

Faaid cowered behind his chair, hanging on. "Fire! Fire!"

Bannon squeezed the trigger, firing.

Bridget zig-zagged the wheel. The boat swerved left, then right, then left again.

Bannon went tumbling across the deck again. His aim spoiled. His bullet pinged off the railgun's slide.

Zayd's activated the firing sequence. Bannon saw two red columns climb up the computer screen. "Firing!"

The rails didn't move. There was no recoil. The gun simply made a deep, ear-shattering bang. Thick gray smoke puffed from the two rails that formed what would've been the barrel of a conventional gun. A blast of hot muzzle fire followed a split micro-second later.

The *Oceanic Princess* was less than a mile away.

Ignoring the danger Faaid and the others posed to him, Bannon stood up. In horror, he watched the great flank of the cruise ship. Two hundred thirty feet above the waterline. Over a thousand feet in length. Sixteen-passenger decks.

In less than a blink of an eye—the projectile had crossed the space between ships at seven times the speed of sound—a section of the stern just above the waterline exploded.

The ship tilted from the force of the impact. Like a child's plaything splashing around in a bathtub. Smoke and flames billowed up from the giant hole blasted into the hull, and only then, after, did the sound of the explosion reach those watching from the railgun boat.

"No!" Bannon shouted. "Damn you all to Hell! No!"

THIRTY-THREE

THE CHOPPER FISHTAILED, STRUGGLING to cover the distance between the railgun boat and the *Oceanic Princess*. They were only about a mile away. The engines banged and sputtered. McMurphy had taken control from the computer and was flying her manually. He brought the chopper low over the water. If they couldn't make it, they'd have to ditch in the water.

Tara stood beside him, looking out the window at the approaching cruise liner. "Are we going to make it?"

McMurphy grimaced. "Damn right we are," he said with more confidence than he felt. "But I'd strap in all the same."

Tara slipped into the co-pilot seat and snapped the five-point harness into place. "Anything I can do?"

"Pray."

"Done."

The question in McMurphy's mind was where to put the bird down, fore or aft deck? Each had the space. He angled toward the bow. Fewer people were milling about watching their approach.

"Get on the air. Tell 'em to clear the bow. We're coming in, and it ain't gonna be pretty."

Tara snatched up the radio. She broadcast on all emergency bands, assuming, hoping, the captain of the *Princess* would have his personnel monitoring that for instructions and updates from the Coast Guard.

The cruiser ship was coming at them fast. McMurphy had seconds to decide—water landing or crash the *Princess's* party. He angled the chopper's nose up. All or nothing. The aircraft shuttered with the effort. McMurphy looped the chopper up over the deck. Below them, people scattered. Several got pulled out of the way by uniformed crew members of the *Princess*. Others, with their phones out, videotaped the approach.

Seriously, McMurphy thought. He'd never seen so many billabong shorts, bikini tops, and ugly Hawaiian shirts in his life.

He managed to get the chopper over the ship's railing. One engine conked out with a cough and a shudder. They hovered above the deck. McMurphy struggled with the controls. "Hold on. This ain't gonna be gentle."

A second engine stalled. The chopper listed then lurched.

He'd gotten them to just ten feet above the deck when the last engine failed. They dropped like a stone. "This is gonna hurt."

They hit the deck—hard. McMurphy's head snapped back, hitting the padded headrest. He felt the impact all the way up his spine. The five-point harnesses held them in place but chafed as they pulled tightly across their shoulders and thighs.

The left skid snapped. The chopper lurched forward, then settled at a cockamamie angle, like a car with a flat tire. Smoke rose from the console. The cockpit smelled of burnt wires. The cabin was filled with hazy smoke. McMurphy looked at Tara.

She looked back. "If you say any landing you walk away from is a good one, I'll break your legs."

He smiled and pulled a cigar from his breast pocket. He stuck it in his mouth, popped his bushy red eyebrows like Groucho Marx, and said, "Got a light?"

Tara shook her head but couldn't resist giving him a grateful smile. She hit the release on her harness and climbed out of the wrecked helicopter. McMurphy did the same.

A man in a captain's uniform rushed up to them. "I'm Captain Herron, skipper of the *Oceanic Princess*. Are you two all right?"

"Never better," McMurphy said around his cigar.

Captain Herron looked at his bandaged forehead and blackened eye, then at Tara as she came around the other side of the chopper to join them. His gaze rested on her field-dressed wounded arm. Blood had soaked through the elastic wrapping. From his expression, he found McMurphy's claim was dubious at best.

"Warrant Officer McMurphy." He shook the captain's hand. "This is Tara Sardana. I hate to tell you, but this ship's still in grave danger."

"We're aware. We've altered course and increased speed as much as we can. A ship this size doesn't turn on a dime. We're not built for evasive combat maneuvers."

"We need to get your people up on deck," Tara said.

"Start loading the lifeboats on the starboard side." McMurphy pointed toward the railgun boat. It was just a mile away. Off their port side. "That's what we need to worry about."

Several crew members and passengers were standing around, listening. A clamor of concern spread through the passengers within earshot. The crew began to herd the passengers, moving them away from the crashed chopper and toward the lifeboats.

"You heard them," Herron said to his people, reiterating Tara and McMurphy's instructions. "Go! Move!" To McMurphy and Tara, he said, "We've already begun the evacuation protocols. We can have all the passengers in lifeboats and launched within thirty minutes. But that'll require all the lifeboats."

"Your point?" McMurphy asked as they crossed the deck to the port side.

"Half the lifeboats are on this side," Herron said.

They stood, gripping the railing. They stared at the boat racing toward them.

"How bad is it?" Herron asked.

"There's a state-of-the-art weapon on that boat," Tara said, "with the capacity to sink this ship with a single shot."

Herron visibly blanched at hearing that.

"Don't sugar-coat it, Blades."

"He needs to know." She turned her attention back to the railgun boat.

"We've got a man on board trying to stop them," McMurphy said.

What happened next happened almost instantaneously.

Tara shouted, "TAKE COVER! EVERYONE TAKE COVER!"

A puff of white-hot fire and dark smoke erupted from the barrel of the railgun. Instantaneously, they felt the explosion. The sound was horrifying. The ship groaned and yawed starboard. Those milling around were swept off their feet and sent tumbling across the deck. Fire alarms went off. Klaxons sounded.

The explosion first, then they heard the bang of the railgun firing seconds after the missile had already struck.

Tara slid across the deck. She reached out for the broken helicopter skid and grabbed the wrecked metal, cutting her hand on the twisted metal. Worth it, she thought, since it saved her from plunging over the side of the ship. A crewmember slid past her. She grabbed his arm, arresting his slide off the ship, too. A white-hot pain flared in her injured arm. She winced and ignored it as she pulled the young man up until he could grab the skid for himself.

Panting, he thanked her. Over and over.

McMurphy and the Captain had grabbed the railing in time, preventing them from getting pitched over the side of the boat. Two crew members and three passengers weren't so lucky.

Their screams could be heard as they fell to the water below.

Under them, the *Princess* began to right itself.

Tara climbed to her feet and pulled the crewman up with her. "Thank you, ma'am. I thought I was a goner for sure."

McMurphy and Herron helped other crew and passengers get to their feet.

From deep within the ship, more explosions rumbled. Tara felt them rumble through the deck. The muted blasts, like the boom of a bass drum deep in her chest.

Herron called out to his crew. "People need our help. Let's go. Move. Move!"

THIRTY-FOUR

BRIDGET BARNES SPUN THE wheel of the railgun boat, aiming it once more for the cruise ship. As they raced toward the cruise ship, Bannon looked past her and saw the smoke billowing from the large black hole in the *Oceanic Princess's* hull. They were close enough now for him to see the fires raging inside the ship. Several decks were exposed. Iron girders had been torn apart like balsawood. Live wires hung like writhing silver snakes. Snapping and sparking. Water gushed over the ragged end of the floors, the result of an overwhelmed sprinkler system, fighting and losing against the bright flames that were only getting more out of control.

Blind rage burned inside Bannon, brighter and hotter than the fires raging on the *Oceanic Princess*.

Zayd went about the business of loading a second missile into the holding chamber of the gun. Done with that, she limped over to the firing console and again began keying data into the keyboard.

Bannon fired at the computer. He hit it. The screen exploded in a geyser of sparks and smoke.

Zayd jumped away and turned toward him, a look of horror on her face. "No!"

He didn't know if that was enough to disable the gun, so he lined the Beretta's forward sight on Zayd's forehead.

About to pull the trigger a second time, Bridget shot him, hitting him in the shoulder. The impact forced Bannon back a step. He clamped a hand to his bloody shoulder and did his best to ignore the pain. He swung the Beretta in Bridget's direction. She ducked. Faaid body-slammed him, spoiling his shot and sending them both toward the rear gunwale. They both nearly tumbled out of the boat.

Bridget shoved the throttle forward. "Fire again!" she shouted at Zayd. "Fire again!"

The boat leaped, skimming over the water on a collision course with the flank of the *Princess*.

Faaid shoved Bannon back, arching his back over the gunwale, ocean spray soaking his face. The terrorist punched Bannon in his wound. Bannon howled in pain. He threw a right hook, using the butt of his Beretta to coldcock him. Faaid ducked and twisted, avoiding the blow.

As they struggled, Faaid shouted, "Fire again! Blow that ship apart!"

Bannon drove a fist into Faaid's gut, driving him back. Faaid raised his gun, but Bannon charged. He slapped Faaid's gun hand away, using his injured arm—a burning pain shot through his shoulder—then swung the Beretta, gun butt first, raking across Faaid's jaw. The man cried out and stumbled to the left.

Bannon charged toward Bridget, her hands gripped tightly on the wheel. She spun it, sending the boat into a sharp turn. In the bow, Zayd grabbed for the console. Her hands slipped.

She stumbled toward the gunwale, grabbing the railing she saved herself from being pitched over the rail.

The *Princess* was crippled. Another shot would destroy her.

Bannon grabbed Bridget's arm. He tried to pull her from the pilot's berth. She pushed him away and turned the boat to the right, putting them on a direct collision course with the *Princess*. They were so close now the ship's shadow loomed over them. People lined the top deck. They looked down and pointed.

Faaid grabbed Bannon from behind. Bannon shoved him back. The terrorist's feet slipped out from under him. He landed on his ass and slipped across the wet deck, crashing into the corner.

Zayd was back up at the computer console, entering data into the keyboard even though the screen was smashed. The railgun moved, repositioning, responding to her commands. The railgun was still in play.

Bannon grabbed Bridget by the shoulder and ripped her away from the wheel. She stumbled to the side. He grabbed the wheel and swung it hard to the left. He thrust the throttle all the way forward. The Bowrider responded quickly. The bow rode high. The backend fishtailed hard, leaving a deep, frothing wake behind them.

He continued to spin the wheel to the left, putting the boat on a parallel course with the looming *Princess*—as the railgun with its target acquired continued to swivel toward the hull of the big cruise liner—Bannon pulled the throttle back to all-stop.

Behind him, Faaid was getting back up, searching for his dropped gun. The sudden reduction in speed pitched him forward. He landed on his knees and slid forward like a baseball player sliding headfirst into second base. Bridget crashed into the space between the bridge console and the co-pilot's seat, tumbled, and fell to the deck.

To keep them off-balance, Bannon threw the throttle full forward.

In the bow, Zayd stumbled as the boat leaped forward. Her injured knee collapsed under her. She plunged over the side as Bannon's erratic piloting skimmed them across the cruise ship's hull, tearing a rending gash into its side while Zayd's body, caught between the fast-moving Bowrider and stationary ship's hull, was ripped in two. Blood and gore painted the side of the cruiser liner. Exposed steel plates and fiberglass were shredded, ripped, and torn. The slashing sound was like a thousand fingernails scratching across a hundred blackboards.

Bannon turned away from the mess.

Hung up on the peeled-back metal plates where the missile had ripped through the hull and exposed the interior to the outside, the railgun boat hung at a severe angle. The boat's twin Merc engines smoked, sputtered, and died.

Bannon turned toward Faaid and Bridget. Faaid had regained his footing. With a bloody gash over one eye, he pointed his handgun at Bannon in a steady, two-handed grip.

"You will not stop us," he said. Blood dripping along his scarred face.

TARA STOOD AT THE top of a stairwell leading up from the midsection decks below. Bloody, tired, and disheveled—that was putting it mildly—she had an M16 strapped to her back and a Beretta weighing down the pocket of her oversized coveralls. Blood had soaked through the wrapping around her arm, and her arm ached. She kept finger-combing her hair from her face. Disgusted by how matted and sticky it felt and how much she smelled like an overflowing toilet.

Lights flickered, experiencing shorts and other power interruptions. But the emergency lights had kicked in. The hazy stairwell glowed red. She directed passengers coming up the stairs, telling them to gather at the forward observation deck for further instructions. Most of them were doing their best to remain calm. Parents put on brave faces for their children, who looked around wide-eyed and scared. Young ones were cradled in their mother's arms, wailing inconsolably. Tara couldn't blame them. Few of these passengers were injured. Most of them had been in areas away from where the missile struck and exploded.

That wasn't to say they weren't injured. Many were. A lot of them. Tara knew the cruise ship had two doctors and a team of nurses on board, and the crew were all first-aid trained, at least. The medical staff was as close to the blast site as they could get, performing triage.

"This way," Tara said repeatedly, directing passengers to a line of crew members waving them toward the starboard side where lifeboats were being loaded with the women, children, and wounded first.

The line of passengers shuffled along the port side of the ship. A few stopped and were looking over the railing, something having caught their eye. The progression was backing up. Frustrated, Tara called, "Please, keep moving. We have a lot of—"

Several of the gawkers gasped and pointed.

Tara moved through the crowd and pushed her way to the railing. When she did, she gasped as well.

The railgun boat was speeding straight at them at what looked like top speed, on a direct course to slam into the hull of the *Oceanic Princess*. Bannon was wrestling Bridget Barnes for control of the boat. Faaid was thrashing around like a fish on a deck. Zayd clutched her computer podium. It looked like she was trying to activate the railgun, preparing to fire again.

"Get away from the rail!" Tara shouted. "Move! Move!"

Many of the passengers did as they were told, some pushing and shoving to get out of harm's way, regardless of who they plowed through. Still, others remained. Either too scared or too fascinated to turn away.

Tara grasped the railing and watched. Bannon had gained control of the boat. He jerked the throttle to stop, then gunned it forward. The boat spun to the side at the last minute. Safiyyah Zayd fell overboard seconds before the boat skidded across the hull of the *Princess*, crushing the woman between the scrapping hulls.

Several people pulled back at the sight, horrified.

The railgun boat skinned the hull. The bow lifted into the air as it caught and rode a peeled-back section of steel plating. It jerked to a stop. Hung up on the side of the ship.

Faaid held a gun on Bannon. He said something Tara couldn't make out.

She didn't care. She pulled her Beretta and leaned awkwardly over the railing.

FAAID AIMED HIS GUN at Bannon. "You will not stop us. This is where it ends, Commander."

"Finally, something we can agree on," Bannon said. "But it's not my end we're talking about here."

Bridget Barnes backed away from the bridge. Her green eyes darted around. Bannon could see the wheels turning in her head. She was looking for a way to escape. She wasn't the immediate threat. Faaid was. He'd deal with her later.

"Unfortunately, Commander," Faaid said. "I can only kill you once, though you deserve a thousand deaths for what you did to me." He waved a hand vaguely at his scarred face.

"You ask me," Bannon taunted. "It's an improvement."

Faaid tightened the grip on the gun. He'd just started to apply pressure on the trigger when a bullet pinged off the engine cowl. A quickly fired second shot struck him in the stomach. He clutched at his wound, staggering back.

Bannon glanced upward to see who his benefactor was, knowing it would be one of two people.

TARA FIRED TWO QUICK shots at Faaid. Her second round hit the terrorist in the gut. He staggered back. Bannon rushed at him after a quick look up at her.

But it was Bridget Barnes who had Tara's attention.

The redheaded woman used the opportunity to climb through the opening from the bridge to the bow section of the boat. She reached the gunwale and pulled herself forward. Tara lost sight of her, unable to lean out far enough to see her without tumbling off the ship.

But she didn't need to see to know what the woman was up to.

She was going to climb into the cruise ship through the hole blasted into it. Her plan was probably to lose herself in the crowd. In the confusion, blend in with the passengers and secure a berth on a lifeboat.

"Not gonna happen," Tara vowed. She turned around and pushed through the crowd. The stairwell was jammed with passengers still streaming up from the darkened bowels of the ship. She fought past them, making her way down, determined to put an end to her tormentor once and for all.

BANNON LOOKED UP THE massive wall that was the hull of the *Oceanic Princess* to see Tara leaning over the railing. She stared down at him, gun still in hand. From the corner of his eye, he noticed Bridget scramble over the side of the boat, climbing up the ragged edge of the hole in the *Princess*.

One problem at a time. He returned his attention to Faaid. He was leaning against the rear gunwale, holding his stomach, blood leaking through his fingers.

Bannon advanced on him.

Faaid looked around for a means of escape. From his expression, Bannon saw him even contemplate jumping overboard. Go ahead, Bannon thought. "Bleeding like that, you'll be shark food in a New York minute."

"Stay back," Faaid said, his eyes dark with contempt.

He raised the pistol still in his hand and squeezed off a shot. Bannon was already diving through the air at him. He tackled Faaid, driving him back against the gunwale behind them. The impact jarred the gun loose from his hand. It went spinning out over the side of the boat.

Faaid landed a solid blow against Bannon's kidney. Bannon grabbed him by the throat. Pain flared through his shoulder, but he held on and pummeled Faaid's face with his closed fist. After more punches than were completely necessary, his own bullet wound stinging like crazy, Bannon dragged the semi-conscious terrorist up to the bow of the boat. There, he grabbed a length of rope tied to the end of a rubber bumper. He used it to tie Faaid to the railgun.

Done, he tugged on it to make sure it was secure.

"What now?" Faaid said through a bloody lip and a half-swollen shut eye. He'd lost a tooth. His front was soaked in blood. "Leave me here until you can turn me over to your authorities?"

"Hardly." Bannon stood over him, staring down. "You get to enjoy a long-standing maritime tradition. An honor you don't deserve but seems fitting all the same."

"What?" Faaid spit out blood.

"You get to be a sea captain that goes down with his ship." Bannon squatted and got close to the mass murderer's face. "And this time. I'll get it right."

Faaid's eyes widened. He pulled frantically at his wrists bound to the railgun's base. "You can't!"

Bannon retrieved the saucer gun from under the co-pilot's console. With it in hand, he followed Bridget Barnes' lead up the shredded hot metal and climbed into the bowels of the *Oceanic Princess*. Fires still raged behind him. Smoke fouled the air. Bannon climbed up a broken girder two decks higher than the wrecked railgun.

"Wait," Faaid cried out, panic in his voice. "This isn't over."

"Oh, believe me, it is," Bannon shouted back down. "Especially for you."

"No. Listen to me. This…this was simply a test. There's more."

Bannon's patience had run its course. "Tell it to the devil when you see him, Faaid. You and your damn railgun are going to the bottom of the ocean."

He aimed the saucer gun at the railgun boat's fuel tanks.

"No!" Faaid shouted. "You're making a mistake! Ghaazi Alvi will…"

The rest of what he had to say was lost to the sound of hot, spitting bullets from the crazy weapon Bannon fired and the large explosion that followed as the boat's fuel tanks blew and a black, oily fireball roiled up into the sky.

What was left of the railgun boat's bow section, rocked by the explosion, slipped off its ragged perch and slid into the sea. It drifted away from the cruise ship, away from all the death and destruction it had caused and slipped under the gentle waves of the Atlantic Ocean, taking Faaid's dead and burned body along with it.

Bannon watched until nothing was left. Then waited some more. When the last random air bubbles had ceased popping up through the scattered debris, through the flaming black oil slick, only then did Bannon toss the saucer gun into the water and watched it sink, too.

"It's done, O'Neil. We won, son. We won."

Bannon turned and disappeared into the crippled *Oceanic Princess*.

CHAPTER THIRTY-FIVE

McMURPHY MOVED THROUGH THE lower decks of the cruise ship with a team of *Oceanic Princess* crew members, one of their nurses, and three passengers who refused to go topside and instead remained to help. Armed with a flashlight, a purser named Baker led them down and through the ship, getting them as close to the blast site as possible in their search for survivors.

The lights flickered, more on than off, with bright white emergency lights illuminating the way. The haze grew into heavy smoke the deeper they went down and toward the stern. Along the way, as they came across passengers, they were directed to make their way to the forward promenade to check in and wait for their lifeboat assignments. For those who were injured or too frightened or distraught to continue on their own, Baker assigned crewmates to accompany them.

They passed the casino and stepped into the Tiamat Bar & Grill.

U-shaped leather chairs were turned over and strewn about the place. Bar stools were tipped over. A flat-screen TV behind the bar played a carousel video of beach pictures with palm trees and sailboats. A large crack ran through the screen and the images flickered erratically. The worst defilement to McMurphy was all the shattered booze bottles fallen from the glass shelves, still backlit with electric blue light.

"This way," Baker said.

He pushed through a door, taking them into a large space that resembled a hotel lobby. There were club chairs and sofas around built-in cocktail tables. More padded seats surrounded large potted trees, and a wide, sweeping staircase with open treads and enclosed in waist-high glass led up to the next deck.

McMurphy looked up.

"Passenger accommodations," Baker explained.

A hole had been blasted through the ceiling and the lobby's far wall, exposing the cabins above. Many of the cabins were destroyed. Others were missing a segment of wall or floor, making them visible to the rescue team solemnly looking up.

Here, the ship was oppressively hot. The smoke had grown so thick McMurphy's eyes stung. From the floor, he picked up several washcloths that had fallen from the cabins above, along with towels, blankets, pieces of beds, cabinets, and various wall decorations like sconces and pictures.

He handed the washcloths around, placing his against his nose and mouth.

According to Captain Herron, the missile had slammed into the *Princess* in a section aft of the engine and boiler rooms. The subsequent explosions after the initial blast had been the result of fuel tanks and overheated generators blowing up. The fire suppression system was top of the line, Herron assured McMurphy. The good news, the captain went on to say, if there could be any in such a situation, was the section that received the heaviest damage was the laundry area, the fresh water tank, and cargo holds, thus less populated areas and minimized the number of casualties.

If we're lucky, McMurphy groused, not feeling hopeful as he stared at the hole blown through the hull ahead of him. A steel girder lay at an angle. Around it, large sections of the wall, blasted into chunks, littered the area along with piles of rubble and other debris. A fluorescent light fixture hung from the ceiling, one bulb still glowing, the other one sputtering in an attempt to stay lit and failing.

He moved closer and gazed down at the gaping hole. He could see seven exposed decks across from them. He didn't see any movement, but through the thick smoke, that wasn't a surprise. Several fires continue to burn.

The others gathered around him. He looked at Baker. Through the washcloth held to his mouth, he said, "We should spread out."

Baker nodded when the nurse called out. "Look! I see someone."

McMurphy and Baker crowded around him and followed where he pointed through the hole two decks down.

A figure was climbing up a section of girder. With all the smoke and McMurphy's eyes tearing as bad as they were, it was hard to get a clear view of him. The man's progress was slow. He was struggling and was only using one hand to pull himself up.

When he got closer, McMurphy said to Baker, "Give me a hand."

He climbed over the girder. With Baker holding his left hand, McMurphy stepped down the incline formed by a section of wall. He reached his other hand out as the figure, with his head down, concentrating on finding solid foot-and-handholds, climbed closer.

"Hey, buddy. Grab my hand."

The guy reached up and slapped his hand into McMurphy's. He looked up and grinned. "We've got to stop meeting like this, Skyjack."

Brice Bannon's soot-smudged face was a welcome sight. McMurphy returned the smile with one even bigger. "Of all the cruise ships in all the world," he quipped, hauling his friend up to safety for the second time in as many days. Then he scooped him up in a giant bear hug. "Brice! Jesus! You're okay."

Bannon winced. "Arm."

McMurphy put him down and leaned back, noticing his bloody shirt. "You've been shot."

"It's only a flesh wound."

"You always say that. You and Blades. I'll be putting that on both your tombstones. 'It's only a flesh wound.'" McMurphy looked around. To Baker, he said, "Where's that nurse?"

At McMurphy's suggestion, the ad hoc rescue team had split up and moved to the far corners of the room, calling out for survivors.

Baker said, "He's over—"

Bannon held up a hand. "Don't sweat it. I'm fine." He wished that was the case. The bullet remained lodged in his shoulder. He felt it every time he moved his arm, which

290

wasn't much at all. He looked around. "Besides, you all have your hands full."

"Zayd?" McMurphy asked.

"Dead."

"Faaid?"

"Deader."

"The railgun?"

"At the bottom of the ocean. With Faaid."

McMurphy gave him a look. "You're sure about that?"

Bannon nodded. "It's over except for one more thing."

"What?"

"The other woman, Bridget Barnes, she got away from me. She's on the ship somewhere. And speaking of that. Where's Blades?"

McMurphy shrugged. "When the missile struck, we came down here to help. We got separated. Last I saw her, she was up top helping passengers get to the promenade where they're checking them off and loading lifeboats." He patted Bannon's good shoulder. "Come on. I'll help you find her. Find them."

"Over here!" a crewman shouted. "We found one."

The voice had come from the space behind what looked like a reception counter. Teak and beautiful if one could get past the deep gouge carved through its face and top.

"No," Bannon said to McMurphy. "You stay here. Help these people. I'll get Tara and deal with the Barnes woman."

McMurphy didn't argue. He moved toward where the rescuers were busily clearing debris, digging deeper into the smoldering wreckage, and removing large sections of plaster and wallboards off the leg of a balding man in his fifties. He grabbed a large section of buckled bulkhead and cleared it away. Baker and the others pulled the man free. The nurse knelt beside him and popped open the first aid kit.

When McMurphy looked back, Bannon was gone. He silently wished his friend good luck and said, "Okay. Where to next?"

TARA RACED DOWN A badly damaged, previously opulent winding staircase to the lower decks. She pushed through passengers urging her to go back up. She ignored them.

Finding Bridget Barnes was the only thing on her mind.

As she moved further aft, she ran into a small group of passengers congregated near a raised, tiled hot tub. Large palm trees stood at attention over the half-empty tub. Its contents spilled out on the floor. The crowd stood looking and pointing out to sea. A murmur of speculation buzzed among them.

They'd spotted several ships on the horizon.

A few hoped they were ships coming to rescue them. Others voiced concern the ships represented more trouble.

"They're Coast Guard ships," Tara assured them. "They're coming to help."

"Why should we believe you? We don't know who you are," a large man with a beer gut said. "You could be one of them."

Next to him stood a woman, equally overweight, her face sweaty and smeared with mascara and tears. With them was a young boy around seven. He wore a New York Yankees jersey.

"I'm not. I'm helping with the rescue."

"You look like you could be a terrorist," the man said.

"Because I'm dark-skinned? Because I'm from the Middle East?" Tara stepped close to him and fisted her hand. "You know what they call that?"

Before the man replied, his wife hit him in the shoulder. "Ignorant. That's what they call that. Shut up, Harold." To Tara, the woman said, "What should we do?"

"Head to the front of the ship. Get to the upper deck promenade. There, the crew will check you in. They're making sure everyone is accounted for."

"Thank you," the woman said.

As the crowd started to break up and move toward the stairwell Tara had descended, she called out. "I'm looking for someone," she said. "A woman. She's got red hair. Really pale skin. Deep scratches on her cheek. If anyone's seen her, please let me know. It's important."

A few people shook their heads. A couple looked at each other as if checking with each other. No one spoke up.

Tara asked the racist and his wife. "What about you two? Have you seen her?"

The man shook his head. "We need to go." He tugged at his wife's arm. She clutched her son's hand and pulled him along. The man looked further aft. "Whoever she is, if she was back there when this happened, forget her and get yourself off this death trap of a ship."

Tara watched them join the line of people moving up the staircase. She saw the boy's jersey was 99. She called out. "Hey, Yankee."

The boy turned around.

She smiled. "I think the Yankees are pretty cool, too."

When they reached the top of the steps, he looked down at her and waved.

Tara waved back, then she turned and looked out at the small fleet of Coast Guard ships. They would be here soon. That was good.

But first, it was time to think like a terrorist. If it had been Zayd or Faaid she was after, zealots like that might be determined to finish the job they'd started, which was to sink the *Oceanic Princess*. She didn't think that would be the case with Bridget Barnes. She wasn't a zealot. Sure, she had her reasons for working with Faaid and the others, for hating America as much as the others did. Tara didn't know what her reasons were, but she sensed the woman wasn't prepared to die for them.

No, she'd come aboard the *Princess* to escape. The only way to do that would be to hide among the passengers. Blend in and escape on a lifeboat.

Determined not to let that happen, Tara returned to the upper deck and headed for the starboard side, making her way toward the promenade, where passengers were lined up in a relatively calm and orderly fashion. Crewmembers were checking off names from a passenger list. Others were escorting women and underage passengers to a stairwell that would take them to the lifeboats.

Tara pushed through the crowd. Twice, she saw redheads. Her heart leaped, but neither turned out to be Barnes. Frustrated, she wondered how she'd find a single person among five thousand passengers. She was glancing around again when she heard a commotion near the front of the lines.

"I'm sorry, ma'am. But according to this, your name's already been checked off the list."

"Well, that's a mistake. I'm right here. I need you to let me on one of those lifeboats," a woman's voice said.

Tara moved toward the arguing voices. As she got closer, moving people out of her way, she saw the woman arguing with the crewman. She wore a colorful scarf over her head and big dark sunglasses.

"If you could just show me some ID," the crewman said.

With two lines of people between them, a gust of wind caught the woman's scarf and nearly tore it from her head. She caught it and kept it at bay, but not before it revealed the woman's bright red hair and three deep scratches down her cheek.

Tara pushed a man to the side. He pushed back. "Wait your turn, lady."

The commotion caught Bridget's attention. She turned, saw Tara, and ran.

"Damn it." Tara shoved the man back so hard he stumbled and fell, knocking three more people down like bowling pins.

Tara ran.

Bridget had a big head start.

Tara pushed and shoved more passengers aside. In return, she was on the receiving end of some pretty nasty—and deserved—comments. Tara ignored all that and broke through the lines, clearing them in time to see Bridget duck through a door and re-enter the *Princess's* interior.

Tara ran after her, yanked the door open, and plunged into the darkness of a passageway.

Fifty feet ahead of her, Bridget ran through another door.

Tara went through it, too, ending up inside a restaurant. Large enough to serve two thousand people. Tables and chairs were turned over and had tumbled back and forth in the room before settling into a jumbled, broken mess. Tara navigated through the maze of tables, broken dishes, glassware, and scattered cutlery. Table linens and napkins littered the floor. The smashed china and glassware crunched under her feet as she ran and leaped over overturned tables and chairs, heading for the door closing on the other side of the hall.

She pulled her Beretta from her coveralls' pocket, burst through the door, and scanned the area with her eyes and gun.

Rather than running away, Bridget Barnes stood her ground, waiting for Tara to appear. "I knew you'd never stop," she explained. "Not unless I stop you."

"I'm the one with the gun."

Actually, Tara had two. The M16 was still strapped to her back as well.

"You're just going to shoot me? Payback for me being mean to you."

"Being mean? You killed people."

"Like you haven't. Like your people haven't. I know all about you, Tarakesh Sardana. Go on. Just shoot me then and get it over with."

Tara considered the gun in her hand. It was a stupid, rash, impulsive thing to do, and she knew it. Still, she tossed the weapon aside and fisted her hands. She needed to do this.

Bridget did the same. And smiled.

Tara advanced on the terrorist. Trained in several fighting styles, even weak from two days of captivity, a lack of water and food, and a bullet wound in her arm, Tara had no reason to believe she couldn't take Bridget in a straight-up fight.

She should have rethought that.

They charged at each other.

A street fighter, Bridget fought tough, with a hard-hitting boxing style, dirty and savage. As it turned out, she could take a punch and give one even better.

Bridget grabbed Tara by the front of her coveralls. She spun her around and slammed her hard into the bulkhead. Tara's back hit the wall. The blow took her breath away. The M16 strapped diagonally across her back dug painfully into her flesh. Tara screamed out. Bridget threw a punch, but Tara moved her head. Bridget's fist smacked hard into the bulkhead. She cried out. Tara kneed her between the legs.

Bridget staggered back.

Tara charged at her, but Bridget dropped to the floor, planted her foot in Tara's stomach, and rolled, throwing Tara over her and down the passageway. Bridget spun and got up. She pounced on Tara, who was still on the floor. Bridget rained punches down on Tara's sides, back, and the back of her head. Tara curled up and covered up, absorbing the blows as best she could until the opportunity arrived. She could kick out her left foot.

Her sandaled foot smashed into Bridget's knee. She heard bones crack and the knee pop. Bridget cried out in pain. She grabbed her leg and opened herself up. Tara swung a punch that snapped Bridget's head around and sent a fan of blood flying from her mouth.

Tired, bloody, and exhausted, Bridget tried to backpedal away from Tara. She got up on her good leg and hobbled a few steps back toward the restaurant. Tara kicked out her feet, caught the escaping woman's ankles, and tripped her. Bridget fell to the carpeted floor.

She scrambled away on her hands and knees, cursing every time her injured knee crashed into the floor. Tara was confident she had her until Bridget reached the tossed-away Beretta.

Bridget grabbed it and flipped over onto her back.

Tara had been advancing on the woman, thinking the wounded terrorist could get away. Now she faced her own gun pointed at her.

With the gun held in both her hands, pointed at Tara between her bent knees, Barnes started to squeeze the trigger.

Tara unlashed the chain around her waist, her constant companion since the start of her captivity. She swung the chain. The heavy cuff slammed into Bridget's hands. The metal cut a deep gash in the back of her hand and sent the gun flying out of her hands.

Tara stepped over her and swung the M16 around from her back in one smooth, practiced move. She pointed the barrel of the weapon at Bridget's throat. "No more games."

"Go ahead. Kill me. You think that finishes it."

Tara gave her a grim smile. "It finishes you."

"Tara! Don't!" Bannon appeared at the doorway to the restaurant. He held a hand out to urge her to stop.

Tara adjusted her grip on the rifle. She'd sworn to kill the woman, and she had every intention of carrying out that vow. She'd wanted to do it with her bare hands. But this would do.

"Do it," Barnes urged. "But then you'll never know. Not until it's too late."

"Know what?" Bannon asked. "Faaid said something similar." He looked at Tara. "We need to know."

Tara tightened her jaw. "Lies. A desperate gambit to stay alive."

"I thought so, too. He said it wasn't over. That this…this was a test. Tara, we need to know what he was talking about. We need to be sure."

"I'll tell you," Barnes said.

Tara hesitated. The weight of indecision weighed heavily on her. She glared at Bannon. "Oh, come on. You got to kill yours, Brice."

"I didn't realize what he was saying meant anything, not until now. If she knows something important, Tara, she's the only one left."

Barnes held her hands up at Tara, waving then at her. Blood coursed down the back of her injured hand, a river of red running down her arm. "I know things you'll want to know, Tarakesh. I swear."

Tara groaned with anger and frustration. "What things?"

"Who's behind this? All of it."

"We know who. You and Zayd, with Faaid in charge."

Barnes snorted a laugh. "He wished. He was never more than a minion. No. I can give you the real person in charge.

You know him, Tara. You both do. I told you. You and I, we've got a connection."

Bannon stepped closer. "Who?"

"He calls himself *Munaqadh*."

"Faaid mentioned that name before he died, too," Bannon said. "What does it mean?"

"Savior." To Barnes, she said, "Seriously?"

"You know him by another name. You know him as Ghaazi Alvi."

Tara stepped back and lowered the rifle. The name was like a punch to her stomach. "That's impossible. You're lying." She stepped forward, raising the rifle again. "Tell me you're lying."

"I'm not. Why would I?"

Tara adjusted her grip on the rifle. "To keep me from killing you."

"Tara," Bannon said.

Barnes shrugged her shoulders. "It will only delay the inevitable. I'm guilty of terrorist murder. I'm dead sooner or later."

"It can't Ghaazi," Bannon said. "He's—"

Tara looked at him, her eyes wet with tears. "My brother."

Barnes said, "And he's most definitely not—"

"Shut up. Liar." Tara spun her rifle around and slammed the butt across Barnes's jaw, knocking her out cold. She dropped the weapon at Bannon's feet and walked away.

CHAPTER THIRTY-SIX

A FEW HOURS LATER, on the deck of the *Oceanic Princess*, Bannon, Tara, and McMurphy were reunited. McMurphy had a thick cigar lit in his mouth, happily puffing away, and a Styrofoam cup in his hand. Bannon strongly suspected it contained whiskey.

Bannon had his arm immobilized in a sling. The ship's doctor had taken a look at his gunshot wound, patched him, and told him he'd need surgery to get the bullet out. He redressed Tara's flesh wound, telling her to keep it clean and take it easy for a few days.

She hadn't said much since Bridget Barnes revealed the identity of the mastermind behind the terrorist plot. Bannon had no brothers or sisters. He'd grown up in the system. An orphan subject to a series of foster homes. Some had been good. Others, not so much. None became a family he would call his own. Close ties like brothers and sisters came to him through the military, not blood relations. He wondered what it would feel like to feel that level of betrayal.

The three of them were dirty, bloody, disheveled—in a word, they were a mess.

At their feet, Bridget Barnes sat Indian style, her hands secured in handcuffs behind her back.

The deck was busy with crewmembers and Coast Guard personnel rushing back and forth. Around the crippled cruise ship were a dozen Coast Guard ships and other smaller vessels in the area that had also responded to the distress call the *Princess* put out early on.

They'd aborted the launch of any lifeboats. The hole in the hull from the railgun was above the waterline, so they'd secured that section. It was determined the ship could limp back to Boston Harbor under its own power and the watchful eye of several escort Coast Guard ships.

Captain Herron approached them. "Just wanted to take a minute to thank you all." He looked at Bannon. "If that nut job had gotten a second shot off, we would've been goners. We owe you our lives."

Bannon shook the captain's offered hand. "He didn't. That's what matters." He looked around. "Your crew really stepped up, Captain. You should be proud of them."

Herron beamed. "Yeah, they did. We train for this sort of stuff, but most of 'em, they never imagine they'll ever use it. We deal with seasickness and drunken idiots mostly." He nodded. "I am."

To McMurphy and Tara, Herron said, "I can't thank you two enough for what you did. By getting people away from the port side of the ship before the attack, you saved hundreds of lives. And your help afterward, dozens more."

"Glad we could be here to help," McMurphy said. They each shook the captain's hand.

"You have a casualty count yet?" Bannon asked.

Somber, Herron said, "Seventeen crewmembers, nine passengers, and three unaccounted for. The injured list is holding at a hundred and two. Search and rescue are flying the most serious back to the mainland now. None of those appear to be life-threatening."

Bannon frowned. "We're sorry for those you lost."

"If not for you all, it would've been a lot, lot worse. On a positive note. TSB's on board, and they've declared it'll take a while and some work, but they believe the *Oceanic Princess* will live to sail another day."

After another round of handshakes, the captain backed away, returning to the job of tending to his ship, his crew, and his passengers. They were still trying to account for the last few still missing.

Grayson approached them, pocketing her phone as she did so. She glanced at the damaged Marine helicopter but didn't mention it. McMurphy turned away and took a healthy gulp of whatever it was he was drinking.

"That was the President. He's asked me to extend my congratulations to you all. Job well done."

"They polishing up our commendations?" McMurphy asked.

She looked at the helicopter, frowning this time. "You know that's not how this arrangement works, Chief."

McMurphy cleared his throat. "Yeah. Right. All guts, no glory, and a phone call *'atta-boy'* from POTUS."

"So, what now?" Bannon asked, trying to save his friend from digging his hole any deeper with Grayson.

"The Coast Guard Cutter *Defiant* reported in," Grayson said. "They've boarded the *Dauphin* and taken the crew into custody without incident. The FBI's sending Laboratory Services personnel out from Quantico to gather whatever evidence, forensically or otherwise, they can from her before she sinks."

Bannon wished them luck but didn't hold out much hope they'd find much.

Grayson looked at Barnes, sitting with her head hung low.

"We begin talking to this one," she said of Barnes. "And to you, Ms. Sardana."

"Me? About what?"

"Ghaazi Alvi. Your brother."

"There is nothing to say. It is a name my brother assumed when we needed to…disappear."

"When you became Tara Sardana?" Grayson clarified.

"Yes." Tara stared at her. Defiant. "Whoever she's talking about, he is not my brother. My brother is dead."

Grayson let it go, for now. But Bannon knew it wasn't the end of the subject. Not for any of them.

"We'll be talking at length very soon, Ms. Barnes," Grayson said. "But for now, answer me one thing."

"Give me my deal," Barnes said, looking up. Her jaw was bruised, her mouth still caked with blood. "I'll tell you everything."

"There'll be time for that," Grayson said.

"Now, or I say nothing."

McMurphy grabbed her by the collar and hauled her to her feet.

304

"Hey! Let go!"

He half-carried her to the side of the *Oceanic Princess*. Barnes squirmed in his powerful grasp but had no more luck breaking loose than a kitten caught by the scruff of the neck did.

"Answer the nice lady, or I toss you in," McMurphy said. "Handcuffed." He hauled her precariously over to the railing. "Oops, terrorist overboard."

Barnes twisted in his grip. She looked to Grayson and the others. "You can't let him—"

In unison, the others turned their backs.

McMurphy shoved her closer to the railing. "Say hi to what's left of Faaid down there."

"Okay. Okay!"

McMurphy dragged her back to the others. He shoved her so hard she tripped and rolled across the deck, stopping at their feet.

Grayson looked down at her. "Tell us about Ghaazi Alvi, whoever he is. What is he planning next?"

"This." Barnes struggled to get back up into a sitting position. She turned to look one way and then the other, indicating everything around them. "All this was simply a test. A test to prove the railgun could operate as promised."

"Faaid said much the same thing," Bannon said. "Did you think you would get away? That you'd get another chance to use it?"

"We didn't have to."

"Why not?" Grayson asked.

"Because it's not the only one."

Bannon felt his stomach hollow. There were more of them. Out there where?

"Zayd wasn't brought here just to bring this weapon online," Barnes explained. "She was here to demonstrate its ability to destroy this ship and everyone on board, yes, but more importantly, she was here to show others how the weapon worked."

"Guess she won't be doing that," Bannon said, sounding more confident than he felt.

McMurphy chimed in. "Not with half of her fish food and the other half scrapped off the hull into a Tupperware evidence tub."

"You're all so arrogant and foolish," Bridget said. "While she was on the *Dauphin,* she recorded everything she did. She created a complete how-to instruction podcast that she transmitted to Alvi before we left. You lost before we ever left the *Dauphin*. He has everything he needs."

"To do what?" Bannon asked.

Barnes sneered. "To strike again. There are more railguns. In the hands of people who have the knowledge and means to use them. You won the battle, but the war's already lost. They cannot be stopped. *Munaqadh* cannot be stopped."

EPILOGUE

Three days later

THE SKY WAS APPROPRIATELY overcast. The priest read a prayer, standing at the head of FBI Agent Trejo's open grave. The ground around it and the nearby pile of dirt were covered with carpet remnants of green Astroturf. Beyond the crowd of mourners stood four cemetery workers casually leaning on the big tires of the backhoe that had dug Trejo's final resting spot. One smoked a cigarette.

In addition to family, friends, and casual acquaintances, those gathered to mourn Agent Trejo's passing were law enforcement personnel from every federal, state, county, and local police agency from Maine and as far south as Pennsylvania and beyond.

Not among the crowd were Brice Bannon and Skyjack McMurphy.

When he'd heard they planned on paying their respects, Agent Dan Pierce formally and forcefully requested that they not attend the service or the one for Agent Acosta earlier in the day. Pierce had eventually learned it was Bannon and McMurphy who'd broken into the federal building. That they'd kidnapped Safiyyah Zayd and left him and his team spinning their wheels for the next three days, looking for an escaped terrorist and leaks in their organization that didn't exist. He did make it clear he didn't blame them for Trejo and Acosta's deaths.

He just didn't want to ever see either one of them again.

Bannon suspected the agent feared their presence would remind him of how badly he'd screwed up. That it had been his poor decisions and his rushed actions that caused the deaths of his men. That was a burden he would have to shoulder for the rest of his life.

Too damn bad.

Like at Acosta's service earlier, Bannon and McMurphy came dressed in black suits and remained back by the line of cars. But they were in attendance. This day was about remembering two brave men and the ultimate sacrifice they'd made, not their supervisor's bruised ego.

When the priest finished speaking, and the family began to toss flowers into the grave, Bannon and McMurphy turned and left. They had one more funeral to attend.

IN HIS WILL, SEAMAN Troy O'Neil had stipulated his desire to be buried in Massachusetts National Cemetery, adjacent to Joint Base Cape Cod, his home for the past year. In attendance was every Coastie not on duty from Maine to New York City. Other branches of the military were well represented, too, as were others of law enforcement personnel.

When the Coast Guard Chaplin finished speaking, the rifle party fired a three-volley salute. A woman close to the casket cried. Then, a lone bugler stood on a nearby rise and played taps. The men and women in uniform presented their final salute while the mournful notes played. A six-member honor guard removed the flag draped over O'Neil's casket. They folded it thirteen times into a tri-cornered shape and presented it to CPO Johnson in his dress blues. He turned smartly and knelt on one knee before Troy O'Neil's mother. With white-gloved hands over and under the flag, he presented it to her.

"On behalf of the President of the United States, the United States Coast Guard, and a grateful nation, please accept this flag as a symbol of our appreciation for your loved one's honorable and faithful service."

Too upset to take it, her husband leaned over and took the flag from Johnson. He gently laid it in the woman's lap.

Johnson returned to attention, snapped a salute, and smartly turned away, effectively ending the service.

Bannon, McMurphy, and Kayla were in their dress whites. Tara wore a simple black dress. Grayson remained beside the Chaplin, wearing her Army Service Uniform, a midnight blue coat, and skirt. She'd delivered a beautiful eulogy about heroism and young men and women that didn't leave a dry eye. As the mourners slowly, reluctantly it seemed, began to disperse, Chief Johnson came over to Bannon. He touched Bannon's arm, getting his attention.

"Commander," he said. "Seaman O'Neil's parents would like to meet you."

"Of course." Bannon excused himself from McMurphy, Tara, and Kayla and followed Johnson back to where the couple remained by the casket but now on their feet.

Mrs. O'Neil clutched the flag to her chest with two hands.

"Mr. and Mrs. O'Neil," Johnson said. "This is Commander Bannon."

Bannon shook their hands. "I am so sorry for your loss."

Mr. O'Neil nodded. "We understand you were with Troy when he…when he died."

"Yes, sir, I was. I had the great fortune of serving with your son. Side-by-side. If only for a little while. He was a good man. A brave man. He saved my life."

"Commander—"

"Brice, sir. Please."

The older man forced a smile. "Brice. Ever since Troy was a little boy, he loved being around water."

"That boy came out of the tub all pruned up every time from staying in for too long," Mrs. O'Neil added, dabbing a tissue to her eye but smiling at the memory.

Bannon smiled.

"He had it in his head to join the Coast Guard since the day he learned how to swim," Troy's father said. "I don't know where he got that from. I didn't serve, I'm sorry to say."

"No need to apologize, sir."

He nodded and gave Bannon a sad smile. "I'd never seen that boy happier than the day he graduated from boot camp. He…I…I've never been prouder of him."

Bannon placed his hand on the man's shoulder as he bowed his head to cry.

"He exemplified what it meant to be a Coast Guardsman. He died a hero, saving not only me but protecting thousands of others." Bannon waited until they both looked at him again.

"I can't go into details, but believe me when I say that's no exaggeration. You should be proud of him. We are."

Bannon glanced over at Johnson, who nodded his agreement.

Mr. O'Neil nodded. "Doing what he loved. Guess you can't ask for more than that."

"Respectfully, sir, you can. You can make a difference. That's what your son did. He made a difference."

Grayson walked over and again extended her condolences to the grieving parents. When they walked away, she said, "I've done this hundreds, thousands of times. It doesn't get any easier."

"Let's hope it never does. I never want to be that numb," Bannon said.

They joined Tara, Kayla, and McMurphy, and together, they stepped carefully through the wet grass, making their way back to the line of cars snaked through the hilly cemetery. It would take a while to clear the cemetery of traffic, and truthfully, none of them was in much of a hurry.

As they walked toward Bannon's F-350 and Grayson's government SUV, she pulled a letter-size white envelope from the inside pocket of her dress coat.

She handed it to McMurphy. "Might as well give this to you now."

He took the envelope from her. His name was written in pristine handwriting across the front. Her handwriting. Chief John "Skyjack" McMurphy. He opened it and shook out the single piece of paper inside.

"What is it? I win the lottery or something?' he asked before reading it.

"Not exactly," Grayson said. "It's a bill from Uncle Sam."

McMurphy knotted his bushy red eyebrows. "A bill. A bill for what?"

"For the CH-53 King Stallion helicopter you destroyed."

He stopped walking and silently read the invoice.

"One hundred twenty-two million dollars! Are you serious?"

He looked up with his mouth hanging open. The others had continued walking, smiles on their faces.

"You can't be serious," he called out. "I didn't even total that bird."

They kept walking toward the cars.

McMurphy continued to shout. "I can fix it. The skid. It's just a little bent. Easy. And the bullet holes…putty and some paint." He shook the paper over his head. "Oh, come on. Lizzy? Guys!"

THE SUN HUNG HIGH in the bleached out sky. A white orb searing a stretch of paved road running through the barren landscape south of the NATO-controlled Kandahar Airport. The acrid desert rolled out on either side of the road like a lumpy dirt carpet of brown, the dreary monotony of bumps and berms only occasionally broken up by patches of sage bush and brushwood and ribbons of dark rocky ridges.

Nothing moved until a desert-tan, high mobility multipurpose wheeled vehicle, commonly referred to as a Humvee, sped along the highway at a steady thirty-five miles per hour clip. Mounted with an M2 Browning .50 caliber machine gun, it crewed with four personnel. The gunner was in position wearing a dark ballistic vest, a tan camouflage helmet, and large orange-shaded goggles. The vehicle provided security for the close-column convoy that followed.

Traveling forty meters behind their security escort, a light-armored vehicle served as convoy lead to three medium tactical vehicles, one M925 5-ton cargo truck. The trail vehicle was a second Humvee.

Sergeant Josh Starling drove the trail vehicle with Specialist Jon La Rosa riding shotgun—literally. Born in

Sedona, Arizona, Starling was no stranger to temperatures that could reach a hundred and four degrees Fahrenheit and an unrelenting barren desert that offered no relief from the broiling sun and searing heat. Beside him, La Rosa, an olive-skinned Puerto Rican kid who'd lived his whole life in Miami, complained insistently about the heat. Like it would change the more he whined about it.

"How ain't you hot, Sarge?" he asked again, wiping a rolling drop of sweat from his temple.

"Use to it." Starling sped the Humvee up, closing the gap between them and the last tactical vehicle, the M925. A blunt-nosed truck, it was capable of transporting ten thousand pounds of cargo in its seven-by-fourteen footbed, had hinged side racks and tailgate, troop seats, and a tan canvas cover that sagged between its supporting ribs that wobbled as the truck barreled down the road.

"They say it's different," La Rosa said, making conversation.

"What's that?" Starling asked, not caring what La Rosa had to say or thought.

"Dry heat versus tropical heat," La Rosa said. "It's all friggin' hot, you ask me."

Starling didn't respond. That didn't stop La Rosa.

"Least where I'm from," he said, "you've got lots of water to jump into. Cool yourself off, you know what I mean?"

Before Starling could reply, he heard the split-second whine of an RPG and saw the streak of a white contrail flare across the barren landscape ahead of them. A thunderous explosion of sound followed. The blast obliterated the lead

DAVID DELEE

vehicle, a light-armored vehicle. In it had been their company commander and Starling and La Rosa's platoon leader. Oily black smoke billowed into the sky. Proof to Starling there'd be no survivors.

Small arms fire opened up on the convoy from the low desert berms.

The radio crackled with frantic voices, calls for assistance and airstrikes. Curses were shouted over the static as the convoy vehicles moved forward and in reverse, each driver indecisive as to whether to drive ahead out of the kill zone or to back away.

A second shoulder-fired anti-tank missile struck one of the tactical vehicles up ahead.

The impact lifted the truck up onto two wheels before it slammed down again, righting itself. Two soldiers leaped from the cab. They ran for cover away from the burning truck and dove into a low gully beside the road.

An exchange of small and medium arms gunfire raged up ahead.

Over it, Starling could hear the rapid spitfire of the lead Humvee's .50 caliber machine gun.

If there was Hell on Earth, this was it. Starling threw his Humvee in reverse as the 5-ton ahead of them barreled backward, desperate to get out of the kill zone. Starling slammed on the brakes and spun the Humvee around. The roadway behind them exploded in a geyser of macadam, dirt, and smoke.

"Get out!" he shouted to La Rosa. "Get out!"

The overly talkative specialist did as he was ordered, taking his M16 with him. They ran for the gully beside the road and dove for cover.

The 5-ton struck Starling's Humvee, upending it a split-second before another RPG-launched missile destroyed the cab of the truck, engulfing the vehicle in fire and smoke. From inside it, Starling and La Rosa could hear the dying men scream.

The engine compartment burned. The flames inside the cab roared out through the shattered windows and reached the canvas cover stretched over the ribs of the truck's cargo compartment, and soon it was burning hot, too.

From the bed of the truck, voices cried out.

Starling scampered out from the gully. "Cover me!"

He raced for the vehicle, providing his own one-handed cover fire as he ran.

"Sarge! Josh! What the hell are you doing?"

Starling ignored La Rosa. He reached the back of the truck. It was upended at an angle, having crushed the Humvee under its two tires on the one side of the rear tandem dual axle. He climbed up on the hood of his crumpled vehicle and unhinged the tailgate of the 5-ton. He let it slam open and jumped back as the Middle-Eastern men trapped inside the cargo space leaped and scrambled off the Humvee to escape the burning truck.

They tumbled to the ground and ducked as bullets pinged off metal and chewed chunks out of the macadam, spitting dark pebbles around them like shrapnel. The men were dressed in drab green and brown baggy clothes. Most wore a taqiyah. All were handcuffed behind their backs with black zip-ties. In all, two dozen men fled from the back of the truck.

Ahead of them, another vehicle in the convoy explodes. More rocks and shrapnel rain down, pelting them. Starling ducked and covered his head.

One of the men from the back of the truck, a tall, dark-skinned man, stumbled over to Starling. He was very thin with a scraggly black beard and wore a soiled turban. He turned his back to Starling. The sergeant cut off the zip tie restraints with his Ka-Bar knife.

The others approached him, and Starling did the same for them.

When all the prisoners were freed, the tall man in the turban reached out and covered Starling's hands with both of his, cupping them, shaking them. He patted them.

"You saved our lives. You saved my life. You have been a good friend to me through troubling times, Josh Starling. Your compassion shall not go unrewarded."

The sound of approaching attack helicopters filled the air. The fighting around them was fierce. The cries of the dying echoed over the barren emptiness of the desert. More RPGs landed and exploded around them.

"You must go, Ghaazi!" Starling shouted over the latest explosion. "Run! Now!"

Ghaazi Alvi nodded and took off running, joining the other escapees as they ran low and quickly, soon disappearing behind the rolling berms of desert and rocky ridges. Starling watched them go with a grim but satisfied smile. He heard the roar of waiting vehicles and saw a cloud of dust billow up from behind their well-placed concealment. He nodded once and ran back to where La Rosa anxiously waited.

Starling slid back into the safety of their dusty, ad-hoc foxhole.

"Christ, Sarge. What'd you do? You aided those prisoners in escaping."

Starling stared at him for a moment and then said, "I did."

He aimed his Beretta M9 at La Rosa's forehead and pulled the trigger, killing him.

To the corpse, he said, "Let me know if Hell's got a dry or tropical heat."

DRESSED IN TAN SLACKS, a short-sleeve polo shirt, and boat shoes, Brice Bannon walked through the kitchen of his seaside bar, the Keel Haul. A hole-in-the-wall dive located on the strip in the small town of Hampton Beach, a small jewel on the eighteen-mile New Hampshire seacoast. The Key Haul was Bannon's pride and joy.

At least it had been until three weeks earlier when a group of terrorists attacked the bar in the middle of the night, shooting up the place with automatic small arms fire and grenades. Fire, smoke, and a lot of bodies later, the resulting damage had made a soup-to-nuts renovation all but unavoidable. A process the Keel Haul was currently undergoing.

Paint-splattered metal scaffolding was pressed up against one wall near the front of the bar. A worker in painter overalls was taping and plastering the ceiling. There were sawhorses and gang boxes, ladders, and big rubber garbage cans with brooms and shoves stuck in them all around the place. The floor was covered in sawdust. Painters, carpenters, electricians, and laborers filled the bar with more people than Bannon typically served on a Saturday night.

He stepped through the propped open kitchen door just as a table saw buzzed into operation behind him. The noise vibrated his back teeth. He flipped back and forth through papers on a clipboard as hammer guns and power drills added to the cornucopia of construction sounds.

In the bar area, the tables and chairs were stacked in one corner, a canvas tarp draped over them. The booths were all covered in plastic sheets, taped down with duct tape. He walked toward the bar, greeted by more banging and the colorful shouting of construction workers and Garth Brooks singing about his friends in low places.

Bannon glanced up from his clipboard in time to see his best friend, John "Skyjack" McMurphy, step through the open front door. It was open because there was no longer a door there.

Before the attack, the door had been a conversation piece. Salvaged by Bannon from an 18th-century British frigate he'd discovered during a dive off the coast of Rye Beach, just a few miles north of Hampton Beach. He'd lovely restored the door to near pristine condition and even installed an authentic brass porthole in it, complete with dog ears and nuts.

To gain entry into the bar, the terrorists blew the door to smithereens. What little that was left of it was in the thirty-yard dumpster out back.

McMurphy paused in the doorway and looked around. His expression was one of amused bewilderment as he made his way to the bar. He wore gray running shoes, blue jeans, a plaid work shirt, open and untucked, and underneath it, a black T-shirt that reads: 603 LIVE FREE OR DIE. The state's area code and motto.

At six feet tall, McMurphy was as wide as a linebacker and could be twice as mean when he wanted to be. But his unprovoked demeanor was jovial and as self-deprecating as they come. A former career Chief Warrant officer with the Coast Guard. He had dark red hair, which he wore longer now that he was out of the service full-time. As was usually the case, he puffed on a thick stogie jammed into the corner of his mouth.

The stools along the bar were all covered with plastic except for one.

On it sat Captain Floyd, an ancient regular with rounded shoulders who, as near as anyone could tell, came with the bar when Bannon bought it. Floyd was never seen without his sea captain's hat. He looked to everyone like those carved wooden statues of a sea captain they sell in every seaside novelty shop throughout the New England seacoast.

When he wasn't drinking, Floyd covered his mug of beer with a liver-spotted hand to keep the dust from it.

McMurphy grinned. "Should've known you'd be here, Floyd."

"That's cap'n to you, young man, and you can't smoke in here. It's against regulation."

McMurphy gave the old man a mock salute, ignoring his request regarding the cigar. "Aye, Aye, Cap'n, sir."

Floyd grinned approvingly. "More like it."

Bannon stepped behind the bar and dropped the clipboard next to a stack of tumblers also under plastic.

"Some mess you've got here, brother," McMurphy said.

"Tell me about it. These change orders are going to cost a fortune, and they keep rolling in."

Bannon was a ruggedly handsome man in his mid-30s. As tall as McMurphy, his was a trimmer physique, one tailor-made for surfing, which Bannon did a lot of in his younger days, and running, which he still did with religious regularity. Like McMurphy, a former commander in the Coast Guard, he remained in the reserve, but he no longer cut his dark wavy hair to strict military regulation either. A fine coating of sawdust covered it presently.

McMurphy leaned his elbows on the bar, planted a foot on the brass foot rail, and looked around. He reminded Bannon of a cowboy in the old West.

"When do you expect to be done with all this?"

"A couple or three days, according to my contractor, who I just met with." He looked around the bar, too. "Yeah, color me skeptical. Beer?"

"Thought you'd never ask."

Bannon reached down under the counter and dug through the ice to come up with two icy bottles of Coors Light. Bannon handed one to McMurphy.

"Gracias, sir." He tipped the bottle toward Bannon and then sucked half of it dry.

"What're ya thanking 'im for?" Floyd asked. "Service in this joint's been crap for weeks now.

"That's because we're closed, Cap'n. For renovations."

"Didn't ya notice all the construction going on around ya?" McMurphy asked.

Floyd looked around as if seeing it all for the first time, a sour expression on his face. He shook his head. "Naw. Ain't that."

Bannon gave the old man a bittersweet smile. "I miss Tara, too, Floyd."

"What?" The old man furrowed his forehead. His thick white eyebrows bunched together over his nose. "Ya mean that girl hangs around here pretending to be a bartender?" He harrumphed. "Don't make me laugh. She a pain in my—"

"Speaking of Blades, you hear from her?" McMurphy asked, drinking his beer.

"No. She's basically MIA." Bannon leaned on the counter and used his thumbnail to tear a rip in the silver label. "Learning her brother was alive after all this time thinking he wasn't. It hit her pretty hard."

"Not to mention finding out he's the evil terrorist mastermind who tried to kill nearly six thousand people. Including us. Multiple times." McMurphy shook his head. "That'd mess with anybody's head."

"Yeah, then there's that."

Bannon didn't have a brother or any siblings, so he'd never know the hurt that kind of betrayal would cause, not from a blood relative. His parents had been killed when he was very young. He had no memories of them. He'd grown up in the system. His earliest memories were of being bounced from foster home to foster home until he turned eighteen. That day, he joined the Coast Guard, where he found a family at last.

"She went to go find him, didn't she?" McMurphy asked.

"That'd be my guess."

"I would've helped if she'd asked."

"That's why she didn't ask. She figures this is her problem to fix."

McMurphy nodded. "You worried?"

Bannon gave the idea some thought. He shrugged. "Tara can take care of herself."

McMurphy nodded. "Yeah. Me, too."

The three of them were brothers and sisters in arms. That made them closer than family. So, of course, he was concerned for her. "Tell you the truth, though. It's Ghaazi Alvi's well-being I'd worry about once Tara catches up to him."

"Amen to that, brother." McMurphy finished his beer. "You ask me, the little weasel deserves everything she gives him."

"Want another?" Bannon asked, indicating his empty beer bottle.

McMurphy slapped the bar. "No. Thanks. I've gotta run." He stepped back. "But, the reason I stopped by. The Seacoast Penguins. We've got a game tonight. Six o'clock. Wondered if you wanted to tag along? We're going up against the Saltwater River Cats. The division leaders. We're gonna crush 'em."

McMurphy coached a little league baseball team in the Hampton Beach organized youth league. He'd done it for years, and Bannon often went along and helped out. It was fun. He loved baseball, and the kids were great. A lot of them were sons and daughters of deployed servicemen and women. As such, much of the coaching came down to consoling the broken hearts of those missing their loved ones.

"Would love to but can't." Bannon held up his cell phone. "Grayson. I've got a meeting with her later today in Boston."

Elizabeth Grayson, a former US Army four-star general and the current Secretary of the Department of Homeland Security, for whom they worked on occasion. The two men and Tarakesh 'Blades' Sardana formed the core members of a small team of specially-trained, highly skilled operatives she'd brought together for unique, sensitive, and, if necessary, secret missions outside the normal channels of either Homeland Security or the Department of Defense.

When she first approached him, Bannon called it black ops, and Grayson bristled at the term.

"Secret, yes, but not black ops," she insisted. "A single unit that's small, efficient, and nimble enough to respond to and investigate specific, targeted threats to the homeland, threats that can't be effectively handled by standard operating means or a normal military response."

In other words, she said, selling him a chance to make a real difference in this scary world, to get things done when the lumbering behemoth-sized political bureaucracy can't or won't.

The three of them had agreed to her terms. And she to theirs. A few hiccups notwithstanding, the arrangement had worked well so far.

"Lucky you," McMurphy said. "What's she want?"

"Didn't say, specifically," Bannon said. "I'm hoping there's been some progress in locating the other railguns."

Three weeks earlier, Bannon and his team had tracked down a group of terrorists led by a zealot named Aziza

Faaid. He and his cell had managed to get their hands on a scaled-down, portable version of a devastating weapon called a railgun. Typically, the size of a battleship mounted sixteen-inch, 50-caliber naval gun, the sort that weighed two-hundred-sixty-seven-thousand pounds, with a sixty-six-foot long barrel length.

Faaid's scaled-down railgun fit on the bow of a thirty-five-foot-long Bowrider.

Based on state-of-the-art technology, the weapon had been capable of delivering a seven-pound projectile to seven times the speed of sound and generating muzzle energies of nearly fifty megajoules. Put in perspective, that was the kinetic energy equal to the impact of a five-ton bus traveling at over three hundred miles per hour.

Faaid had planned to use the railgun against a passenger cruise ship called the *Oceanic Princess,* under sail with over six thousand guests and crew onboard. Bannon and his team defeated Faaid, but not before twenty-eight people were killed, and over a hundred more were injured in the attack. Also, two FBI agents and a Coast Guardsman named Troy O'Neil were killed trying to put a stop to the horrific plan.

Only after the weapon was destroyed and the terrorists were either killed or captured did Bannon and his team learn the railgun they'd sent to the bottom of the Atlantic Ocean was only a prototype, one of four. Three more operational railguns were out there, somewhere in the United States, waiting to be used, and no one had a clue where.

McMurphy handed him his empty beer bottle. "Better you than me. Maybe ask her again why she benched us rather than have us help in the search. After all, it was us—we—who saved the day, as I recall." He slapped the bar and turned for the door. "Just saying. Have a good one. You, too, Captain Floyd."

Floyd held up a single finger.

McMurphy laughed. "You're a hoot, old-timer. Always good for a laugh, Cap'n."

When he reached the door, where there was no door, McMurphy turned. He took a Seacoast Penguin's baseball cap from his back pocket and mashed it down on his head. He mimed opening an imaginary door, stepping through it, and then closing it again. Once he was on the imaginary other side, he leaned in. He called out over the construction noise. "Might wanna see about getting a door *before* you try and lock up tonight. Just a suggestion."

"It's being delivered in an hour, wise guy," Bannon shouted back. "Good luck. I've seen your kids play. I love 'em, but you're gonna need it."

McMurphy feigned horror and placed a hand over his heart. "Ouch!"

Bannon waved him away with a smile. "Get out of here."

Want to keep reading? Grab book 3 in the series,
Strike of the Stingray

ALSO BY DAVID DELEE

Grace deHaviland Bounty Hunter series
Too Far
Stare at the Moon
Takedown
With Intent to Deceive
Pin Money
Fatal Destiny

Brice Bannon Seacoast Adventures
Crimson Storm
Siege at Tiamat Bluff
The Yakuza Gambit
Strike of the Stingray
The Oceanic Princess
Facing the Storm

Nick Lafferty Crime Thrillers
Cold Cases
Out of the Game
Crystal White

Flynn & Levy Police Thrillers
Between Truth and Lies
While the City Burns
Moral Misconduct

ABOUT THE AUTHOR

David DeLee is the author of the Grace deHaviland Bounty Hunter series, including the novels *Fatal Destiny, Pin Money, With Intent to Deceive, Takedown,* and *Too Far*. David's also written many short stories featuring Grace, most notably *Bling, Bling*, which appeared in the anthology *The Rich and the Dead* edited by Nelson DeMille.

David's other work includes the novel *Crystal White,* which SUSPENSE MAGAZINE called "...a dark portrayal of the evil that men—and women—can do." the second novel in the Nick Lafferty thriller series, *Out of The Game*, and *Moral Misconduct,* his Flynn & Levy police procedurals, and his Brice Bannon Seacoast Adventures.

A member of the Mystery Writers of America and the International Thriller Writers organization and a former licensed private investigator, David also holds a Master's Degree in Criminal Justice. He makes his home in New Hampshire.

For more information, check out David's website: www.daviddelee-author.com